Dangerous Waters Trilogy, Book 2:

Ghost of a Chance

By Dee Lloyd

Writers Exchange E-Publishing

http://www.writers-exchange.com

Dangerous Waters Trilogy, Book 2: Ghost of a Chance
Copyright 2018 Dee Lloyd
Writers Exchange E-Publishing
PO Box 372
ATHERTON QLD 4883

Cover Art by: Jatin

Published by Writers Exchange E-Publishing
http://www.writers-exchange.com

As his headlights sliced through the thick, dark night, Bret rammed the volume control higher. The driving beat of Shania Twain's defiant taunt rattled the windows of his pickup. The stimulus of loud music pounding on him was what he needed. Tonight's hospital visit with his father had left him totally drained. Will was not taking the prospect of a lengthy recuperation well.

Forget about that! Give in to the beat! His broad palm smacking the steering wheel in time to the music felt good. Yeah, right Shania! Bret agreed. Not many things impressed him much either!

He turned off the air conditioning and opened his window. Maybe the warm, moist Florida air flowing in and whipping around him would soothe some of the tension out of his muscles.

The quiet blackness of the night and the aggressive musical therapy seemed to be doing the trick but Bret felt the back of his neck tighten again as he approached the abandoned construction site. Resolutely, he kept on thwacking the steering wheel in time to the music. Mind over matter. That's what he had to concentrate on.

But it didn't work.

And it hadn't for almost a week. The moment he hit the property line of the projected retirement community, the temperature in the cab plunged and, no matter what kind of music he was playing on the stereo, the wailing of a saxophone sliced through the air. Piercing and sad, it replaced every other sound. It silenced the rumble of the pickup's engine and Bret could swear that his own breathing was soundless. The saxophone sang alone...and stopped when he reached the far property line. Once or twice, he thought he'd caught a glimpse of someone walking along the side of the road. A woman he thought. But that was only imagination. He'd allowed himself to be spooked by some kind of freaky radio waves that seemed indigenous to this spot.

Bret speeded up. He shivered. The chill was deep and intense. It didn't dance on the skin like a cooling breeze but rather began at the marrow of his bones and radiated outwards. This short stretch of road always seemed endless, the piercing wail of the saxophone interminable. He had almost reached the end of the long curve in the road that edged the site when he saw her.

This time she was right in the middle of the road--not twenty feet in front of his truck--a gleaming white figure in the headlight beams. In the split-second that he was able to focus on her, he thought he recognized that slender build and dark hair. Then he was too busy swerving onto the shoulder to avoid hitting her to get a really good look.

But what on earth would Yvette be doing out here?

The moment his wheels skidded and sank into the soft loamy shoulder of the road, Bret flung his door open and leapt out. Vaguely aware that the air was even colder outside the truck, he verified his first impression. It was Yvette, all right. Apparently, she had been in some kind of accident. That was definitely blood on her white jacket and she was missing one shoe. Even from a distance he could see scrapes on her bruised face.

What the hell had happened to her? Her features were so battered that he could barely recognize the pretty Maid of Honor who had smiled at him last week at his cousin's wedding.

In spite of her limp, Yvette was moving very quickly away down the highway.

"Hey," he yelled as he began to run after her. "Wait up."

She turned and looked at him over her shoulder without slowing down a bit. Her pale, serious face was streaked with blood and her dark hair seemed to be matted with it. The last time he had seen her, she had been witty and animated. Her face hadn't worn that gray, desperate look.

She didn't seem to recognize him. Bret stopped, not wanting to frighten her further.

Her movement ceased when his did. Her cold, blank stare conveyed nothing.

"It's Bret," he called. "I'm not going to hurt you, Yvette."

She shook her head slowly, then put her hand to her throat. "Danger," she said in a hoarse whisper. "Please."

She worked her mouth as if she were trying to say more but could not make the sounds come out. Finally, she croaked, "Warn her."

The hoarse whisper reached him just before her spotlit figure in its stained and bloody suit vanished.

"Wait." The word was too late.

The road, brightly lit by the headlights of Bret's pickup, was completely empty.

When he climbed unsteadily back into the cab of the truck, he found it strangely quiet. Both the sexy country singer and the jazz saxophone were silent. Except for the insistent whispering of the breeze through the long needles of the lanky Australian pines at the side of the road, all he could hear was the pounding of his heart and the sharp intake of his own breath. He growled a disgusted epithet. His body might be almost healed but his nerves were sure shot to hell.

He dragged his fingers through the thatch of blond hair that was longer than it had ever been in his adult life. Well, he wasn't about to sit here on the weedy shoulder of a deserted road and allow his imagination to get the better of him.

Lord! It was desolate. Where was the endless stream of noisy, smelly semis he usually cursed? The road was always clogged with them, day and night. This emptiness wasn't natural.

The Bar and Grill that Buzz had inherited it from his uncle was somewhere around here. Buzz had gone on at great length about his plans to make it into "the best damned bar and grill in Florida" as soon as he could leave the service. Well, there would never be a better time for a stiff bourbon with an old buddy. Maybe that would get the icy chill out of his bones.

Who'd believe that Bret, the dependable, unflappable anchor of Greco's special task force could be spooked like this? And by what? An attractive woman he'd conjured up who had suddenly vanished into the mist? He took a deep breath and turned the key in the ignition. Buzz's place in Pioneer Grove was about a quarter of an hour away. The pickup moved down the road like a dream.

Thirteen minutes later, he was parked in the next to last parking space in the lot. He hadn't been out this way since his return but he'd heard that Pioneer Grove was no longer the little down-at the-heels collection of buildings he remembered. It had been razed and resurrected as an upscale retirement community. The results were impressive.

He had expected Buzz to be running a casual blue-collar bar, not a sprawling glass and brick showplace like The Grove. The property he'd inherited from his uncle was a lot more extensive than Buzz had let on. Adjacent to the restaurant, a prosperous-looking strip mall boasted some professional offices, a bank, a Salvatore's Salon, and a trendy coffee house. The restaurant seemed to be doing great business. Good for Buzz!

Bret pushed open the heavy glass doors and stopped dead in his tracks. He really was losing his mind! Dominating the lobby was a six-foot-tall, glass-framed photograph of Yvette. But this was Yvette as he had never seen her. He figured she must have worn a wig and some strategic padding for this photo because, in it, her dark hair reached her waist and the plunging neckline of her blouse revealed a cleavage that had not been apparent in the bikini she'd worn at Kit's pool party.

The flash across the picture announced, "Saturday nights in the piano bar, our own Emilienne Pelletier."

Bret swallowed hard. Pelletier was Yvette's surname. He hoped to hell she was alive and singing in that bar. But he doubted it.

Milly was not in a singing mood tonight. She was exhausted from lack of sleep and depressed by the black and bloody dreams that plagued her every night for almost a week. Spending her nights struggling with a faceless attacker and fighting for breath as his fingers squeezed the life out of her, was a lousy preparation for singing at the piano bar. Above all, she was desperately worried about her sister. She knew the dreams were somehow connected with Yvette. And Yvette had disappeared.

However, in spite of the dreams, she was going to sing tonight. She owed it to Buzz's memory to keep up the Saturday night tradition that brought back their regular customers week after week. She checked her reflection in the mirror behind the bar and tucked the formfitting, sleeveless blouse with its plunging neckline into the waistband of her long black skirt and smoothed non-existent wrinkles out of the silky fabric that skimmed her hips. This was the moment that Buzz always used to give her a gentle swat on her bottom.

"Go get 'em, Honey." She could hear Buzz's rough voice encouraging her as she made her way to the piano bar.

He had understood the tug-of-war between her love of singing and her aversion to the spotlight. It wasn't stage fright. She would have been fine performing on the radio. But until she actually began singing to the audience, she was uncomfortable being stared at. Unfortunately, Buzz was gone.

She sat down on the familiar piano bench. She had taken to wearing her long hair parted in the middle so that when she leaned forward to play the introductory notes to her song, the dark veil covered part of her face. In those brief moments before she became totally involved in telling the story of her song, she felt more secure with that silky moving curtain between her and her audience.

Tonight, the bar was packed. Conversation and laughter filled the room. Quite a number of New York accents carried over the softer southern voices. That reassuring murmur of voices sparked the first stirring of excitement. The customers were involved in their conversations and she would have to work hard to entice their attention away. She enjoyed the challenge and the need to intensify her own emotions to reach them. These days, she felt truly alive only when she was making an audience yearn, or cry, or laugh.

On impulse, her fingers began the driving rhythm of That Old Black Magic. The sexy old standard felt right tonight. She let the lyrics sweep her into a dark world of passion and surrender. Her husky voice began to work its own magic to seduce her audience. For these five minutes, she could feel sexy and powerful and involved in a fantasy world far different from her everyday life. She looked at faces around the room. Many of them familiar, most of them turned towards her.

Few of her audience were young, but most were fiercely determined to deny that fact. The women's animated faces were artfully made up. Diamonds flashed on male and female fingers and earlobes. Heavy gold gleamed dully. Almost without exception, they were watching her now.

Yes, she had them. Men and women alike were succumbing to her spell. The noise level had dropped to almost nothing. Any words that were spoken were soft, intimate. Milly felt a flash of envy for the lucky couples who were sharing that moment. Of course, there were always a few men who gazed at her with lust in their eyes, but that was not the kind of romantic spell she yearned for. For six years, she had been loved and truly cherished. That should be enough for anyone, but the little girl in her--the one who had loved fairy tales--wished for the Old Black Magic that she was singing about. Was it actually possible to be so possessed by a man that you were swept away into a swirling vortex of love?

As if the black magic had conjured him up, a tall, fair-haired man appeared under one of the little recessed lights in the archway that separated the piano bar from the main restaurant.

The spotlight turned his blond hair into a brilliant halo. He was well built and good-looking in a rather conventional way. His hair was thick, his features darkly tanned and regular. But it was the peculiar tension in the way he held his head that caught her attention. And he was staring at her.

There was nothing romantic or even sexual in the way he was staring. He looked startled. He might even, for a split second, have looked afraid. He regained his composure quickly but his eyes did not swerve from her face.

The intensity of his gaze was unsettling. Milly inclined her head and bent a little further over the piano so that her hair screened part of her face again. She decided it was time for a change of mood and launched into an upbeat medley of show tunes.

At the end of the set, Milly left the stage quickly, needing to get away from those penetrating eyes. She smiled and waved at her regulars as she brushed past their tables but didn't stop to chat as she usually did.

"I'll be in my office for a few minutes," she told Stu who was polishing glasses behind the bar. "Call me if you get too busy out here."

She closed the office door behind her and, feeling a little silly, breathed a sigh of relief. What was the matter with her? Granted, those horrible nightly dreams were making her edgy, but why would she be concerned about one stranger staring at her? She should be used to that. There were always strangers out there on Saturday nights.

It must be that he looked so out of place. Why was this blond Adonis in a bar out here, in the western part of Palm Beach County instead of trolling for women in one of the martini bars in City Place or maybe beach front on Atlantic in Delray?

She missed Buzz. She especially missed his solid, loving presence behind the bar when she sang. He used to tease her about having to beat the men off when she wore her "Tempation outfit". She sighed again. Buzz used to love to remove those silky blouses... But she mustn't go there. Buzz was gone.

And Yvette was missing.

"Milly," Stu's rough voice came over the intercom. "I have a customer here who wants to talk to you." It was unlike Stu to interrupt her wind-down break. "He asked for Buzz first," he added. "Something about being in the service together."

It said a lot about the kind of man her husband had been that even two years after his death people wanted to pay their respects to his widow. Milly took a deep breath, raised her chin and brushed her hair over her shoulders so that it hung down her back. This was always hard.

It came as no surprise that the man waiting at the bar was the tall, blond stranger. His startling blue eyes seemed to be searching her face.

"You're really not Yvette! Your eyes are gray! No, they're green," he announced with a relieved smile that lit up his face and made his blond good looks anything but conventional. "I saw 'Emilienne Pelletier' on the poster in the lobby but I thought maybe Yvette was using another name."

Hope flared. "You know Yvette?" she demanded. "Have you seen her? Do you know where she is?"

An odd look crossed his face. He paused for a moment, then said, "I don't know where she is. I haven't talked with her since my cousin's wedding a couple of weeks ago."

She must have made some kind of signal that his mention of the wedding clicked with her. Bret raised a questioning eyebrow.

"Oh, yes," she said, "Yvette was maid of honor at Kit's wedding. You are one of the cousins...?"

"Where are my manners? I'm Bret Thornton. When I saw you at the piano tonight, I thought for a moment you were Yvette." He extended his hand and added, "You're Buzz's wife?"

His warm hand engulfed hers in a firm handshake. In spite of his tanned beach boy good looks, his hard palm told her that he was no stranger to hard work. He did not relinquish her hand immediately and she was oddly reluctant to withdraw hers.

"Yes, I'm Milly. I was married to Buzz," she said quietly, "but he died almost two years ago."

"He died?" Bret placed his left hand over their joined hands and gave hers a sympathetic squeeze. She realized how long the contact had gone on and broke it.

"I can't believe it," Bret was obviously shaken by the news. "I ran into Buzz when I was in town for the holidays two years ago. He seemed to be in good health and happier than I'd ever seen him."

"How did you know Buzz?" she asked.

She couldn't remember Buzz ever mentioning Bret Thornton but the man did seem genuinely upset. At closer quarters she could see that Bret was older than she had first thought. Faint lines around his eyes and mouth showed that he was probably in his mid-thirties. And she wondered how he got those odd scars on his neck and jaw.

"We were in the service together." Bret seemed about to say more but instead withdrew into silence. The closed look that came over his face reminded her of Buzz's reaction whenever the subject of his connection with that virtually unknown government agency came up.

"Let me buy you a drink," Milly offered.

"Bourbon on the rocks," was his terse reply as he nodded his acceptance. "If you don't mind talking about it, I'd like to know what happened to Buzz."

Milly made a quick decision. She rarely invited anyone into her office even on business but she wanted to talk to this man. His reaction to her resemblance to her twin sister had been strange to say the least. She needed to find out what he knew about Yvette.

"Stu," she said to the massive ex-fighter who was hovering a couple of feet away on the other side of the bar, "this is Bret. He was in the service with Buzz a few years back." Stu offered a large scarred hand which Bret accepted.

"Yeah?" Stu said, obviously waiting to hear more.

"Stu was tending bar here when Buzz bought the bar ten years ago," Milly said. "He's been the backbone of the place ever since. And a dear friend."

Stu's battered face melted into a smile at her words but his eyes on Bret remained cold and skeptical.

"We'd like drinks in my office," she told Stu. "Bourbon on the rocks and my usual." She suspected that she would need the clear head that the club soda and lemon would allow.

Buzz's scarred old walnut desk dominated the little office. It was a utilitarian room. The leather couch along one wall, an extra wooden captain's chair, and two filing cabinets filled almost every inch of floor space. She hadn't redecorated the room since it ceased to be Buzz's domain. He had loved those garish red tartan curtains and she hadn't had the heart to replace them.

She was having second thoughts about inviting Bret in here. He exuded a disturbing amount of vitality. Perhaps it was just his size and height that were intimidating in these tight quarters. Even standing five foot seven inches herself, she felt dwarfed by him. She sat in the captain's chair and gestured towards the couch. She hoped that having him seated below her would give her the psychological advantage.

"Do sit down," she said.

It took all Bret's self-control not to run from the room and from this all-too-appealing widow and apparition-look-alike. She was too graphic a reminder of the hallucinations he had come here to try to put out of his mind. He must focus on the differences between the twins. Milly and Yvette weren't identical twins. The eye color wasn't the only difference. Milly was a couple of inches shorter and a bit more generously endowed. Their personalities were certainly different. Yvette was talkative and vivacious, while Milly appeared to be quietly serene. And, sexy. He couldn't leave out sexy after hearing her rendition of that steamy old torch song.

"Emilienne Pelletier." Bret rolled the words on his tongue. "The name confused me."

"I use my maiden name when I sing. That's what I'm known by. Besides," Her smile lit her whole face. "even Buzz felt that Emilienne Brzezynski would be a bit mind boggling on a poster."

A man could have a worse goal than earning Milly Brzezynski's smiles. His mind flashed back to grim, blood-smeared features that were the mirror image of Milly's.

He forced himself to concentrate on the topic they were here to discuss. Buzz. His death. Death was not a pleasant subject but it was part of the real world.

He assumed a relaxed pose on the leather couch. "So," he began, "you were going to tell me about Buzz."

"Buzz was shot in an attempted robbery two years ago New Year's Eve. He didn't do what he'd always insisted I should do if someone tried to rob me at gunpoint." There was still some anger there. "He did press the alarm button without the thieves noticing but he didn't go along with their demands. When they told him to open the till, he refused and pulled out the handgun that he kept under the bar instead. He wasn't fast enough."

Milly's words might be cut and dried but he could see that she did not utter them easily. Her shadowed gray-green eyes showed how much her loss still affected her.

"I'm sorry. Buzz was a great guy. This doesn't seem right after all the tight spots he fought his way out of. He took me under his wing when I joined the agency," Bret offered. "He saved my bacon more than once."

At that moment, a busty blond wearing a form-fitting tuxedo arrived with their drinks. Stu had added a bottle of bourbon to the tray.

"Just leave the tray on the desk, Eva," Milly told the woman.

"Sure thing," the waitress said, flashing a bright smile at Bret as she left the office.

Milly handed him the glass, being careful that their fingers not touch. She didn't know why but she felt vaguely threatened by Bret Thornton.

"To Buzz," she said.

Bret raised his glass, then drank deeply. "One of the good guys," he said. "Did they ever catch the man who shot him?"

"There were two of them. They were tried in Georgia where they were wanted for a couple of other robberies. They'll be old men before they ever get out of jail." She made no attempt to keep the satisfaction out of her voice.

"Tell me about Yvette. Were you expecting to see her here?" The words were casual but he sensed an urgency underlying them.

"No," Bret answered quickly. "The last time I saw her was last Sunday morning on my cousin Kit's boat. But I was below, working on the engine most of the time and didn't say more than a few words to her. I haven't really spoken with her since the wedding."

"You're a mechanic? I thought Yvette said that you and your brother worked for some Trade Commission or other. She was bragging about being Maid of Honor with two good-looking and terribly distinguished Best Men."

Bret fingered the scar on his jaw. "I did. Bart still does. Right now, I'm doing some Security consulting. But I've always liked to tinker with engines. Kit asked me to do a tune-up that day. I was sorry not to have a chance to talk to Yvette on Sunday. We were thrown together a lot over the wedding and got along well." He cleared his throat. "You must know Kit then."

"I met Kit and her husband years ago." By her tone of voice, Bret gathered that the experience hadn't been totally pleasant. "She and Yvette roomed together in college."

"I didn't know Kit and Ronald had known each other that long," Bret said, vainly for a topic of small talk.

"I don't believe they did," she said.

Milly looked him for a moment, apparently considering what she was going to say next. Bret had never had so much difficulty maintaining a conversation.

"I won't keep you," he said. However, he was reluctant to make the move to leave. It had been years since a woman had intrigued him as much as this one did. "I know you have another appearance at the piano in a few minutes. Thanks for the drink."

"It was my pleasure," she said, beginning to rise from her chair. Her thickly lashed pale eyes were definitely anxious.

He did not leave as he should have. He had no business here. Instead, he reached for her hand. Milly gave him a questioning look.

"Warn her!" the hollow whisper echoed in his mind. "Of what?" he countered silently.

His face must have shown his confusion and concern because Milly blinked back tears and blurted, "I haven't been able to reach Yvette since she left here Sunday morning."

Bret's years of masking his emotions in tense situations came to his aid here. He wanted to be open with her. But what could he say? He couldn't explain why he thought he'd seen Yvette on the road earlier.

"I know she's been out of touch only six days," she continued. "But it's not like her. Ever since Buzz was killed, she calls me two or three times a week. I'm really worried that something's happened to her."

Bret tried to think of something reassuring.

"Maybe she decided to take off for a few days and forgot to tell you."

That was pretty lame.

"Not likely. Yvette was headed back to her office after a two week absence. Right after the wedding, she took our aunt for a five-day cruise out of Lauderdale. Believe me, that's as much holiday as Yvette can stand."

"I did get the impression that she loves her work." Bret remembered the enthusiasm in Yvette's voice when she said that she and her partner were planning to hire on a junior when she got back to New York.

"She lives for it," Milly agreed solemnly. "But she does fly down from New York for a day or two a couple of times a year to check on Aunt Florence...and me." Milly's voice caught. "She's a real mother hen."

"Firstborn twin, I guess," Bret said. "I know the feeling."

Lord! Could he possibly sound more fatuous? He wondered how she would react to what he was really thinking. *Well, Milly, I saw your sister walking down the highway a couple of hours ago. But I think she's dead. Why? Because her face was ashy gray, her clothes were covered in blood, and she vanished before my eyes after telling me to warn you.*

He would have to add that he was afraid that he had lost his grip on reality. She would give him no argument on that.

"Yvette's partner expected her to be in the office on Monday morning for an important appointment." Milly carried on. "I've called all her friends in New York. My aunt has called everyone she knows. No one seems to have any idea where Yvette could be."

"Did you talk to Kit? Yvette might have mentioned something to her."

"All Kit could tell me was that Yvette was staying overnight at the new airport hotel because she had a seat on the first flight out Monday morning. I checked with the airline. She wasn't on the morning flight."

"You've made a Missing Person's report to the police." It wasn't a question.

Milly's gray-green eyes were glistening with unshed tears. "Right after my aunt and I called everyone we could think of."

Bret was silent for a long moment. He didn't believe in ghosts. As a matter of fact, he didn't believe in much. But he knew with a leaden certainty that Milly would never see her sister alive again. And, although it defied all logic and all the rules of common sense, he had a sick feeling that Yvette's determined spirit wasn't going to let him opt out of Milly's doomed search for her.

He nodded slowly. Like it or not, he was going to have to deal with this.

"All right, Milly," he said, draining the last drops of bourbon from his glass and getting to his feet, "This calls for concerted action and you can't do it alone. Here's the plan. I will make arrangements to meet with Kit and Ronald in the morning as early as we can. As far as we know, they were the last people that we know who talked to Yvette on Sunday. If we want to catch them before either of them takes off for the day, you'd better be ready to be picked up at eight. "

"Why on earth should I?" He was glad to see defiant, angry sparks in her eyes. Indignation was much easier to deal with than incipient tears. "I simply asked you if you had any information about my sister. You didn't." Her voice shook with anger. "Where I go from here is none of your business."

"You need my help," he informed her firmly, somehow knowing that was the wrong thing to say. Emilienne Brzezynski would resent help. Where did he ever get the idea that she was the more serene of the twins?

"Questioning people was part of my business for a long time, Milly. Kit might have information she doesn't know she has. She'll talk to me and tolerate more from me than she would from you or a policeman. Then, after we talk to her and Ronald, we'll see what we can learn at Yvette's hotel."

Milly shot to her feet. "Thank you for your concern," she bit out through her teeth. "But Yvette is my sister and this is my problem. I'll make my own inquiries. Please do not bother coming back in the morning."

"It's no trouble," he assured her. Those fascinating eyes were flashing fire. "See you at eight!"

To prevent himself from doing something really stupid like taking her into his arms and assuring her that everything would turn out all right if she would only trust him, Bret turned and made a fast but relatively dignified escape, swiftly closing the door behind him.

He couldn't make out the words, but whatever she said to his disappearing back was loud enough to echo several times off the heavy oak door.

For the first time that evening, he felt like smiling.

Milly was still catching her breath when Eva burst in the door.

"Are you all right?" she asked. "What did that guy do? I could hear you yelling at him all the way from the bar."

Milly rolled her eyes heavenward and raised her arms in supplication to whatever gods protected unappreciated, intelligent females from domineering males.

"God! I hate know-it-all men who don't ask how a woman intends to deal with a problem. Just assume they're the only ones who can figure it out. Then tell her what to do."

"So the hunk pushed the major button, did he?" Eva's broad smile didn't lessen Milly's annoyance. "Hey, send him my way. A guy that gorgeous can order me around all he likes."

Eva had worked for Buzz since the day he opened the piano bar. When Milly had arrived for the three week singing contract that had turned into a permanent position, they had hit it off. Eva's easy-going personality was a nice balance for her own admittedly up-tight nature. Eva perched on the edge of the desk and leaned over to peer into Milly's face. Refusing to give in to her distance vision problems, Eva never wore her glasses when she was on duty in the bar. She insisted that she got much better tips without them.

"You really are upset. Oh, Milly, there's no need to get frantic because some guy tries to boss you around. You're in charge. Just tell him to butt out."

Milly ignored Eva's suggestion. She had major complaints to air.

"I don't know the man from Adam. He walks in here, says he knew Buzz in the service, has one short drink and then... Tells me what WE are going to do. Tomorrow morning, he's coming to get me and we are going to find out what has happened to Yvette. Oh, yeah, he'll let me tag along while he traces her movements after she left here last Sunday. As if I hadn't done that already!"

Milly took a deep breath and uneasily stated the truth of why she was upset. "I don't trust him, Eva. There's something strange about him. About the way he looks at me."

She thought she'd seen sympathy in Bret's blue eyes. Had she imagined the flash of guilt? He knew something. She was convinced of it. What was the real reason Bret Thornton was determined to accompany her on her search for her sister?

"Milly," Eva said with a knowing smirk, "lots of guys look at you strangely. You have that effect on the male beast. How did he know Yvette was missing?"

"I told him."

"You told him?" Eva grinned again and shook her head in disbelief. "And now you're insulted because he decided to give you a hand!"

Milly was beginning to realize that she might have over reacted to Bret's authoritative manner. She was spared having to admit that to Eva, however, when Stu announced over the intercom that she had three minutes to get to the piano for the second set.

As always, work was her salvation. She always enjoyed the second set. This late in the evening, the audience was loose and ready to enjoy the music. Their good humor was contagious. Milly sang mostly requests, old favorites that she could almost sing in her sleep. And there was no sign of Bret Thornton. By the time she stopped singing, it was well after midnight and she had worked out her bad temper.

After the last customers finally left, she and Stu quickly ran through their daily closing routine. She cleared out the till, put the proceeds in the office safe and was ready to head out to her cottage by the time Stu had tidied behind his bar. The cleaners would arrive in the early morning to do the rest. As usual, Stu waited to get into his car until she was safely inside the bungalow behind The Grove which she and Buzz had shared. Hers was closest to the restaurant. The other two, Aunt Flo's and the little guest bungalow, were farther back.

When she flipped on the ceiling light in her kitchen, Stu tapped his horn and left.

She went straight to bed, resigned to the fact that she would be spending a good part of Sunday with one of the most overbearing, maddening and challenging men she had ever met. She almost looked forward to it. His tall, muscular presence made her feel more alive than she'd felt in a long time. But, she definitely wasn't looking for a man. She had decided that she had a better chance of finding out what had happened to Yvette with him along than on her own. Whether she liked it or not, Bret had an air of competence about him. But she couldn't figure out why he was so determined to help her find Yvette. Those intense blue eyes hid secrets.

Thinking, wondering, even fantasizing a little about Bret Thornton, Milly didn't fall asleep for quite a while.

Her heart pounding, Milly struggled toward consciousness. Hoarse screams and fast, loud saxophone music echoed in her ears. The screams were coming from her own throat. It was becoming impossible to make any sound with those strong fingers pressing on her windpipe. The hard driving music pounded at her eardrums.

With every ounce of her energy, she tried to push away the hands. Thumbs pressed harder on her throat. She fought for breath. Her vision was clouded with a red mist. She couldn't make out where she was or who was attacking her. A man's heavy body was holding her down. She could hear his rasping breath and his curses. The sharp, heavy scent of nervous perspiration and citrus cologne were the last things she was aware of as she broke out of the nightmare.

Milly's flesh felt icy and she was shaking as she gasped in large gulps of warm night air. The dream had been so real that she ran her trembling fingertips over her throat, feeling for bruises.

She and Yvette had always sensed when the other was sick or in trouble. And she was positive her twin was having more trouble right now than either of them had ever experienced. It was even possible that Yvette was dead. No. Milly wouldn't accept that. Surely, she would feel Yvette's total absence. She had the strong feeling that Yvette urgently needed her to do something to save her. But how could she do that if she didn't know what her sister wanted her to do or where she was?

"Oh, Yvette," she whispered. "Please let me know. Are you still alive?"

Without a definite sign, she wouldn't accept the answer that pounded in her every heartbeat.

Last Sunday, when she had the dream for the first time, she awoke weeping and calling for Yvette. Every night since, she became more convinced that something dreadful had happened to her twin. More details in the nightmare were becoming clear but she still had no idea of the identity of the man who was choking her. Something about him, though, was vaguely familiar. Tonight was the first time she had smelled his cologne. That was something. She would recognize that scent.

She must get up. A door slammed across the courtyard. Flo had probably heard her screams all the way from her bungalow. Milly didn't want her aunt to find her curled up in bed, sobbing. The woman who had been a mother to her and Yvette for most of their lives was worried enough without that.

Milly was on her way to the kitchen when Flo rushed into her cottage.

"You okay?"

"I'm fine, Flo. I'm sorry I woke you." She was proud that there was no quaver in her voice. "I was just about to put on a pot of coffee."

"I had to get up to start the baking in a few minutes anyway. Why don't we go right over to the restaurant and make some coffee there?" Flo was obviously doing her best to sound bright and normal.

"You had that dream again," she said. Her normally lively gray eyes were bleak.

Milly nodded and tried to keep her lip from trembling.

"Still the same?"

"I still couldn't tell where I was. Or who was attacking me."

Flo opened her arms wide and Milly went to them. Flo gave her a quick, fierce hug and then a hard swat on the bottom.

"Well," she said, gruffly, "there's no point in dwelling on it. Let's hit the kitchen. Might as well get a few minutes' head start on the day."

Flo was an energetic, trim woman in her mid-fifties who usually looked and acted at least a decade younger. Soon after Milly and Buzz were married,

Buzz convinced Flo to sell her restaurant in Niagara Falls and come to Florida to run the kitchen of The Grove for him. The arrangement had been ideal for all three of them. Buzz had his chef, Milly had her dear aunt Flo nearby and Flo had a brand new state of the art kitchen. This morning, however, she looked every one of her fifty-six years. This week had taken its toll on her, too.

The two women had a fast cup of coffee then went about their regular morning routines. Soon, bread and rolls were rising in the warming ovens and Flo had the day's pastries ready for baking. About seven-thirty, Milly and Flo sat down with their toasted multigrain bagels and coffee and stared at each other across the table.

"Well, what is it that you are trying to decide whether or not to tell me?" Flo opened the conversation as she spread cream cheese on her bagel.

Why did she ever think she could keep anything from Flo?

"You remember Yvette telling us about the gorgeous twin best men?"

"Kit's cousins," Flo acknowledged, taking a bite of her bagel.

"Well, one of them, Bret, turned up here last night. Apparently he had served with Buzz and dropped in to see him. He hadn't heard what happened."

"Oh, ma petite!" Flo's pale eyes filled with understanding. "That is always so hard for you."

The two women were silent for a moment.

"For a minute," Milly said, "he thought I was Yvette. When he discovered I wasn't, he seemed almost relieved. His reaction was really odd."

Flo shrugged. "The state you are in about Yvette, I imagine he thought your reaction to being mistaken for her was a little odd, too."

"Could be."

"I dropped by the piano bar last night for a nightcap and to hear you sing. Eva was amused about your having a roaring head to head with a gorgeous man last night. What did he do? Ask you for a date?" Milly caught the sarcasm. Flo never missed a chance to insist that she get on with her life.

"No." Today's mission was not a date. "The minute he found out Yvette was missing, he announced that he was going to find her. He's being nice enough to take me with him to trace her movements. He didn't ask if I wanted his company. Or if I needed it."

"Are you going to accept his help?"

"Bret Thornton is a steam roller. He said he'd be here at eight o'clock this morning and didn't give me time to argue. I planned to tell him where to go when he got here. But I may not, now I've had time to think about it."

"You can't do everything alone."

"I haven't been alone," Milly snapped. "You and I both called everyone we knew."

"We didn't get one lead about where she might be," Flo stated.

Milly sighed. "I know we didn't. Much as I hate to admit it, Bret can probably get more information out of his cousin and Ronald than I can. He saw Yvette with them on Sunday."

She stared into her coffee cup. "I guess I have to face it. I'm going to spend the day being ordered around."

"Wanting to run the show isn't evil, Milly. You loved Buzz and he sure liked to issue orders."

"There's no comparison. Buzz always asked my opinion about what we were going to do."

"And you always chose what he wanted." Flo shrugged. "Let's see what this Bret is like to work with."

Well, Flo was right about one thing. Buzz had always been first in the chain of command. Of course, Buzz had been twelve years older than she was. He'd lived all over the world, known all kinds of people and was the most trustworthy human being she had ever met. He had every right to expect her to rely on his judgment. Nevertheless, two years of widowhood had taught Milly to relish being in charge of her own life. She and Flo had always given each other total support and plenty of personal space. All the same, she hoped that Flo would find something really offensive about Bret Thornton.

His tendency to take charge was annoying. She wanted to think it stemmed from conceit. A niggling little voice whispered that it could just as easily be concern or a genuine desire to help her. No. There was something else. She couldn't escape the feeling that Bret somehow felt guilty about something that had to do with Yvette. Could it be as simple as a brief fling over the wedding weekend? In spite of Yvette's blithe comment that she hadn't met anyone who set off sparks at the wedding, Milly wasn't sure that her twin hadn't simply wanted to keep her feelings private for a while.

What had Yvette really thought about Bret? She and her sister weren't usually attracted to the same men. What was she thinking? She wasn't at all attracted to Bret. He was too...self-assured.

At this moment, he was also standing in the doorway to the kitchen. Wearing cut-off jeans that were softened and faded by many washings, a blue tee shirt the color of his eyes, with his feet bare in once-white deck shoes, she had to admit he looked even better than he had last night.

"So, there you are," he said, looking around him with interest. "Good morning. Smells wonderful in here."

"It's supposed to," Milly bit out, getting up to greet him. "It's a restaurant kitchen."

Bret moved past her to the table where Flo was sitting. "And this must be the amazing Flo. Yvette told me a lot about you."

Flo took his hand. "Well, all she said about you was that you and your twin were the best looking best men she'd ever seen. Identical, too."

Bret fingered the jagged scar on his neck. "Easy to tell us apart these days," he said.

"Must have been a terrible accident," Flo prodded.

"Work-related."

As Bret was obviously not going to go into any more detail, Milly stepped in. "Would you like some breakfast?"

"Thanks, but I had something before I left home."

"A cup of coffee, at least," Flo insisted.

"Thanks, but I really would like to get on our way." He turned to Milly almost apologetically. "I know I'm a bit early, Milly, but I told Kit we'd try to meet her at the boat between nine and nine-thirty. She and Ronald are planning to do a little deep-sea fishing today."

"Yvette mentioned they cut their honeymoon short because your father had a coronary. How is he?" Flo asked.

"His condition apparently is stable enough that his doctors decided to move him out of the Intensive Care Unit yesterday. Kit thought it was safe to spend the day with her new husband and wait until this evening to visit him."

"I appreciate her putting herself out to talk to me," Milly said. She wasn't as eager to see Kit's new husband.

"Kit's concerned about Yvette, too. Before we go," he added, "do you mind if I use your phone to check on my dad?"

Milly gestured to the little telephone desk in the corner of the kitchen. He was put through to his father's private nurse who informed him that Will was improving rapidly and getting more testy by the moment. Bret asked her to report that he wouldn't be in to see him until late that afternoon.

About twenty minutes later, they were in morning traffic which was moving relatively smoothly towards the stretch of road that Bret was learning to dread.

"Could we put on some music?" Milly asked.

He suspected that she was feeling a little awkward about the way she had shouted at him last night. He wished he didn't have to risk turning the stereo on. He had no idea whether having it on was essential to making the ghostly saxophone's riff blast through the car. Unfortunately, he couldn't think of a logical reason to refuse.

"Why not? Play whatever you like," he said indicating the storage bin built into the leather dash of his dad's Jaguar.

Milly started to sort through the CDs, then turned to look at him quizzically. "This is a wild collection. There's everything here from classical to hard rock. Did you choose it all?"

He had to smile at her amazement. He wondered what kind of tastes she expected him to have. For that matter, aside from torch songs like the ones he heard her sing last night, what kind of music did she listen to?

"All mine," he admitted.

When she popped a CD into the player and the swelling strains of a Beethoven symphony filled the car, it was his turn to be surprised.

"It's a Pastorale morning," she said with a contented sigh.

She was right. In the brilliant morning sunshine, even the scrub palms and Australian pines dotted amongst the sparse vegetation along the sides of the road could be considered attractive. The countryside was anything but lush, but it was a contrast to the traffic.

Bret found it hard to believe that his weird evening experiences had ever happened. The resemblance of the vital dark-haired woman who was sitting beside him to the ghostly figure he'd seen on the road was, however, still unsettling.

Milly's long dark hair was bound in a long, thick French braid. She wore neat, relatively modest navy shorts that still displayed a tempting length of gorgeous leg and a crisp, sleeveless, white cotton top. Even playing down her sensuality like this, she was every bit as sexy as she had been in the piano lounge last night.

But, her every movement reminded him of her sister. When he looked at Milly, Yvette's image was there in the background, either laughing and dancing as she'd been at the reception or in whatever dismal form she'd been in early last night. Why had Yvette chosen him to warn her sister? Even though Kit had thrown them together every chance she got, he had never known Yvette that well. True, she had mentioned a twin sister in their brief conversations, but neither of them had any reason to expect he would ever meet Milly.

They were half way around the curve of the road that skirted the construction site before the saxophone slashed through the symphonic music. It lasted five or six seconds; then, at the southern boundary, it was gone.

"What was that?" Milly's face had gone pale. "Where did that come from?"

"Some kind of freaky radio waves I think," Bret replied in a matter-of-fact voice. He wasn't about to admit that it was part of his recent hallucinations. "That's happened here before."

He glanced over at her. "Hey, are you all right?"

Milly was wide-eyed and looked absolutely terrified.

"You're trembling."

Bret pulled off the road and reached for her. She lunged into his arms. He was surprised at how natural it felt to be holding and trying to comfort her.

She pulled away too soon.

"I'm sorry," she said. Her voice was shaky and she couldn't seem to look him in the eye. "I feel so foolish. But that tenor sax riff. I've heard it before."

"Here?" Bret asked. He immediately felt guilty at the surge of relief that someone else shared this weird experience.

She shook her head. "In my dreams," she told him. She shrank back against the passenger door. "Every night."

"Can you talk about it?"

To Milly's own surprise, the hazy, dreadful details of her nightly dreams began to pour out of her.

"The saxophone is playing. Someone...a man is holding me down and choking me. He's on top of me. So heavy. I can't see his face."

Bret slid across the seat until he was right beside her.

"I don't know who it is," she couldn't keep the sob out of her voice.

Bret opened his arms and she snuggled against his chest again.

"You don't have to talk about it, if you don't want to," he said. One strong arm held her close and the other and the other gently stroked her back.

"I think I need to," she said. With her cheek against his warm chest, she could handle this.

"It's always dark. Pitch dark. I don't know where I am. I fight him but he's too powerful. He hits me across the face. Then he starts to choke me. No matter how hard I struggle, I can't get his hands off my throat. The pressure gets stronger and stronger. I can't breathe at all and everything goes black. And that saxophone keeps on screaming."

She was on the verge of doing some screaming herself but, somehow, telling Bret slackened the nightmare's grip on her. She pulled back far enough to look at him. His blue gaze was fixed on her. She could see her own horror reflected in his eyes.

"And you endure that every time you fall asleep?" he whispered.

Once again, she found herself held tightly for a brief moment in Bret's muscular arms. It felt much too good. She made herself pull a little away from him.

"How did that music get on your stereo? It cut right through the Beethoven."

"I wish I knew." Bret still had one arm loosely around her shoulders but his fingers stopped stroking her upper arm. "It does that almost every time I drive by here. And it doesn't matter if I'm driving the pickup or one of the cars."

For a moment, she thought he was going to say something more but, instead, that closed, almost guilty look came over his face. What was he hiding? He couldn't possibly be the man who attacked her in her nightmare. Nothing about him was right for that role. He was strong enough but much too tall.

Finally, he spoke again. "You probably don't feel up to talking to strangers now. Ronald and Kit might be more than you want to cope with this morning."

Milly noted that he didn't seem to consider himself a stranger. Oddly enough, she felt the same way.

"I can talk to them and follow up any leads I get from them. That would probably be best." He apparently had come to another decision about what she was to do. "I'll take you home and call you tonight to let you know anything I find out."

That snapped her out of her self-pity.

"Not on your life," she said, sitting up and straightening her clothes. "Nothing has changed. I'm going with you."

Without a word of argument, Bret turned the key in the ignition and eased the Jag back onto the road.

"Kit said she'd have the Sprite at my dad's dock by the time we get there. It's in West Palm. That's closer for us than her place over in South Palm Beach and they were stopping by to pick up a picnic lunch before they headed out to sea anyway."

His voice was brisk. It was as if the last few minutes had never happened. That was fine with her. She didn't want to think about the wild music and Bret's connection with it either.

"Kit couldn't tell me anything about where Yvette might have gone when I talked to her last Monday," Milly began, "I knew she had called Yvette at my place on Friday to ask her to put off her flight back to New York for a day or so."

"Did Yvette tell you why?"

"All she said was that Kit wanted her to draw up some papers for her and that she wanted it done in a hurry. Of course, she wouldn't talk about a client's business but I could tell she was angry. Yvette hates to change her plans."

"The rush doesn't mean the papers were important. Kit's always in a hurry," Bret told her. His fond smile told her how he felt about his cousin. "Let's go over any details you know about Yvette's movements on Sunday."

"She left my place on The Grove property first thing Sunday morning. She canceled her Saturday flight and was extremely annoyed when she discovered that every seat was booked on the Sunday evening flights. She had an important meeting Monday morning. Having to buy a First Class seat to get on the first flight out Monday morning didn't help her mood. Then she had to spend more money for an expensive room at one of the airport hotels Sunday night to take a pre-dawn shuttle to the airport. Yvette isn't cheap exactly but she hates 'paying for unnecessary frills'."

Milly's expressive hands flew even more than usual as she unconsciously imitated her sister's speaking style. Then she swallowed hard. "I called the hotel. She made it that far. But she never checked out. And she didn't make the flight. That's all I know."

"Then her luggage is still at the hotel?"

"I didn't think to ask."

"We'll pay them a visit after we see Kit."

Milly had lived in the area for almost six years now but she had never been in the elegant area of West Palm Beach that Bret drove through this morning. Some of the homes in this little tucked away section, close to the Lake Worth border wouldn't have been out of place in South Palm Beach. All she could see through the formidable gates and walls around the mansions they guarded was the occasional glimpse of carved stone, molded concrete or vast sheets of glass. Bits of bright tiled roof peeked through the foliage of tall shade trees. She found everything expensively lush and green and a little intimidating.

Yvette had mentioned that Kit had inherited a major trust fund from her mother and when her father died, she'd been left extremely wealthy. But it was Bret's family home they were headed towards. Had he, too, been brought up in this kind of neighborhood? It was sure a far cry from Niagara Falls.

Bret wheeled off onto a long curving driveway through elegantly landscaped grounds to a large, white, colonial style building that could have graced the grounds of Tara. He brought the car to a stop at a side entrance.

"Excuse me a minute," Bret said, as he slid out of the car. "I just want to pick up a hamper lunch from Anna."

Anna? She should have known there would be a woman in his life.

"Will's housekeeper," Bret explained over his shoulder.

Milly' looked away from him at the expanse of greenery. A couple of hundred feet down the way, she could see a medium-sized bungalow with white siding and a red tiled roof. Beyond it, she caught the glisten of the blue-green waters of the Intracoastal Waterway.

"On second thought," His voice came over her shoulder as he opened the passenger door. "Why don't you come in and meet her? She's going to pester me until I explain who you are anyway."

He extended his hand to assist her out of the low-slung car. She felt like Cinderella for a moment before she remembered that she had a real and serious mission here. This was not about her. She needed to find out every tiny bit of information that anyone in this elegant place had about Yvette's recent activities.

A tall, comfortably built woman with short, faded blond hair appeared in the doorway. Her face was wreathed in smiles and she was bearing a large wicker basket on one arm.

"So you finally made it, boy!" she said. "And who is this? Your lady at last?"

Bret shook his head and laughed. "Anna. Behave yourself. This is Milly Brzezynski. She is a friend and is not here to be harassed."

"I am not going to harass anyone. It's about time you brought your lovely lady to meet me. The insulated coolers for Kit are in the hallway. I will talk to Milly while you get them."

Bret shrugged and actually disappeared into the house. Milly felt like calling him back. She didn't belong here.

"Bret says that you don't have time to visit but..." Anna made a kind of dismissive but affectionate noise. "You will have some iced tea with me."

Milly smiled. Anna's authoritative manner reminded her so much of Bret. Had this woman had something to do with his upbringing?

"Oh, no, you don't, my sweet!" Bret put down the two coolers he was carrying and gave Anna a hug and a solid kiss on the cheek. "Turn my back for a minute and you countermand my orders. Who's the boss here?"

Anna gave Milly a wink. "That doesn't dignify an answer," she retorted with a straight face.

"I'm afraid Milly and I have important business, Anna. Kit should be waiting for us at the dock. I'll bring Milly back another time to visit with you. Kit says thanks for making the brunch," he said, picking up the two coolers. "Will you get the basket, Milly?" he said over his shoulder.

Milly shot an annoyed glare at him but he was facing the other way.

"Aye, aye!" she said as she followed him out to the car.

He was single-minded and bossy but she had to be honest. He was very easy to talk to and had taken just the right tone about her nightmare. She dismissed his strange tie-in with the frightening music. Bret certainly seemed to understand her horror when she had awakened calling Yvette's name. She guessed it was being a twin.

Then too, it was impossible to ignore that he was tall, broad-shouldered, and did more for a pair of denim cut-offs than any other man she could think of. If she was going to pad along behind him like an obedient little serving maid, she thought with an appreciative grin, she might as well enjoy the view.

As they continued down the paved drive to the dock, Bret pointed out the one-story white house with the red roof that she had noticed earlier. "That's my place," he said. "The caretaker used to live there but when he died, Will hired a property maintenance company. So it was free for me when I moved back last summer."

The house looked more suited to a small family than a bachelor. The u-shaped building surrounded a large patio and swimming pool that should have children splashing in it.

Two good-sized yachts were tied up at a long concrete dock.

"The smaller boat is Bart's and mine. Actually, Bart's the one who has always been crazy about boats but he's trying to turn me into a yachtsman,"

Bret told her, indicating a sleek, forty foot, gleaming white fiberglass boat with a royal blue tarp shading the top deck. He hoped that Bart would surface soon from that mysterious mission he was involved in. He had a bad feeling about that. He dragged his thoughts back to the boat. "We named it The Two. Sounded less cutsey than Twins. I'll give you the tour if we have time."

He returned the wave of the blond woman on the deck of the larger, more traditionally shaped yacht. "And that is The Sprite, Kit's boat."

As Milly and Bret left the car and started up to the dock, Kit hurried to the railing and called out to them. The moment they came on board, she hugged Bret and kissed him lightly on the lips.

"Is Uncle Will any better this morning?" she asked.

"The nurse tells me he's so cantankerous that he must be improving," Bret told her.

Milly had forgotten how tiny Kit was. She looked like a child in Bret's embrace. This morning she was wearing her shoulder-length platinum blond hair in a ponytail and was the picture of designer casual in white shorts and a golden sunburst tank top. And she hadn't added one ounce of fat to her five-foot-nothing frame. Milly resisted the urge to tug her shorts down farther over her not exactly model-thin thighs.

Milly looked around her at The Sprite. Over the years, Yvette had regaled her with stories about the long sun-filled weeks that she and Kit had spent together on this boat, cruising the Bahamas and the Caribbean Islands. It was truly lovely. Sixty feet of gleaming white hull with glowing wooden railings and decks. These people did live in a different world.

Milly shifted her attention to the man who had once been so important to her. Ronald made no move to greet her. In fact, he didn't even look at her. But she looked straight at him. And felt nothing! Not one nostalgic twinge.

Even though the pounds he had put on looked good on him and he didn't seem to have lost any of his dark hair, somehow, Ronald just wasn't the imposing figure that she remembered. What had seemed sophisticated to her ten years ago now seemed pretentious. That heavy gold pinkie ring whose huge diamond was gripped in the fangs of an elaborately carved cobra looked ridiculous with his casual denim rip-offs. The snake head setting that held the diamond in its fangs was bizarre.

Ronald was shorter, less vital in her present view. Perhaps Bret's presence diminished him.

Bret's firm hand at the back of her waist urged her forward.

"Ronald and Kit, you both know Milly," he said.

Ronald cast a practiced smile just past her right ear. "I suspect we must have met when your sister and I were in law school together," he drawled. "So, hello again, Milly."

He might not be as dynamic as he had been when he swept her off her feet but he seemed to be every bit as devious. Strange that he was so determined that Kit remain ignorant of their past relationship. She couldn't see any reason why Kit should care about a brief affair he'd had ten years ago.

"Sorry, Ronald," she said, "I probably should remember you." She shook her head, then beamed the most disarming smile she could manage at him before she turned to Kit. "Of course, I remember Kit, though."

"Tell me, Milly," Kit asked, "how long has it been since we've actually seen each other?"

Kit's pale blue eyes were shrewd above her smiling lips. Milly suspected she hadn't been taken in by the phony by-play.

"Yvette's law school graduation. I guess that's about six years."

"Have you heard from her?" The anxiety in Kit's voice dispelled what little hope Milly held.

"Not a word. Not since she left my place last Sunday morning."

Kit, impulsively, wrapped her arms around her and gave her a quick hug.

"Come on. We don't have to stand here in the sun." She led them to some deck chairs in the shade of a large striped awning that had been opened over the aft deck.

"Where do you want this stuff?" Bret indicated the containers that Anna had sent.

"Ronald, would you help Bret put the supplies in the galley?" She turned back to Milly. "Anna sent some bits and pieces that could serve for a brunch for all of us and supper for Ronald and me. I don't know what any of us would do without that woman."

"I only met her briefly," Milly said. "But Bret seems very fond of her."

"She's been with the family forever. She was their housekeeper in Colorado before their mother left them. I spent a few skiing holidays with them when I was a kid."

Bret and Ronald emerged at that moment bearing four tall sweating glasses.

"I made an executive decision and brought iced tea," Ronald said, bending over and brushing a kiss on Kit's lips as he handed her a glass.

Kit's adoring smile gave Milly a twinge of apprehension. Perhaps Ronald had matured and was more capable of caring for someone than he'd been when she knew him. He'd put on a good show then, too. Of course, she'd been young and inexperienced and had probably read too much into his declarations of love.

"I've called Yvette's office several times and no one there has heard from her. Marie...she's Yvette's law partner," Kit explained for Bret's benefit. "Anyway, Marie is beside herself. She even asked me if Yvette had fallen for some man at the wedding and taken off with him. She knew it was a long shot but she'd explored every other possibility she could think of."

"I don't suppose Yvette did meet someone?" Milly's hopes perked for a moment.

Kit gave them a wry grin. "I was trying to set her up with Bret - for all the good that did."

"Bart and I kept her pretty busy. Even when Bart turned on the charm full power, he got nowhere. I don't think she had time to connect with anyone else."

Bret took a small notebook out of his pocket. "All right. Let's get down to it. What do we know? Milly saw Yvette last at about..."

"Nine o'clock Sunday morning," Milly filled in.

"She got here not long after ten-thirty and spent most of the day with me," Kit said. "The legal work that I wanted to discuss with her took quite a long time. Yvette was determined to put in some provisions that I wasn't happy with. But by about four o'clock we had a rough draft done. She said she'd get the paperwork back to me right away."

"Did she say anything about where she was going from here?"

"She booked a room near the airport at The Inn. I tried to get her to stay here with us and have Ronald's driver take her to the airport in the morning but she said she wasn't about to interrupt a couple of honeymooners any longer. You know how independent she is. She insisted she was going to make an early night of it anyway. I didn't get the feeling she was planning to meet anyone.

"She did let Gord--he's Ronald's driver--take her to the hotel. He says he dropped her off in the lobby at about five-thirty. She wouldn't let him take her bags to the room. Insisted on having the bellman look after them. And that's the last contact we had with her."

"She tried to call me at seven o'clock but I wasn't home," Milly offered. "She didn't leave a message but I found her hotel number on my call display when I got home at about ten o'clock. I returned her call but there was no answer in her room and she must have turned off her cell phone. She didn't call you that night?"

"There was no one at the house to take her call. We'd given the staff a couple of weeks' holiday because we'd planned to be in the Bahamas."

"Kit joined me at the hospital about seven. Things were still pretty dicey with Will that night," Bret explained.

"What time was it they shooed us out of the ICU? About nine?" Kit prompted.

"That's about right."

"I didn't hurry back. Ronald was at his office doing some paperwork he didn't manage to finish before the wedding."

"I did the bare minimum at the office," Ronald cut in. "Then I thought I'd earn some brownie points with my mother and drove up to her condo to see how she was. I knew her blood sugar had been acting up. Waste of time though. She was out playing bridge. I imagine you've reported Yvette missing to the police, Milly."

"I waited until Tuesday," Milly told him, "but they still didn't seem to be too concerned about a single woman in her thirties who might have simply decided to be out of touch for a couple of days. Flo badgered a family friend who works for the sheriff's department to send someone out to The Inn. However, when the man they sent didn't find any sign of violence there, I think they shelved the case for a while."

"More than likely chalked it up as another tourist who chose to take some extra holiday time," Ronald commented. "They're hoping that someone will report her missing in her home state and they won't have to use their personnel to handle the case."

"Marie got the New York police involved as soon as we discovered that Yvette wasn't on the Monday morning flight."

"Police are understaffed everywhere," Ronald said. "But let's try to be optimistic. Maybe you're both wrong and she is just taking an unscheduled break."

"I hope you're right, darling," Kit said.

"While we're waiting, I guess you and I will have to take up the slack, Milly," Bret said. "We can make the time to concentrate on finding her."

Kit sighed. "I wish I could give you some kind of lead but I was so determined to get my own way about the changes I wanted Yvette to make when she was here that I didn't even ask what was going on in her life. All the time she was here, I fought her and accused her of being unreasonable."

"Can you tell me what you were arguing about, Kittle?" Bret asked.

"I'd rather not," Kit said. "I can't see how that business could have anything to do with Yvette's disappearance."

"Okay. Let's try this angle. Do you remember what you talked about over lunch or after the business was finished?" Bret was determined to get every crumb of information he could.

"Let me see. We talked about her cruise a little but Yvette didn't want to talk about that. Believe it or not, she kept turning the conversation back to our honeymoon. She wanted to know every little detail."

"That doesn't sound like Yvette!" Milly's disbelief was obvious.

Kit laughed. "No. No. Not that kind of detail." She flushed and exchanged a glance with Ronald. "But she kept coming back to where exactly we anchored The Sprite and what the weather was like and if there were any yachtsmen she and I knew around."

"She seemed to be particularly interested in where we went in Nassau," Ronald added. "And who we saw there."

Kit opened her mouth to say something but apparently thought better of it.

"Probably," Milly suggested, "she wanted to switch to a topic you were happier with than the legal matter you were arguing about."

"True," Kit said. "Then while I was below making sandwiches, you were exchanging anecdotes about your law cases, weren't you, Ronald? It seems to me when I came back on deck, you were laughing about a crotchety old man trying to save the natural habitat of some exotic reptile - a bloated toad or something. Yvette made quite a story of it. The landscape was already torn up, but he was turning it into a case of revenge for his beloved toad. He'd shut down a construction site on one of Yvette's clients, hadn't he?"

"More likely he was tired of the noise and dust. Yvette was able to laugh about it because she had got the injunction set aside," Ronald said. "She found out that the old guy had invented the Wildlife preservation society whose letter he'd used to get the injunction in the first place."

"Right," Kit agreed. "She'd had a lot of run-ins with the pompous little guy and was gloating about not having to deal with him anymore. She was cheering about the construction company finally being able to pour the foundations the next morning. But that was finished business. She wouldn't have any reason to meet with any of those people."

"That was the only case she mentioned. She mentioned the arson case I have coming up. Oh, Yvette did say that she and Marie were thinking of moving to a newer office building."

Kit looked at her watch. "Is anybody hungry?"

"Not really," Milly murmured.

"I think Milly and I should get on our way. We'll get something to eat later."

"I thought you'd stay for Anna's brunch," Kit said.

"I'd really like to check at the hotel as soon as possible. If some of the same staff are working this Sunday, someone might remember when Yvette left and who she left with. At the very least, you can claim her luggage, Milly. There might be some clue there."

"What about Yvette's journal?" Kit exclaimed. "She's always jotting something down in that thing. She always drove me nuts with it when we went on holiday."

"Of course! Her Book of Words, she calls it." When Milly smiled, thought Bret, she was breathtaking. "I have the feeling if we can find that book we'll have a lot of answers. Yvette works out a lot of problems in those little red books. She can't function without one. The minute she finishes one she starts another. Oh, Bret, maybe it's in her luggage!"

"We'll check it out. Thanks for everything, Kittle, but if you're going to get out on the water before high noon, you two will have to get moving."

"Kittle?" Milly asked.

"Anna called her that when she was just a toddler." Bret grinned. "It's a Scottish word that means ticklish and unpredictable."

"And it's still delightfully true," Ronald teased. "Isn't it, sweetness?"

"I've found a couple of your weaknesses, too." Kit's reminiscent smile made Milly's doubts about their relationship look silly.

"But, Bret, all that food!" Kit wailed.

"Tell you what, Kittle," Bret replied. "We'll share. Come below with me and help me scrounge enough for a picnic lunch. Milly and I can enjoy that after we've talked to the staff at The Inn."

That quickly, Milly found herself alone with Ronald in the shade of the awning. The flow of easy conversation stopped. The awkward silence wore on until Ronald finally broke it.

"The years have been good to you, Mill," Ronald said with a practiced smile. "You are even lovelier than you were at twenty-one."

"Thank you," she replied with a surface smile of her own. It was hard to believe that she had ever thought she was in love with him.

Long pause.

"Yvette mentioned that you had lost your husband. I'm sorry."

She couldn't bear to talk to him about Buzz. "I was surprised to hear that you were marrying Kit," she said. It was better to attack. "Last I heard, you had eloped with the daughter of one of the partners in the firm you were articling with." Ten years ago, that news had shattered her.

"Jenny passed away five years ago."

That surprised her. "I didn't know," she said. She had assumed that he was divorced.

They were spared any further stilted conversation by the return of the cousins.

"We have a feast in here, Milly." Bret grinned and indicated the cooler he was carrying. "I'll let you know what I find out, Kit," he said, turning to leave. "And don't hurry back off the water to visit Will today. I'll be dropping in on him later this afternoon. I promise to give him your love and report in full tonight."

"Come to think of it," Ronald said. "I should give Mom a call, Kit. She told me she was fine last night but I'd feel better if I talked to her this morning. I won't be a minute. All right with you if I use the boathouse phone, Bret?"

Even though the only emotion Ronald aroused today was well-founded distrust, Milly was glad to see the last of him when he left them at the end of the dock. She didn't like to be reminded of what a naïve fool she'd been. She had believed his hints about getting married when he finished articling. Of course, if she hadn't felt the need to put some distance between them, she wouldn't have convinced her agent to book her into small clubs all along the Atlantic seaboard. And she would never have met Buzz.

The Inn's lobby was impressively modern. In spite of the airport hotel's semi-quaint name, its entrance was created of vast expanses of glass, chrome and tubular steel. The ambiance was softened by huge vases of cut flowers and potted trees everywhere you looked but, in spite of their best efforts, the result was anything but restful.

At the front desk of The Inn, she and Bret were referred to an efficient, round-faced woman who was wearing a name tag that read, "Esther Silver, Assistant Hotel Manager".

"I wish I could be more help," she told Milly, looking intently at the monitor on the gleaming black marble counter, "but the only information we have in the computer is a record of one room night secured by credit card with no official check-out."

"You do still have her luggage?" Milly asked quickly. That luggage was rapidly becoming the only link she had with her sister.

Keyboard keys clicked rapidly.

"Yes, we have two bags in storage for Yvette Pelletier. Would you like them sent to her home address?"

"Could you arrange to let us take them with us?" Bret asked.

When she hesitated, he took an official-looking card from his wallet. Then, he turned the full force of his smile on her. Milly had to admit that was one potent smile.

"It would be such a hassle to have to go to New York to find out what is in those bags. Please, Esther, there might be something in them that could tell us where Milly's sister is. She's been gone almost a week now."

Milly watched the by-the-book assistant manager become a flexible woman under the power of Bret's blue gaze. She didn't blame her. He was hard to resist.

"Well, I suppose it would do no harm," the woman paused, then capitulated. She smiled up at Bret. "Yes. After all, Mrs.," she looked down at the business card that Milly had given her, "Mrs. Brzezynski, you are Ms. Pelletier's sister. I'll print off a form that will indicate that you have taken possession of the luggage."

Bret moved a step closer to her and gently tilted her chin up to look into her eyes. His deep blue eyes, filled with concern, were hypnotic. Standing that close, she was intensely aware of his heat and the scent of soap and healthy male that was uniquely his. If he bent ever so slightly, their lips could touch. She almost raised her chin to meet him halfway. She caught herself just in time.

"You holding up all right?" he asked.

She nodded wordlessly.

What was the matter with her? Bret was simply being friendly. She was overtired. Life would return to normal after they found Yvette.

If she had wanted to fool herself that Bret had felt something, too, she could have made something of the fact that he was slow to break off eye contact before he turned to speak to the assistant manager on her return.

Almost immediately, the bellman arrived with the bags from storage.

"Yes," Milly said, checking the tags on the medium sized suitcase and a fairly large computer case, "these are Yvette's. That big laptop bag doubles as a briefcase and a carry-on when she travels."

While Milly signed for the luggage, Bret chatted with the assistant manager.

"Milly," he said, handing her his car keys and the bellman a healthy tip, "would you take this man to the car and lock the luggage in the trunk for me?"

She was about to ask him where he was going to be in the meantime but Bret had turned back to his new friend, Esther, and was involved in earnest conversation.

When Milly returned from the parking lot, it was obvious that he had used the time well. Esther was delving into the telephone records to see what calls had been charged to Yvette's room.

There had been two outgoing calls. One had been to Milly's number and the other to the airport - more than likely to confirm her flight.

"How about incoming, Esther?" he asked.

"None at all. I'm sorry."

"Is there any way we could find out the name of the maid who actually packed up the items in Yvette Pelletier's room?" Bret asked.

"I can get that information for you."

And Esther was good as her word. Within minutes, she had the name of the maid who had packed Yvette's things. Unfortunately, Consuela was not working that day. She would, however, be doing her rooms on the tenth floor tomorrow morning.

"Thank you for all your help, Esther," Bret said. "We'll be back in the morning."

"Did it ever occur to you to consult me before you told people what we were going to do?" Milly grumbled as they stepped out into the brilliant sunshine.

He looked at her in surprise. "I couldn't think of any reason you'd object to returning to talk to the chambermaid. But I can come back alone if you like."

"I was thinking that you wouldn't need to come back at all," Milly snapped. "I appreciate your help with Kit and with getting the luggage, but you don't need to put yourself out any more. If you like, I can keep in touch about what I discover."

"I want to help." Bret looked at his watch. "It's past time I fed you. Do you have any favorite picnic spots?"

"Buzz is the one who was brought up around here and he wasn't a fan of picnics. He said he had enough of sitting on the ground to eat when he was on active service."

Bret punched the remote on his key chain to unlock the car and again to start the engine.

"I like to start it up and get the air conditioning working as soon as I get within range," he said. "That car is going to be an oven."

"Would you pop the trunk lock, too? I want to get the computer case. I'd like to check if Yvette's journal is in it. I can do that while you're driving."

"Good idea. Now here's a plan." Bret grinned and cocked an apologetic blond eyebrow at her. "Sorry. I meant to say, what do you think of this plan?"

She couldn't help but laugh. "I'm sorry, too," she said. "I'm being ridiculously touchy."

Bret took her hand and held it as they walked along. It felt good.

"O.K. If you wouldn't mind waiting while I drop in at the Healing Springs Hospital to check on my father, we could have our lunch on the grounds. Healing Springs has acres of grounds and they've set up lots of attractive picnic sites for their visitors and staff. Kit and I took our sandwiches out there one day to get out of the hospital for a while."

"Why don't you drop me off at home, Bret? It's not far out of your way."

"I was hoping that you would let me help you go through your sister's luggage when we finish at the hospital. And we can do some planning."

Milly decided that she had been difficult enough for one day. That heavy cloud of doom was closing in around her again. With every passing minute, it became more difficult to convince herself that Yvette was ever going to be found alive. Having Bret around kept the gloom at bay.

"I'd like the help," she admitted. But a tiny warning skittered through her brain. The man was too good to be true. Why was he so determined to stay right with her?

The temperature in the Jag was almost livable when they got into it. "That air conditioner is a marvel," Milly said, glad to have something positive to say as Bret placed the computer carrying case beside her on the seat.

She stared at the black bag. She desperately needed to know what it contained but just could not bring herself to undo the first zipper. What Yvette's journal might contain was too important.

She had a dark premonition that she wasn't going to find it in the case. Hating her uncharacteristic refusal to face facts, she gritted her teeth and made herself lift the bag onto her lap. This was the most likely place for Yvette to have put her Book of Words. But it was hard to be optimistic in the face of the overwhelming dread that swept over her as they drew near the place where they had heard the notes of the anguished saxophone.

Bret drove with his eyes firmly fixed on the road ahead, his face expressionless. She was surprised to see, though, a definite tension in the set of his jaw and in his grip on the wheel. He seemed to share her dread of a repetition of this morning's experience.

"Well, here goes," she said, opening up the first compartment of the computer-case.

Lying flat on top was a file folder labeled in Yvette's distinctive printing, "Kit – Changes". She was tempted to see what kind of changes Yvette had been making but Kit had not volunteered the information and she knew that Yvette would never forgive her for breaching the confidentiality that was so important to her. She hoped against hope that Yvette was not beyond caring about any of this.

Neatly stowed in individual sections were Yvette's laptop, its power cord and telephone connector. Nothing else. She took out every item, then carefully checked its slot for openings to secret hiding places before replacing it. Yvette had always been secretive about her little red volumes.

The other large compartment contained the small make-up case that she had given Yvette for their last birthday, a yellow blouse, a nightie, a change of underwear and a small electronic organizer.

"No journal," she announced. "It is not here, Bret. I have checked every pocket and sleeve in this damned carrying case twice and Yvette's journal is not here."

Milly's voice was so flat and lifeless that that he hardly recognized it.

"We'll find it." Bret reached over and squeezed her hand.

"What's that?" he asked, more to distract them both from the fact that they were coming to the construction site than from any real interest in the object she held in her other hand.

"A pocket computer," she told him. "Yvette enters her appointments on it and keeps it loaded with novels. She travels so much..."

Milly's voice trailed off and she stared off into space. He didn't try to continue the conversation.

He was mightily relieved when their drive past the construction site went without incident. In the noonday sun, the site was simply a large piece of torn-up real estate with a couple of silent hulks of construction equipment parked on it. No saxophone blasted; no sudden chills filled the car; no pale woman appeared, then disappeared. He wondered what had kept the strange sights and sounds at bay.

The only difference he could think of was that another vehicle had joined them on the long curve. He felt absurdly grateful for the existence of the beat-up white van that had been behind them most of the way from West Palm. The rest of the traffic seemed to have evaporated but the van had stayed with them.

However, his surge of relief was short-lived. He looked over at Milly to share the moment's elation with her and saw that her cheeks were wet with tears.

"Milly, we'll find the journal," he said, wishing he could think of something more encouraging to say.

"It's not only the journal," she told him so quietly that he could hardly hear her. "All of a sudden, I know we're not going to find her alive. Until a moment ago, I thought I could sense her somewhere needing me. But, I can't feel that any more. Yvette's gone."

For the second time that day, he pulled off the road and cradled Milly in his arms. This time she was not shaking with terror. Her body was wracked with heart-rending sobs.

"Sweetheart," he found himself saying, "I'm sorry." He didn't beg her to stop crying; she needed to cry. He didn't tell her she was being foolish; he had enough experience of the strong communication between some twins. He didn't want to imagine the void he would feel if Bart were to die. All he could do was hold her and murmur nonsense into her dark hair.

Besides, he already knew that Yvette was dead. The rational side of him still occasionally insisted that he was having some kind of mental breakdown but Bret knew that he had not imagined Yvette on this road. Her ghost walked here. And it wanted him to warn Milly.

He wished he knew what the hell he was supposed to warn her about!

He should tell Milly what he had seen. But he didn't want to tell her about the bloody and battered, pale figure just yet. Or the warning. Her dreadful dreams gave her enough to cope with.

Anna might as well not have bothered preparing her famous picnic lunch. The fried chicken, sugar cured ham, spicy sausage, homemade crusty bread, coleslaw, potato salad, five bean salad and special jellied citrus salad could have been a take-out hamburger for all the attention Milly was paying to her food. She was making an effort to eat but Bret could see how little food appealed to her.

Her sad eyes were red-rimmed and her heavy dark lashes stood out in wet peaks. Bret wished he could do something to erase that desolate look from her face. She was still the most attractive woman he'd ever seen but the verve and the sparkle were missing.

"Have you finished with that?" Bret reached across the picnic table for her plate.

She looked at the fork in her hand and stopped pushing at the bit of potato salad she'd been toying with. "Yes. Thank you," she murmured.

Having parked at the far end of the parking lot in the shade of a tall stand of coconut palms, he had plenty of time to think on his way back from stowing the cooler in the trunk of the car. Until this past week, he would have said that he was an exceptionally unimaginative and pragmatic man. That was before he was confronted by Yvette's ghost. The experience had shaken him up thoroughly. Then, meeting Milly had finished the job of turning his world upside down. He couldn't dislodge the haunting image of Milly at the piano singing about Black Magic from his mind.

The nightmares Milly described were vivid and violent. Although it went against every logical brain cell that had always ruled his life, he was as sure as Milly was that Yvette had been strangled. More than likely she had been killed Sunday evening in the vicinity of the abandoned construction site.

He didn't know quite how he was going to manage it with absolutely no physical evidence but he was going to find out who had killed her. One thing he did know for sure was that he was not going to let Milly out of his sight until the murderer was behind bars. If Yvette felt that her twin was in danger, Bret was going to do more than warn her. Besides Yvette had already alerted Milly through the dreams. What the devil did the dead woman want him to do?

Milly was still sitting dejectedly at the picnic table when he returned from stowing the cooler in the trunk of the car.

"I'll wait for you while you visit your father," she said. "This is a nice spot here in the shade."

It was, in fact, a beautiful location overlooking sweeping lawns and beds of brilliant flowers. But he was not leaving her alone anywhere right now.

"I'd rather you came with me," he said. It was a sign of how upset she was that when he took her hands and pulled her to her feet, she did not resist.

She did offer one feeble protest. "Bret," she said, "I shouldn't. In my present frame of mind, I couldn't brighten anyone's sick room."

"You won't have go in to see my dad if you don't want to. There's a little anteroom with a desk and armchair where Will's nurse hangs out when he needs a little privacy. I've read a lot of magazines there in the last few days."

"You mean there's another room inside your father's hospital room?"

"This place caters to patients who can afford to be pampered," Bret explained. "Will complains loudly but he loves to be pampered. He would come here to have a hangnail trimmed."

"I'll wait in the anteroom," she decided.

"I saw Yvette's organizer on the seat and thought I'd bring it along," Bret said. "While I'm talking to my father, you can check her calendar."

"Good idea. That is if I can figure out how to work the thing."

"You'll figure it out," he said and leaving Milly to puzzle out the workings of the pocket organizer, Bret entered Will's room.

His father was sitting in an armchair glaring out the picture window. Milly might as well have joined them. Not even her sad face would have changed Will Thornton's mood.

"It's about time! Where have you been? For God's sake, get me out of here," he greeted his son. "That tiny jailer you hired won't let me use my laptop or even use the phone."

"You're looking much brighter, Will." Bret ignored his father's complaints. "And Mrs. Foster is only following Dr. Zellman's orders. You're supposed to avoid stress. You've only been out of Intensive Care for a few days."

"You don't think that all this frustration is stress?" Will exploded. Mrs. Foster's morning phone report had sure been right on target about his frame of mind.

"I have a couple of deals that will go right down the tubes if I don't act on them immediately."

"George tells me he's right on top of everything," Bret assured him.

"But they're my deals," Will muttered.

"And George is your partner. The business isn't going to lose out."

"Can't you at least authorize my laptop so that I can check the stock market?"

"Will, you know what Dr. Zellman said. 'No phone. No internet. And limited television'."

"I need a new cardiologist. Dammit, Bret. I need to keep in touch."

"And we'd like to keep you around for a while." It was time to change the subject. "I brought you half a dozen movies last night, Will. Have you watched any of them?"

Mrs. Foster had entered the room on silent nurse's feet. "Just one," she said. "But we're going to watch another as soon as Mr. Thornton has his afternoon walk down the hall and a little nap."

"Bret, get on the phone and tell that quack I need to go home. If he insists, I'll even take the jailer with me." Will resented having his orders ignored but his earlier belligerence was fading. The slight threadiness that was already creeping into his father's voice told Bret that he had probably stayed long enough.

"I'll try to be here for his morning rounds tomorrow. We'll talk to him together," Bret told him. "Try to relax. I'll see you then."

He paused in the archway to the little nurse's office and beckoned to Milly. When she joined him, he took her hand and led her one short step into the hospital room.

"Will," Bret called.

The silver-haired man with the ferocious scowl looked up impatiently. Milly could see where Bret got the eyes.

"I mean it, Bret." Then he spotted her. "Yvette," he said

His welcoming smile showed a hint of the animation and drive that had made him such a successful businessman. "What a pleasant surprise. There's nothing like the sight of a beautiful young woman to cheer up an old man."

Milly approached his chair. "I'm not Yvette, Mr. Thornton."

"Yvette had to leave after the wedding," Bret cut in. "This is Milly. Yvette's twin sister. Milly and I are involved in some fairly time-intensive business together and I thought this would be a good time for you to meet her. I'll bring her back for a chat when you're in a better frame of mind."

"Well, well, well," he chortled. Will's smile broadened. "I would be delighted to see you again, Milly. Have Bret bring you...to the house." The scowl returned when he looked at his son. "Where I intend to be very soon."

"I'd like that," Milly said. And she meant it.

Bret made no comment on the interchange. The second they cleared the doorway, he asked, "Any information on the organizer?"

"I was able to open the calendar but it didn't have any appointments on it that Marie hadn't already mentioned over the phone. Nothing that wasn't strictly related to the law firm. I didn't have time to look at all the functions of that little gadget."

As they continued through the halls to the side exit, Bret told her a bit about Will's state of health.

"This is his second coronary," he said. "Right after I arrived home a little over a year ago, he had his first. I was still involved with quite a lot of physical therapy myself and we recuperated together."

"The 'work-related injuries'?" Milly asked as they emerged into the bright sunshine.

The jagged Z-shaped scar stood out white against the tan of his jaw. A similar long white line curved down the side of his throat. What kind of trade commission work got a man's throat cut?

"Yes," was Bret's only reply.

They walked in silence for several minutes.

Yvette is dead. Yvette really is dead. The words had not stopped echoing in Milly's head since she had realized it a little while ago. Her sister was gone. Milly stopped in mid-stride.

"It wasn't just a dream, you know. Yvette is dead. The man in my nightmares strangled her," she stated quietly. "And that jazz saxophone was playing while he did it. You probably think I'm suffering from delusions."

Her expressive eyes begged for confirmation of the strange knowledge she had received. This was a perfect opportunity to tell her about his encounter with Yvette's ghost. But he still had no idea what it was that Yvette wanted him to warn Milly about. And why she had chosen him to do the warning. Telling Milly would accomplish nothing. He would make sure she was safe. She didn't need to have an additional worry about her own safety.

"From what I've seen of you, Emilienne, you are not the kind of woman to have delusions," he said. "I don't deny that this is strange but your nightmares are very convincing. I think someone did kill your sister. And we will find out who he is."

"Then, let's go," she said, setting out with a determined stride towards the parking lot. "We'd better get that suitcase to my place so that we can look through it right away. The chambermaid might easily have found the journal in the hotel room and shoved it into one of the bags. And who knows what we might learn from the files on Yvette's laptop."

The grounds between the hospital and the parking lot were dotted with huge octagonal beds of hibiscus shrubs covered with brilliant red blooms. Around each were green wooden benches set in concrete.

Rounding the edge of one of these massive planters, they came in sight of the parking lot. Milly was remarking on the amazing size of the scarlet blossoms as Bret aimed the remote control in the general direction of the Jaguar which was parked about a hundred yards away.

She saw a blinding flash and, almost simultaneously, found herself flat on the ground with Bret on top of her.

Her first reaction was to push him off. The frightening sounds of glass shattering and pieces of metal crashing onto pavement distracted her. Another two explosions shook the ground she was lying on. A few yards away, a woman screamed. From the direction of the hospital, she heard men shouting. Running footsteps seemed to be all around them.

She struggled to get out from under Bret but he pressed her face into the grass. Now she could hear the roar of flames and smell oily smoke.

"Stay down," he yelled in her ear. "More cars could go."

She lay there with Bret's considerable weight pressing her into the hard ground and spiky grass digging into her cheek. Her heart was pounding so wildly that she could hardly catch her breath, much less think.

Good Lord! The Jaguar had blown up. Had there been a major short in the electrical system? Or had somebody rigged a bomb to go off when Bret started the engine? The realization hit her. Whatever had caused the explosion, if Bret hadn't used the remote control, they would both be dead.

Finally, Bret let her up.

"You okay?" His eyes searched her face urgently.

"Just squashed," she replied. "You?"

"I'm fine," he replied.

A small line of blood trickled down his forehead. He raised his hand to wipe it away,

"Don't touch it," she commanded. "I can see bits of metal on your skin. And your hair's full of it."

She looked around for her purse and retrieved it from the hibiscus bush where it had landed. She took out a tissue and gingerly she removed the slivers from his forehead.

"Close your eyes and bend over," she said, trying to brush the tiny particles from his hair.

"I wish I had some disinfectant," she muttered, dabbing at the tiny cuts at his hairline.

Bret tolerated her attentions for only a few seconds.

"Stay here," he said, heading towards the fire. "I'm going to see if anyone is seriously hurt."

"Fine," she said, running to keep up with his long strides.

From the bits of glass and debris that crunched under their feet as they ran across the lawn, she could see how lucky they had been. Bret's flying tackle had flung them down behind the tall hibiscus shrubs whose branches had shielded them from most of the flying debris. She shuddered to think what might have happened had they been in the open.

The area at the far end of the parking lot where the Jaguar had been parked was one huge, towering blaze that belched black smoke. From what she could see, at least two other cars had been involved in the explosion. Flames were shooting up at least fifty feet in the air from what was left of the vehicles. The half dozen palm trees that had formed the northern perimeter of the lot apparently had caught fire immediately.

Fortunately, most of the visitors' automobiles were parked at the end of the lot closer to the hospital and appeared to be empty at this time of day. The shock of the explosion had shattered a lot of car windows and there was glass everywhere. So far, no more cars had blown up.

An elderly woman was weeping loudly and trying to comfort her female companion who was lying very still on the grass not far from the edge of the parking lot. Both women were covered with blood.

The only other person in sight was a man who was sitting on the lawn with his bloody head in his hands. His arms, too, were bleeding.

A flood of frantic visitors and white-clad medical personnel began to pour out of the hospital.

Two emergency vehicles with sirens screaming reached the lot before Bret and Milly did. More quickly than Milly thought possible, the well-trained firefighters were training streams of chemicals on the blaze. More sirens drew near and another fire truck and several police cruisers arrived. The police had their hands full keeping the crowd at a distance from the fire. Some people were simply attracted by the spectacle and others were determined to get to their cars to remove them from the vicinity.

Tentacles of fire swirled up the last standing palm tree. The spiraling action of the flames twisted the tree off its roots and hurled it like a flaming caber onto the lawn. Fortunately, the direction of its fiery course was away from the crowd. Firefighters with portable extinguishers were on it right away.

The next couple of hours passed in a blur. The police took the names and addresses of the owners of the drivable cars and gave them permission to clear them out of the lot. That thinned out the crowd considerably. As soon as they learned that one of the vehicles which had been blown to smithereens had been driven by Bret, he and Milly found themselves in one of the cruisers talking to a middle-aged taciturn man who identified himself as Deputy Purdy.

According to the deputy, the other two cars in the explosion belonged to doctors on duty at the hospital. Fortunately, all three vehicles had been empty.

For an explosion of that magnitude, the injuries were few. Only three people had been hurt. Two of these, the blood-covered man Milly had seen sitting on the grass and the screaming woman, had been cut quite badly and had been rushed inside the hospital. The third person had been struck on the head by a piece of flying metal and was still in a coma. For the rest, apart from the cars involved in the explosion, the damage had been restricted to blistered paint and broken windows on a few cars.

"Who knew you were coming to visit your father this afternoon, Mr. Thornton?" Deputy Purdy asked.

"I'm here almost every afternoon." It was becoming increasingly difficult for Bret to restrain his temper. He'd already answered this question several times. "And I do not believe that I am the target of this attack."

He certainly wasn't going to mention any of the enemies he had earned during his years with the agency. Besides, he was sure none of them would wait until this moment to try to kill him. He had not been involved in any kind of mission for almost two years. He hated to face the truth but he was no threat to anyone any more.

"I've been trying to tell you," Milly interrupted. "There's a good chance that the explosion was intended to destroy the computer and luggage that belonged to my sister. We had just retrieved it from the hotel where she was last seen a week ago."

"Yes. I've noted the connection with Yvette Pelletier. Sergeant Parsons hasn't let anyone forget that she is missing." Purdy spoke in the soothing tones that one would use with a child or a totally irrational adult. "I'm sorry we haven't been able to trace her, Ms. Brzezynski. We've alerted all the local police departments."

He turned back to Bret. "I understand that the Jaguar is the property of your father, William Thornton. Has his development company had any threats lately that we should know about?"

"Thornton Corp. hasn't had any trouble with environmental groups for years. If you need that verified, call George Miller at the head office. Please don't question my father. He's had a coronary and spent the last week in intensive care. Oh, my God, I'd better get up there and make sure that he isn't getting some kind of twisted story about the explosion."

Abruptly, Bret got out of the cruiser and pulled Milly after him.

"If you need more information, you have our numbers," he called over his shoulder.

Mrs. Foster met them in the hall. "Your father is finally asleep," she greeted them. "His nap was delayed by all the commotion."

"I guess he wasn't too upset by it then," Bret said with relief.

"The blast really rattled the windows," she said, her eyes bright with excitement. "And we could see the black smoke above the trees. Some of the patients were terrified but your father was mainly curious."

"What did you tell him?"

"I checked with the nursing station to see what they were telling the patients. The story is that there was a bad collision on the highway by the turnoff. I heard that there were a few people being treated in emerg but that no one had been killed in the accident. Is that true? I would have thought there would be casualties in the kind of explosion we heard." She looked at him quizzically. "It happened in the parking lot, didn't it? It's very hard to get any information in here."

"You're right. Those cars were in the lot. All of them were empty at the time. I wish I knew how I was going to explain to Will that the Jag I've been driving was one of the cars that blew up."

She was obviously surprised at that bit of news but fixed Bret with a steely eye. "You and I will have to make sure that he doesn't discover that until he is a lot stronger," she told him.

Milly, who had stopped at the nurses' station a little way down the corridor, tapped Brad on the arm.

"Flo will be here to pick us up in a few minutes," she announced.

"Thank God for an intelligent woman! I was afraid we were going to have to convince a taxi to come out here to get us."

They slipped away without disturbing Will and watched the continuing saga in the parking lot from one of the planter-benches close to the hospital while they waited. Darkness had fallen but the decorative light standards that dotted the landscape illuminated the busy scene.

By the time that Flo arrived, all the emergency vehicles had cleared out. In the parking area nearest the hospital, it was business as usual. At the far end of the lot where there had once been a majestic stand of palm trees, there were only black stumps and the charred and jagged hulks of what had been three luxury cars. A flimsy barrier of shiny yellow police tape blocked off the area.

Flo did not cluck over them. She simply took over.

"Tell me all about it when we get to The Grove," she said. "Bret, do you want to come with us? I figure the three of us have a lot to talk about. I can feed you and give you a place to bunk for the night. Or would you like me to drive you home?"

Bret's duty was clear. Yvette had chosen him to look after her sister. Milly was alive now, more by good luck than by good management. He didn't know whether he or Milly had been the targets. Nor did he have any idea who had blown up the car or why. But, now, he was on the alert. The explosion had been no accident. Someone had no hesitation about killing.

"I would appreciate your dropping me off at home, Flo," he said. "I'll pack an overnight bag, get my pickup and drive myself back to the Grove." Besides, he could take a shower and get rid of the bits of glass that he could feel scratching his skin inside his shirt.

With the three of them in the car, the drive past the construction site was uneventful, but Bret was anxious to make the return trip alone. This time he was ready and eager for an encounter with Yvette's ghost. Maybe this time she would tell him something that would help him identify the man who had killed her and had tried to kill him and Milly as well.

Bret was actually on his way to try to contact a ghost. If Bart knew what he was thinking, he'd laugh himself silly. Then he'd have him committed! Unfortunately, Bart wasn't here. Bret could use some of his twin's sense of humor and solid practicality right now. However, what Bret needed more than that was some answers from the only entity he felt had them.

As the pickup crossed the southern edge of the property, Bret tensed, waiting for the music and the dramatic temperature drop. He'd been sure that coming alone would work. Nevertheless, he was almost half way around the long curve and still waiting. The traffic had disappeared but the saxophone remained silent and the warm Florida air did not lower a fraction of a degree. Bret flipped on the radio. The relatively normal sound of energetic banjos twanged in his ears. Was Milly right? Was every trace of Yvette's presence gone?

As he slowed the truck down to a crawl, his headlights caught the sparse branches of some Australian pines at the edge of the road. They were curiously insubstantial - like lanky adolescents whose strength had all gone into producing height. He turned off the headlights and peered into the darkness. As far as he could see, the site was still abandoned. Yvette had apparently been mistaken about the work having started up again. Not a piece of machinery had moved an inch in the last week.

What was that? He thought he saw a flickering light deep in the site and, simultaneously, caught the first faint notes of the jazz saxophone. He pressed more firmly on the brake. Yes. A column of pale light was moving slowly across the broken earth towards him and the saxophone's notes were gradually overpowering the banjos. Bret's instinctive reaction was to stamp hard on the accelerator and get the hell out of there but he forced himself to pull off onto the sandy shoulder of the road.

The wavering light seemed to have stopped about fifty feet away. It was not a column. The fluorescent glow was in constant motion, flickering and changing shape like the northern lights he had seen in Alaska. The chill in the truck, too, reminded him of those cold weeks near the top of the world.

It crossed his mind that he was making a lot of assumptions about a field he knew absolutely nothing about. He assumed that, because the spirit looked like Yvette, it was benign. All he knew about the paranormal he'd learned from wild stories designed to scare the liver out of kids around a campfire. But what if this eerie light really was something evil that he should stay away from? His logical mind told him not to be ridiculous; there were no such things as ghosts.

He had to laugh. Then, what the hell was he doing here?

He took a deep breath, then got out of the truck and started towards the light.

The moment his foot hit the ground, the light suddenly appeared a few feet away from him and metamorphosed into the indistinct shape of a woman. Unlike last night's ghost, this manifestation had no solidity and could never be mistaken for a live woman.

Bret swallowed hard and croaked, "What do you want me to tell her? Who did this to you?"

The being made a hollow keening sound which formed itself slowly into disjointed, almost unintelligible, words.

"Warn..." He got that much.

The next part was several syllables of garbled sound separated by long moments of silence.

Then what he thought was "...both."

The air was filled by more strange growling, guttural sounds. The light's movements became agitated, almost spastic, as if it were sharing the frustration that Bret was feeling.

Then, in a final hissing burst, "...sss dangerous," were the words that came to him from the swirling mist before it vanished completely.

Nerves jangling and totally frustrated, Bret hurried back to the truck. He was out of his depth here. He'd rather face a team of terrorists than deal with these manifestations of whatever it was - the spirit world, another dimension. Hell, he was a soldier, not a mystic.

That encounter had told him exactly nothing! It had merely added another unknown to the mix. Who else was he supposed to warn? Himself? Yvette had said, "both". Did she mean Milly and Flo?

Kit was Yvette's best friend. Could she mean Kit? Or her partner, Marie? Why the devil would a ghost contact him and tell him nothing? Judging by the way Yvette's spirit seemed to be rapidly losing its power to remain visible and audible, this was probably its last appearance.

Look at it from another angle. The man involved was someone both Yvette and Milly knew and would be likely to trust. Milly had said that there was something familiar about the man in her nightmares. This was getting him nowhere. He couldn't do anything until he knew more about Yvette's social life. And Milly's!

Now there was a disturbing thought. He didn't know why he assumed that Milly didn't have a man in her life at the moment. Probably because he didn't want to think of her with another man. He didn't even like to think of her being married to Buzz. And Buzz was dead. Come to think of it, that bartender, Stu, was certainly protective of her. And Saturday night, the piano bar had been full of men fantasizing about her.

Hell, why was he torturing himself like this? This ghost business was twisting his perspective. He was happy without a woman in his life. He had decided long ago that he would die a bachelor. He certainly wasn't looking for a woman now. Not even temporarily. Particularly not a forever kind of woman like Milly. And he got the impression that Milly wasn't interested in finding a man. She sure wasn't interested in him.

When he arrived at Milly's bungalow, he was surprised to find that only a couple of hours had elapsed since they had dropped him off at his house.

Flo ushered him into the inviting living room of Milly's cottage. He didn't know why combining warm indirect lighting, solid panels of green and blue drapes, wildly flowered chintz upholstery and pots of ivy everywhere should feel so welcoming. He only knew that he felt as if he had come home after a long and trying journey.

"Sit right there on the sofa, Bret, and make yourself comfortable," Flo said. "I'm going to dash over to the restaurant to check that the dinner buffet is being handled right."

At that moment, Milly came into the room. When their eyes met, some of the shivery after-effect of the experience at the construction site, evaporated from his stomach. Milly had to be tense and exhausted from her own extremely trying time, but what he read in those green-tinged gray eyes was trust and concern for him. He had an almost overwhelming need to draw her into his arms and hold her close.

"You're here, Emilienne. Good!" Flo said. "I won't be gone long. Pour a glass of wine for yourself and something for Bret. And try to relax. I'll bring back a selection from the buffet for the three of us. Anything you don't eat, Bret?"

"Not if you prepared it," he told her.

Truth to tell, he didn't want food or conversation. He needed to think. He had to put the temptation of Milly's nearness out of his mind and figure out a number of things. How had the murderer known where to find them this afternoon? Had he been watching at the hotel and seen them put Yvette's luggage in the car? Or had Bret read the situation wrong? Was he the target? Was Milly? Most important, how was he going to catch the bastard? At this point, the murderer had as little substance as the ghost itself.

Milly gave him a long searching look, then headed for a cabinet in the wall unit that filled one wall of her compact living room.

"I'm having a glass of white wine but I'll bet you would prefer a shot of bourbon," she said.

"You are a mind reader," he told her. "A short sharp shock of bourbon sounds like just what I need. On the rocks, please."

She poured one shot into a crystal tumbler. Then she gave him a questioning look with those heavily-lashed intriguing eyes and poured another in on top.

"Ice, you say?"

When she tossed in several large ice cubes, some of the liquor splashed onto her index finger. She licked her finger as she handed him his glass.

Milly's unconsciously sexy action jolted his libido into high gear. What wouldn't he give to be able to wrap his arms around that generously curved body and kiss her full lips until neither of them could remember the horrors that plagued them. As his gaze lingered a moment longer on her tempting mouth, he made up his mind that one day, very soon, he was going to do just that.

Milly was obviously fresh from a shower. Her long dark hair was damp and she had changed into a sleeveless blouse and clean shorts. The top button of her white blouse closed over the top of a tempting cleavage which he glimpsed as she leaned over to place her glass of wine on the coffee table. She flipped the long damp locks over her shoulders and gave him a self-conscious smile. "I couldn't stand the smell of oily smoke in my hair and I haven't had time to dry it."

"I like it loose," he managed to say around the lump in his throat.

She sat on the sofa beside him, close enough for him to smell the vanilla scent of her shampoo.

"I'm sorry I've been so difficult today, Bret. I didn't even thank you for protecting me from the flying debris," she said, touching the tiny cuts on his forehead with gentle fingertips.

When he lowered his head to look at her, she, without any hesitation, tilted her face up to press a light kiss on his lips.

The feather-like touch triggered a spark that he was sure Milly had never intended. She jerked back and her eyes widened in surprise at her own reaction to the brief contact. He could not resist returning her kiss. When he did, her arms went around his neck. Before he knew it, Milly's delectable body was pressed tightly against his and she was returning his hungry kisses with an eagerness that was unexpected and wonderful.

When he nibbled at her lower lip, she eagerly opened her mouth as if they had known each other forever. The moment their tongues met, Bret realized that if he did not end the kiss fast, he would be hauling Milly onto his lap and moving on to much more intimate caresses. The embrace was rapidly becoming a preamble to lovemaking.

Milly must have realized the same thing.

"Oh!" she gasped and pulled away from him.

His hold on her hand prevented her from leaping to her feet. "I'm sorry, Milly. I didn't mean to get so intense," he said.

But he wasn't at all sorry that he'd kissed her. That kiss had been coming since the moment he had walked into the piano bar.

"I guess our nerves are supercharged today." Milly looked as stunned as he was.

"Narrow escapes can do that."

She could still hear the explosions that should have killed them. They'd come within seconds of being blown to bits with the cars.

"Oh, Bret, your dad's beautiful car. If you hadn't offered to pick up Yvette's things with me..."

"Milly, you know I bullied you into letting me go with you. Don't worry about the car. Will has insurance. I'm a lot more upset about that bastard destroying Yvette's computer and probably her journal."

"Someone followed us from the hotel," Milly said. "I don't know how they could have known we'd be there but there's no other way anyone could know where Yvette's things were."

"I suppose he could have been watching for someone to pick up her luggage. That's assuming that Yvette's luggage was the target. The deputy seemed to think that the explosion was a warning to Will to call him off some development or other."

"Is that likely?"

"Not from anything he's told me about the deals Thornton Inc. has in the works at the moment."

Milly looked at the jagged scar on Bret's jaw. She couldn't help asking, "I know you don't want to talk about it but this couldn't be related to your 'work-related injuries', could it?"

Bret's frown was probably intended to tell her to leave that alone.

"After all, you were attacked once before. And you are the one who has been driving the Jag and visiting that hospital. Oh, Bret, you could easily have been killed in the explosion."

"Milly," he said, expelling a deep breath, "I haven't been involved in anything that anyone could take exception to for almost two years. And I have been highly visible and accessible, right here in Florida for all that time. It's highly unlikely that anyone would choose this moment to try to kill me. All my old enemies are safely in prison."

"What if one isn't?" She couldn't believe she was having this conversation. Or that she could care so much about what happened to a man she had met only last night.

"I would have been notified." Bret squeezed her hand. "But, I will get in touch with a man who will know if I should be looking over my shoulder."

Bret appeared to be lost in thought for a few moments.

"I wonder if Yvette could have known something that was dangerous enough to call for that kind of drastic action," he said.

"It didn't fit my dream but I asked Marie about that. She told me I was being too melodramatic. She said Yvette's practice was mostly real estate and wills. That kind of thing. Marie was sure that there was no possibility of her having information that was threatening to anyone." She took a deep shuddering breath. "But somebody killed her."

When he drew her gently back into his arms, she went without a protest. When she snuggled close, he smoothed her hair from her shoulders to her waist with light, undemanding strokes. For such a virile man, he could be very comforting.

"We'll find out who killed her, Milly."

"You think she's dead, too."

"I do. About your experience today..." he began.

"I don't think I can talk about it now," Milly said. She sat back and looked into his concerned blue eyes. "You have your own 'Twin instincts' so you understand. That makes me feel a little better."

Bret looked exceedingly uncomfortable. "There's something I want to clear the air about," he said abruptly. "You've been open with me. I should tell you about seeing Yvette."

Her worst suspicions were right. In spite of his denials, Bret had been involved in a relationship with Yvette. She didn't care how short it had been. She didn't want to hear about it. She felt sick enough for imagining that his kiss had been anything more than a pity kiss.

"You don't need to," she said, pulling away from him and attempting to get to her feet. "I'd better set the table. Flo will be back any minute."

"Emilienne." More than his firm grip on her upper arms, the authority in his deep voice held her still. "Listen to me. I saw Yvette Saturday night. Good Lord, that was only last night!"

Stunned by his words, Milly could only stare at him in disbelief. "You're not serious!" she gasped.

But this was no tasteless joke. Bret was in deadly earnest.

"I saw her," he repeated, emphasizing every word. "...her ghost. I was on my way home from the hospital last night and, just as I was passing the site of the retirement home, I heard the saxophone. Then, she appeared in the middle of the road in front of my truck. When I pulled off to the side of the road, she began to hurry away from me. She looked as if she had been in some kind of accident. I called to her but she didn't stop."

Bret paused. "She said, 'Danger. Warn her.' That's all. She didn't say who I was to warn or what about. Then she just disappeared."

"The same saxophone we heard today," Milly whispered. "The one in my nightmares."

"I've heard it several times. Almost every time I passed that spot."

"No wonder you looked so strange when you saw me at the piano."

"I almost turned and ran. But I had to talk to you. I was still in shock from seeing an apparition and hearing it speak. When I saw you at the piano, I had to make sure I wasn't seeing Yvette again. I was afraid that I was going to see her everywhere I turned. I still have no idea why she chose me to speak to. I barely knew her. And I had never met you."

"Why did you come to the Grove last night?"

"I remembered that I had told Buzz I'd drop by for a drink. And after having that weird experience, I really thought I could use one. And some conversation with a no nonsense guy like Buzz."

Milly couldn't help smiling. Buzz had been that kind of man. She had loved him and would always miss his common sense and his unwavering, loving support. However, for the first time, she heard the mention of his name and could remember him without feeling the wrenching pain of his loss.

"He would have taken one look at you and poured you a double."

"He taught you well. That's precisely what you did."

"And again tonight." Milly looked at him carefully. His face showed the strain of the last forty-eight hours. "You saw her again on your way here, didn't you?"

"That's what I wanted to tell you. She hadn't left completely but she was much less distinct, mostly shifting light tonight. I asked who had killed her and what she wanted me to warn you about but she didn't answer."

A wave of desolation swept over her. She wondered if she would ever get used to a world without Yvette in it. However, even that would be better than the knowledge that her sister was hovering in some kind of limbo, neither totally alive nor totally dead. She had a strange feeling that if they could find her body and discover who had killed her, Yvette would find peace.

"She didn't say anything?"

"She was having trouble getting any words out. Most of the sounds weren't words at all. I got only three. 'Warn' and 'both' and 'dangerous'." Bret looked tired and discouraged. "Not much help. I figure that one of the people to be warned is you. But who is the other one? And I wish she'd mentioned the name of the man."

"I wish I could raise my eyes to see his face in my dream," Milly said.

"I also wish I still lived in a reasonable world. I can't believe we are trying to figure out the meanings of voices from beyond the grave." He gave her a companionable wink and straightened his shoulders. "We have to get practical, Milly. We are dealing with real violence in this real world. We don't have a shred of evidence that anything has happened to Yvette."

"Well, we sure have shreds of metal and glass that once were Will's Jaguar!" Milly stated. "And you and I both know Yvette is dead."

"And just how do you know that?" Flo demanded from the doorway to the kitchen.

"You'd better sit down, Flo," Milly said, putting her arm around the older woman's shoulders and guiding her to the wing chair near the sofa. "What Bret and I have to tell you is going to be hard to believe."

Bret began, "I presume that Milly has told you about her nightmares... "

That got her undivided attention. "Go on," she said.

Then, beyond the occasional snort of disbelief and some understandable widening of her heavily-lashed pale Pelletier eyes from time to time, Flo let them tell their stories without interruption.

"So, you want me to believe that Yvette's ghost is haunting that construction site. And that you both hear the same music but that only Bret sees Yvette. I don't understand why you don't see her, Milly."

"I wish I could," Milly whispered.

"No, you don't, Milly. Believe me," Bret told her. "Whatever I am seeing is not Yvette. Its shape is similar but it is nothing like your sister. I think it's some kind of imperfect message delivery that her spirit is sending."

"Is one of the messages that her body is there, at the site?" Flo's words came slowly. "Do you think she wants us to notify the police?"

Bret plunged the fingers of both hands into his hair as if he were going to pull the thick blond locks out by the roots.

"Believe me, Flo," he said, "I wish I knew. We have no tangible evidence to give the police. The strange things we've seen and heard at the construction site make me think that is true. But she could have been killed there and her body moved somewhere else. It would be hard to get the police to take us seriously. If they check the area and find nothing now, they'll more than likely dismiss any hard evidence when we do find it."

Flo winced and Milly put her arms around her.

"I'm sorry," Bret said. "I put that more baldly than I should have."

"We have to face facts, Bret. I've been trying to face this one ever since Milly's first nightmare last Sunday night. I did tell Theo about the dreams but he feels Milly is having them because she is so worried about Yvette. I can sit him down and tell him he has to look into this."

"Flo's friend Theo Parsons used to be a golfing buddy of Buzz's. He's a sergeant in the County Sheriff's department," Milly explained. "I agree with Bret, Flo. We should wait until we have something concrete to give Theo."

Flo stood up and straightened her shoulders. "I've set out our supper in the kitchen. It's time you two had something to eat."

"Would you mind if I made a call or two? I want to get a colleague to check a couple of things. Especially what his local contacts know about the explosion."

"Eat first. Those things will keep. And don't bother him about the explosion. I'll get that information out of Theo." One look at Flo's determined face told Bret that this would not be the time to cross her. Adhering to some kind of meal schedule was her attempt to maintain normalcy.

The food was probably very good but Bret wouldn't have been able to say afterwards what he had eaten. And all three of them were so lost in dismal thoughts that conversation was impossible.

By the time they had cleared away their dishes, Bret had assessed their situation. First and foremost, even though Flo's friend in the Sheriff's department might prove valuable as an information source, for the moment, Bret was totally on his own. He had no back-up team. His bizarre contact with the ghost of the murder victim was useless. His experience with criminals and terrorists all over the world and his contacts in international law enforcement agencies were probably going to be of no help to him either. He would have to wing it and depend on his own resources.

Next, although he was going to ask Jim Greco to look into it, he was convinced that this afternoon's attack had nothing to do with his past activities with the now-defunct agency. As soon as Bart had finished what Jim referred to as "this last highly sensitive mission", the agency as they had known it would no longer exist. Bart would probably join him with the security firm Jim had started, and the Thornton twins would become prosaic, respectable businessmen. It was ironic that they would end up doing exactly what Will had wanted all along.

He also doubted that the destruction of the Jag was intended to warn Will off a disputed development project. Will was a canny enough businessman to avoid sensitive issues. Bret would certainly have heard if Thornton's was that deeply involved in a battle with environmental or any other kind of activists.

No, he had a gut feeling that the purpose of the explosion was simply to get rid of any records that might be in Yvette's luggage or on her laptop. Records of what? He wondered if they would ever know.

Some things were evident about the person who had placed the bomb, however. He was ruthless and no amateur. He had attached that device in broad daylight without any compunction about killing him and Milly and anyone unfortunate enough to be in the vicinity when Bret turned the key in the ignition. Whoever he was, he wasn't going to get another chance to harm Milly. Bret was going to make sure of that.

When he noticed both women looking at him expectantly, he realized that one of them had asked him something.

"I'm sorry. My mind was wandering," he said.

"I asked if you would like to be shown to the guest cottage," Flo repeated. "I'm heading off to my bed. Morning comes early around here."

"Buzz had it built for the headliners he intended to have entertain at the bar," Milly explained. "He never did get that program going."

"I shouldn't be that far away," Bret said, slowly. "I'd better spend the night on Milly's couch."

Flo raised an eyebrow and turned to look at Milly.

He could see by the tilt of her head that Milly was going to object.

"Before you say anything, Milly," he said, "think about what happened this afternoon. The murderer took us by surprise and we were almost killed. I'm not going to let that happen again."

"I'm perfectly safe in my own house with the doors locked. Besides, he'd have no reason to want to kill me."

Milly's independent streak was going to be a problem.

"Until we know why Yvette was killed and why the Jag was blown up," Bret explained, "we can't predict what he's going to do next. He may not know that Yvette's laptop was in the explosion. He might come here looking for that. Or for the organizer, which you do have."

"Have you had a chance to look through it?" Flo asked with the first trace of life he'd heard in her voice since that morning at breakfast.

"There was nothing new in the calendar section but that's all I had time to check. I'd almost forgotten I had it," Milly said.

Bret was moving around the room checking the windows and the French doors that led to the patio.

"I'm not impressed with your security, Milly. I'll have new locks and some window sensors installed in the morning."

"Not in my house you won't!" Milly caught up with him and twirled him around to face her. "You take too much on yourself, Bret Thornton. When I want a security system, I'll buy one. You are overreacting here."

"Security is my business," Bret told her flatly. "And I'm telling you that you can't put your life on the line with the lightweight stuff you have here."

"It's my life. And it's my..."

Flo put two fingers into her mouth and gave a piercing whistle. They stopped cold.

"Both of you settle down. You can decide about locks in the morning. Bret, what you say makes sense. Spending the night here on Milly's sofa is a reasonable temporary precaution. You can pull out the sofa bed, then make your phone calls. Milly, get him some linens and take yourself to bed. We're all exhausted and don't need to waste energy quarreling.

"I'm off to bed, myself. I won't need your help in the morning, Emilienne. As a matter of fact, I've made arrangements to cover you at the restaurant for the next couple of days. Good night." Flo left with the measured tread of someone who knew she had everything under control.

"Makes you wonder which one of us is the owner of The Grove, doesn't it?"

"Was she ever in the military?" Bret asked with an embarrassed grin.

"No. Head chefs have the same attitude." She grinned back and heaved a heavy mock sigh. "I guess we'd better follow orders. I do think, though, that you'd be more comfortable in the spare bedroom."

"Thanks, but I like the situation of the sofa. I can see both doors."

"It's your call," she said. As she spoke, she realized that this was the first time she hadn't given him an argument. "I do appreciate this, Bret. I know I'll sleep more easily with you here."

The twinkle in his amazing blue eyes told her that he knew how much the admission cost her. She sent a tiny rueful smile his way and indicated the cordless telephone on a small table in the corner of the room.

"There's a notepad beside the phone and a phone book on the shelf," she said.

He was dialing before she made it out of the room to get the linens.

She was aware of him pacing back and forth between the phone table and the kitchen and heard his low voice rumbling in the background as she made up his bed on the pullout sofa. She couldn't make out his words but had the impression that he was talking to someone he knew well. Not a woman. His voice didn't have that tone. It shouldn't matter to her but she was glad that the good friend and colleague he depended on was male.

As she smoothed the white sheets and tucked them in, her perverse mind insisted in imagining Bret's long, tanned limbs stretched out on them. It was a long time since she had longed to lie in a man's strong arms. And she remembered vividly how wonderful Bret's arms felt around her.

She was standing like a stunned ninny with her hand hovering over the bed, reliving the overwhelming sensations of the kiss they had shared when his words broke through the sensuous fog her imagination had created. It was only then that she realized Bret's pacing had brought him right to her elbow.

"Fine, Jim." He looked directly into her eyes as he continued. "I want it in place tomorrow. Hold on." He slipped his arm around her waist. "My partner can have the guys install your system between ten and twelve tomorrow. Will you let me order it?"

She grudgingly agreed.

"Oh, and do you mind if I have someone leave messages at this number, Milly?"

"Why not?" Her curt response sounded more exasperated than she really felt.

Bret broke off the connection. "It's only for tomorrow, Milly. I'll replace my cell phone on my way to the hotel to talk to the chambermaid."

"On our way," she corrected.

"Right!" His arm tightened in a brief one-armed hug and he brushed his lips over hers. "That's my Emilienne. Never give an inch. Try to get some sleep, love. I have a couple more calls to make. Then I'll hit the sheets myself."

It said something about how emotionally exhausted Milly was that she did not object to his calling her "his Emilienne" or even interjecting that little "love". And she found herself heading directly towards her bedroom.

"Leave your door open," Bret called after her.

If she hadn't intended to leave it open and if she hadn't been so weary, she would have objected to yet another order. She did look back though, and caught his broad grin and the twinkle in his eye.

"Don't be late," she said, returning his grin. "We have a lot to do tomorrow...love."

Now whether her emotional state would allow her to sleep or not remained to be seen.

"I'll make my calls short," he said.

Milly slowly came to consciousness with bright morning sunlight slanting through the lace curtains of her bedroom. She was vaguely aware that something was different. Then she realized everything was different. The curious emptiness she felt told her that Yvette was gone but somehow she did not yet feel the horrible weight of mourning that she knew was waiting to descend on her. Before she could mourn, she had to discover who had killed her sister and find her body.

At least, she hadn't had the Dream last night. It felt so good not to awaken gasping for breath and trying to remove phantom fingers from her throat. Perhaps the dreams were gone for good. But why had she had them in the first place? If Yvette was sending her those dreadful images and sensations, why hadn't she been allowed to see the murderer's face? The scene had become more vivid and detailed every night. Why was there no usable clue to the killer's identity? She no longer had any hope that her sister was still alive but she still could still sense an odd trace of Yvette's presence. Milly would gladly endure one more nightmare experience if it told her something definite.

Her glance traveled idly over the familiar room. She had redecorated the master bedroom after Buzz was killed with an eye to changing the character of the room completely. She certainly had succeeded, she thought. As a matter of fact, the ivory carpet and lace curtains in combination with the deep rose satin drapes and bedspread might even have been overkill. They didn't reflect her style and taste any more than Buzz's masculine furnishings had. But, at least, she had taken charge. She allowed herself a wry smile at her own expense. She had refused help and advice and now she was stuck with this unfortunate bordello look.

Why was her bedroom door closed? She always slept with it open. Then she recognized the sound of water pelting on tile from the bathroom that separated her room from the guest bedroom. How could she have forgotten that Bret had spent the night on the sofa just a few feet away from her door?

The image of Bret's naked body with hot water sluicing over his hard muscles flashed through her mind. She wondered if his body was scarred by the knife that had sliced his throat. Not that that mattered. No amount of scar tissue could reduce the man's sex appeal. For a moment, she allowed herself to imagine Bret, his tanned body still damp from the shower, coming through the door from the bathroom that they shared. In her daydream, he was returning to her bed to make delicious morning love to her.

Judging by her reaction to their one brief kiss, Milly knew that she had never experienced the kind of loving that a woman would share with Bret. And she never would. That kind of passion would demand a level of surrender that would truly test her hard-won independence. Anyway, the way that he had backed off after the high-voltage kiss they'd shared told her that he was no more interested in that kind of involvement than she was.

She stretched languorously and smiled to herself. It was such a lovely fantasy and she hated to leave it. She sat on the edge of the bed and prepared herself to face the reality of the day.

A soft knock at the connecting door broke into her daydream.

"Yes?" she called.

The door opened to reveal the object of her thoughts. He was wearing navy shorts and tugging white T-shirt down over his damp, well-developed chest and taut stomach muscles. She caught a glimpse of three or four inches of whitening scar that disappeared under the waistband of the shorts. For a split second, her eyes followed it down. From top to bottom, he was a thoroughly gorgeous man.

She met his knowing eyes. He hadn't missed her appreciation of his body.

"Morning, sleepyhead," he said. His approving smile told her that his quick glance had taken in her sleep-mussed hair and fairly revealing cotton knit shortie pajamas. "Oh, sorry, I assumed you were up and dressed when you answered my knock."

"There's a coffeemaker on the kitchen counter. Just push the On Button," she said, pulling the sheet over her legs, for whatever good that did. "I'll be dressed and starting our breakfast in five minutes."

"Don't get dressed on my account." His knowing smile got wider as he slowly closed the bathroom door. The sexy smile lingered in the air like the Cheshire cat's.

They were finishing an easy breakfast of bacon and eggs when her cordless phone rang. Bret drew it out of his shirt pocket.

"I'm expecting a call," he said and wandered out onto the patio talking into his hand. Milly cleared the dishes away into the dishwasher, freshened their coffee and followed him outside as soon as she saw him put the receiver back in his pocket.

"Jim tells me the men can be here within the hour to begin the upgrade of your security," he announced. "Do you want to be here while they do it or are you still coming to The Inn with me to see what Consuela can remember about Yvette's luggage?"

Milly made up her mind. "Give me a chance to finish my coffee and I'll go with you."

They sat down at a small round table just outside the sliding doors in the shade of the house.

"Good. We have some planning to do." Bret gave her a crooked smile. "Did you notice that I said, 'We'?"

"I'll begin," Milly said firmly. "As you are insisting on staying here and the work is being done on my locks today, you can move into the guest cottage when we get back."

"Agreed. I'll have to go to the office for a while to rearrange my schedule and pack a few necessities at my house. But I can do all that after I bring you back home. Take the organizer with you. We need to find out the name of the old man involved with the injunction against the construction of the retirement community. The calendar should tell us when Yvette met with him."

"I'll give Marie a call. She'll know his name." Milly was out of her chair and into the house before he had a chance to comment.

What a dynamo she was! All that energy packed into a body that was straight out of his dreams! He watched her slide the door aside and hurry inside. Her shapely hips swayed with unconscious seduction and her bound breasts bounced just enough as she moved. His palms itched to cup those sweet round breasts that he knew would nicely fill his large hands. He didn't know how long he was going to be able to resist the appeal of that body. Everything about her excited him but he was going to have to do his damnedest to keep his distance. He knew instinctively that Milly was not the kind of woman for a brief fling. When she gave her body, she would give her heart. Unfortunately, Bret's heart didn't work that way. It was a purely functional organ. It powered his body but apparently had never been programmed to feel more permanent tender emotions.

This urge to protect Milly must be a leftover from his training and the dozens of rescue missions he had been involved in. Nevertheless, wherever it came from, the urge was real and compelling. They had come much too close to losing their lives yesterday. He would do whatever he could to keep her safe.

"Smithfield. Robert Smithfield," Milly announced triumphantly. "Marie didn't know anything more about him except that he was a retired college professor. His family had owned a sizeable piece of property in what had been a relatively uninhabited area for years. When the professor inherited it ten years ago, he moved in and planned an isolated existence. He was definitely not happy at finding himself with a major development coming in right beside him. Marie stressed that he was difficult to deal with. But we already knew that."

He punched in the familiar numbers of Greco Associates, then Jim's extension.

"Jim," he acknowledged, "I'm glad you're still there. I need someone checked out. Robert Smithfield. I'm particularly interested in any connections he might have that could have done the job on the Jag."

Last night Bret had told his ex-boss about the destruction of the Jag containing Yvette's luggage and computer and Milly's conviction that her sister had been murdered. Although Jim had learned over the years not to dismiss the connection between him and Bart, Bret hadn't wanted to strain Jim's credulity by mentioning his own experiences with Yvette's ghost. Now, he briefed him on Smithfield's connection with Yvette.

Pressing the button to break off the connection, he turned to Milly. "I don't know what Smithfield would gain from Yvette's death but there's no denying his connection with that abandoned construction site."

At that moment a large white van bearing a discreet logo that announced "Greco Associates" pulled up to the house.

"Greco?" Milly asked.

"Jim Greco. He's the front office man. The other partners chose to be silent."

He opened the door to two men in gray coveralls and introduced them to Milly.

"I'll leave you to explain to Mrs. Brzezynski exactly what you are going to do to her house and why it's important." He flashed her an aggravating grin. He knew how much she resented having to admit that she needed the security system.

"If you don't mind, Milly, I'll take a minute to check with Will's nurse. I'm wondering how much yesterday's excitement upset him."

She allowed herself to be led around her own house and lectured by the two enthusiastic young men. When she finished, she found Bret waiting for her at her front door.

The pickup was gleaming black, shiny, and relatively new but still a distinct contrast to the sleek Jaguar that he had been driving yesterday. She told him so.

"Why the pickup?" she asked.

"Some days it suits my mood," he told her. "It comes in handy when I need to pick up a part and I can transport my tools easily when Kit decides it's time I tuned up her marine engine."

"That surprises me, too. I expected you to have more sophisticated hobbies. Sailing, golf, polo..." she teased.

He chuckled. "And wear a monocle, I suppose. I do sail a little. Play golf when Will insists. But I started tinkering with motors and marine engines when I was a kid. Will decided to let me take a few courses when it became obvious that I was going to 'learn by doing' on the family motors if he didn't give in. It got to be expected that I did the tune-ups on the boats and Bart's and my motorcycles when I was home."

Apparently indulging in pleasant reminiscences about motors he had known, he drove along with a little smile tugging at the corners of his sensuous mouth. "Besides, a pickup is more appropriate for some kinds of investigations."

"You do a lot of investigating yourself?" Milly couldn't help but ask.

"That end of the business isn't usually my responsibility," he said. "The pickup makes the right kind of impression when I turn up at a plant to design their security. But, don't worry, I'm not about to assign the investigation of Yvette's disappearance to anyone else."

"I'm beginning to appreciate that. It's amazing how much more clear-headed I feel after a real night's sleep. I'm starting to put the strange things that have happened into some kind of perspective."

"I wish I could. I'm still reeling a bit. But I've wasted far too much time asking myself why Yvette's spirit chose me to communicate with. We simply have to accept that we have both been told one way or another that Yvette is dead."

"All right, what else do we have to go on?" Milly asked.

"We know that there is a connection with the construction site. And that Yvette's client and Robert Smithfield were involved in a bitter dispute over the development there."

"Robert Smithfield sounds like our best bet," Milly mused. "But why would he kill Yvette? According to Ronald, she'd had the injunction removed. What further harm could she do him? But I'd still like to see how he reacts when he sees me. At least that will show us if he knows Yvette is dead."

"Okay. If we get away from the hotel in time, we'll drop in on Mr. Smithfield." Apparently, Bret didn't object to ideas that hadn't originated with him. "I'm curious about something else," he went on. "Either Ronald or Yvette was mistaken. Judging by the look of the site something else is stopping the construction. I hope that Jim Greco finds out something about that and turns up a Smithfield connection who is knowledgeable about explosives."

"I wonder what the police have found out about the bomb," Milly said.

"And I wonder if the guy who set it is satisfied he destroyed whatever records he was after." Bret turned into the entrance to the parking garage. "Well, we'll have a better idea what was in the luggage after we talk to Consuela. How's your Spanish?" Milly asked.

"Passable."

Milly doubted if anything Bret did was merely passable. "If she isn't comfortable in English, I guess you'll have to do the talking. I can barely make myself understood."

Unfortunately, when they caught up with Consuela on the tenth floor of The Inn, that plan had to be set aside. The maid took one look at Bret with his blond, ultra-Anglo looks and military bearing, ducked her head, and switched her vacuum cleaner back on.

"Maybe this would be a good time for you to go down to the lobby and call Deputy Purdy to see what they've learned about the explosive device," Milly said, tilting her head towards Consuela who had vigorously resumed vacuuming.

"I'll only be a few minutes," Bret said, without missing a beat.

Milly pulled the door partially closed behind him.

"Consuela," she said, moving around so that the woman could not help but see her.

The sturdy, dark-haired woman backed away from her keeping the vacuum cleaner between them. She pushed the door wide open with one hand, then made a hesitant kind of shooing gesture at Milly.

"I am Milly Brzezynski. The sister of Yvette Pelletier." That much she could remember from her High School Spanish. She pulled her photo ID out of her purse and shoved it at the maid. "See?"

The woman glanced at it but resumed vacuuming.

"Please. I need your help," Milly said in her halting Spanish. "About my sister."

Consuela turned off the vacuum cleaner and waited.

"She is...." Milly stopped, searching for the Spanish word. How did you say disappeared? Or lost? Or kidnapped?

"Gone," she said triumphantly.

Consuela took pity on her. "The concierge told me you were coming. About the packing."

"Oh, thank God! You speak English," Milly said with a relieved sigh.

"She didn't say you were police." The maid's tone was still hostile.

"We're not!" Milly assured her. "My friend has a private security business. But he is trying to help me find my sister. She checked into one of these rooms a week ago Sunday and disappeared. No one has any idea where she is. I need to know whatever you can tell me about the state of her room when you went in to pack it up."

Putting the facts into words brought all the anxiety back. Milly swallowed hard.

Consuela's dark eyes probed hers for a minute. Apparently, she found what she saw there reassuring.

"I remember," she said. "There was no mess. No one used the bed. Only one suitcase was open but nothing was unpacked. Not even a nightgown."

From the fleeting color that flushed Consuela's face, Milly suspected that the maid had done a little investigating of Yvette's filmy lingerie.

"The only thing out of its case was the computer."

"Was it plugged in?" Maybe Yvette had sent a message! Milly hadn't checked her email since Yvette's disappearance.

"Yes, in the electric outlet. Not the telephone."

So much for that idea.

"Do you remember finding any notes?" Milly persevered. "Anything she had written on?"

Consuela shook her head. "Only the little red book," she said. "It was on the seat of the armchair."

"Where did you put it?" Milly asked.

"In the suitcase. Then I zipped it up. I didn't touch anything else," she said a little too forcefully.

At that point Milly didn't care what Consuela had touched or even if she had taken anything from the suitcase. Yvette's journal was gone - blown to bits with the luggage and Will's car. And with it, the only chance they had to know what Yvette was thinking just before she was lured to her death.

She pressed a twenty-dollar bill into Consuela's hand.

"Thank you," she managed to say.

Bret was standing outside the door. He obviously had heard the last part of their conversation.

"Come on, love," he said, draping one arm around her shoulders, as they hurried down the hall to the elevators. "That wasn't what you wanted to hear but it's pretty much what we expected, isn't it?"

It was dreadfully hard not to dwell on the information they had lost but they did still have things to do.

"Were you able to reach the deputy?"

"No, but I played a hunch and called Flo. She had talked to her buddy Theo and he said that there is no doubt that the bomb was the work of a pro. As a matter of fact, they were able to retrieve a significant piece of the actual triggering device and are looking into the whereabouts of a couple of ex-cons who were known to have used it or something similar in the past."

The rest of the day continued with the same pattern of frustrations. They arrived back at The Grove to discover that the men from Greco Associates had installed the door alarm systems but had run into some problems with one of the components and wouldn't be able to activate the motion sensors until tomorrow or the next day.

"It'll be tomorrow if the replacement piece that's being couriered from Miami is compatible. The day after if we have to have it sent from the manufacturer," was the only explanation offered for the delay.

Milly held on to her temper until the men had gone, then whirled around and confronted Bret. "Well, then, we'll just forget the whole thing," she exploded.

"Nothing has changed, Milly," he stated quietly. "The new locks have improved your security a bit. But you still need the rest of it. I have to go in to the office for the afternoon. There's some paper work to deal with and a couple of appointments that I couldn't reschedule. You'll be here?"

What had possessed her to agree to have him involved with her life day and night?

"Yes," she bit out. "I'm meeting with Flo and Stu in about half an hour."

"Good. We can both get loose ends tied up and clear tomorrow morning for a visit to Mr. Smithfield," he said, scribbling something on the back of a business card. "My office phone number on the front. Cell phone number on the back. If anyone comes around who shouldn't be here, call me right away. Make sure you're with either Flo or Stu until I get back."

She didn't deign to answer but headed into the tiny den to pick up the papers she needed for the weekly planning meeting.

Bret didn't move.

"Well," she said, "aren't you going?"

"Not until you've locked up here and are safely inside The Grove."

"Bret, I'm a responsible adult." She glared at him for a minute then gathered up the folders she needed and bustled past him. "All right! I'm going!"

Bret hadn't even bothered to say that he would have to spend another night or two in her house. He would be simply be here exuding his own brand of male vitality and smiling that infuriating tolerant smile!

Robert Smithfield's neat square house sat at the end of a long, perfectly straight, paved drive bordered by precisely trimmed green foliage. Stretching out back of the house was an intricate pattern of flagstone paths, trimmed shrubs with colorful foliage, and pools complete with little waterfalls. The tiny, tidy house surrounded by sculptured landscaping looked like an illustration in a children's picture book. The short, round, baldheaded man who answered the door fit the picture perfectly.

The scowl on his reddening face, however, didn't. Mr. Smithfield looked anything but welcoming.

"Ms. Pelletier." He was forced to shout to be heard over the furious barking of what sounded to be a pack of little dogs inside house. He seemed to be contemplating slamming the door in her face but a lifetime of good manners stopped him. He eased himself out the door and closed it behind him.

"Josephine and Napoleon are not fond of visitors," he explained. From the look on his face, neither was Mr. Smithfield.

"As far as I am concerned, Ms. Pelletier, you and I have nothing further to discuss. You have certainly done enough to me. You have won. The injunction has been lifted. The dust and the noise will resume." A malicious, self-satisfied smirk curled his lips. "But the labor problems continue, don't they? The machinery is still idle. And quiet."

"I am sorry to disturb you, Mr. Smithfield," Milly began. "But I am not Yvette Pelletier. I am looking for her."

"What are you trying to pull now?" he blustered.

"Your mistake is understandable, sir," Bret interrupted. Milly could see that his respectful form of address appealed to the irate little man. "This is Mrs. Brzezynski. She is Ms. Pelletier's twin sister."

"And who are you?"

"Bret Thornton." Bret produced a business card. "I am a friend of both the twins. And we are trying to trace Yvette Pelletier's recent movements."

"You see," Milly inserted, "my sister has disappeared. No one has seen her since last Sunday. I remembered that she mentioned that she wanted to talk to you. I wondered if she did come back here to see you this week."

"Nonsense! I have no further business with Yvette Pelletier. And she has no reason to want to talk to me. For your information, she has never had any call to come to my home! Ms. Pelletier knows who my lawyers are." He reached for the doorknob and eased the door open. "If you'll excuse me, it's time to walk my dogs."

At the word "walk" the barking rose in pitch and two balls of fluff with sharp pointed noses tumbled out the door.

"Sit!" he roared.

To Milly's astonishment, they did.

"Good day. I'm sorry you wasted your time," he said. "I hope you find your sister," he mumbled a little awkwardly as they got back into the car.

They left him striding down the driveway with the two dogs trotting at heel beside him.

"You agree that he has no idea that Yvette is dead?" Bret asked when they were back on the highway.

"He was angry but not shocked to see me," Milly agreed. "And with that fat little body, he is all wrong to be the killer in my dream."

For the next twenty-four hours, even with Bret sleeping on her pullout sofa, Milly managed not to see him face to face for more than a few minutes at a time.

It took some artful dodging on both their parts. Bret visited his father, then went to the office where he put in time on a lot of things that could have waited or easily been done by someone else. Milly ignored Flo's protestations that she could handle all the preparations for the big reception that was coming up on Friday evening herself. She spent most of Tuesday double-checking everything that Flo had done.

Bret called The Grove at dinner time to say that he wouldn't be joining them because he felt he should stay with Will for a while. His father was becoming even more impatient with hospital restrictions on his activities, he explained.

"You'll be at The Grove all evening?" She knew it was not a question.

"Yes, in my office in direct communication with Stu and with Eva popping in every once in a while. Bret, why are we doing this? No one is after me."

"Milly, we're not sure why the Jag was bombed."

She cut him off impatiently. "And no one arrived to install the security. What's happening, Bret?"

"Sorry, Milly, I have to go. Will's doctor wants to talk. I'll be there in a couple of hours." With that, he hung up.

She didn't know how much longer she could take this house arrest she had accepted. Or her friends' concern. Ever since she heard about the explosion, Eva had hovered over her until Milly thought she would scream.

"So, tell me about your long day with the hunk." Eva slipped off her high heels and flopped down on the leather couch in Milly's office during a lull in the happy hour rush. "I'll bet he didn't lose any of his appeal when you got to know him better."

"Eva, Bret and I spent yesterday covering South Florida like the dew trying to trace Yvette's movements. There is no romance. None. Don't you have something to do in the bar?" she asked pointedly.

Eva ignored the question and downed a good quarter of the glass of ice water she had put on the end table beside her. "He sure is concerned about you. Don't kid a kidder." She took another sip. "I've seen the way you look at him when you think no one's looking."

"It's all in your head. And there's nothing in it."

Eva grinned at the old joke but was not to be deterred. "Are you trying to tell me that you have that sexy guy living in your house and you haven't even thought once about jumping his bones?"

"Eva. Party of six heading for table fourteen." Stu's voice rasped over the intercom.

Milly watched her friend slip into her shoes and dash back out to the bar. Eva could read her too well. She hoped that Bret wasn't aware of how often she had fantasized about doing just that. She didn't seem to have a lot of control over her imagination since Bret had burst into her life. And he would be back here again in a very few minutes.

They had sure been skittish around each other ever since that startling kiss. If she weren't one of the dancers, she'd find the way the two of them were square dancing around each other absolutely hilarious. But, like in a set pattern, they only got a few steps apart before they were drawn back together like two magnets. Oh, Lord! They had better get that security system activated soon. She didn't know how long she could pretend she wasn't attracted to him.

Bret arrived in the stated two hours with his charmer's face firmly in place. He joked with Stu, flirted with Eva and even spoke to Milly now and then.

Milly made her rounds of dining room and bar greeting old customers and making sure that new ones were happy with their treatment at The Grove. As she smiled and chatted, she told herself that she didn't want Bret to focus his attention on her. And that it was only natural that he should flirt with Eva. Eva was an attractive woman who responded nicely to compliments. She wished she could call back her own abrupt reply to Bret's comment that her green dress brought out the color of her eyes. The man made her so edgy.

"You don't have to charm me," she retorted, then regretted not making a more gracious reply when she caught a glimpse of hurt in his eyes.

"Can't help it," he drawled, turning away with a self-deprecating grin. "It's genetic."

She was surprised when he caught up with her about half an hour later.

"Why don't you join Flo and me for a nightcap, pretty lady with the green eyes?" There was an irrepressible twinkle in his eyes.

"Since you ask so nicely, I'd love to," she replied. There! That sounded as if she had been brought up to handle civilized conversation.

They had just seated themselves at Flo's table when Eva led a big, graying man in the uniform of the County Sheriff's Department to them.

"Look who I found," she said with a broad grin. "Thought I should bring him over to see if Flo can bring a smile to that face."

"Sit down, Theo," Flo said. "Bret, I mentioned my friend, Theo."

The two men shook hands. Theo did look particularly grim tonight, Milly thought. He usually looked slightly unapproachable but not like this.

After Eva took their orders, Flo reached over and laid her hand on Theo's arm. "Tough shift?" she asked.

"Just got back from the hospital," he answered. "Domestic call. The boyfriend beat up the kids, too."

"I'll bet you haven't eaten," Flo said. Milly and Bret exchanged glances. Flo saw food as the solution to most problems, physical or emotional. "Bring your drink, and I'll fix you something in the kitchen."

As most people did, Theo obeyed. "Maybe the next time we meet, she'll give us a minute or two to get acquainted," he said to Bret as he followed Flo away from the table.

"For a minute there, I thought this would be a chance to find out something about the explosive device," Bret said.

"If he knows anything about it, Flo will get him to tell her."

They sat quietly, toying with their drinks and listening to the elderly pianist improvise around an old show tune.

"He's good," Bret said.

"Tuesday night is jazz night," Milly said. "We try to get this man at least once a month."

That was about the extent of their conversation but Milly was surprised at how relaxed she was and how much she enjoyed having him with her. But she knew that if he touched her, this lovely secure feeling would vanish in a puff of smoke. She didn't trust herself to keep her distance.

They finally finished their drinks and Milly announced that she was heading for bed.

"Yes," Bret agreed. "It's been a long day. We can plan what we're doing tomorrow in the morning."

Finally, after several long hours of disturbed sleep, Milly drifted into the best dream of her entire life. She was relaxing on the deck of a beautiful boat that was a combination of Bret's yacht and The Sprite, watching the changeable blue of the moving sea. She could hear seabirds and smell the saltiness of the ocean. The motion of the boat was delightfully sensuous and everything was becoming slightly hazy and indistinct.

The color of the water gradually deepened into the blue of Bret's eyes. Then, she was gazing into them and he was lowering his head to kiss her. She reached for him but before his lips could touch hers, the dream began to unravel. She desperately wanted to hold onto it for a few more minutes, but the sunlight faded, the motion of the boat stilled and Bret's image dissolved into formless blackness.

She lay there in the dark limbo between sleep and wakefulness trying to will herself back into the dream. It was not to be. Instead, she heard the first faint notes of the dreaded saxophone. The music was different this time, more plaintive than strident. She tried to shut out the sound and concentrate on bringing Bret back but her willpower was no match for the haunting music.

As the volume swelled, it brought back the too-familiar scents and sensations of the nightmare. But not everything was the same. Tonight the blackness was not total. She could see that she was in the front seat of a car. The lights of the dashboard were extremely dim. The man's weight had her pinned against the car door. The acrid smell of his nervous perspiration and his cologne stung her nostrils.

Hard fingers were squeezing her throat. She beat futilely at his back with her left fist. Her right arm was trapped behind her. She had to get it free so that she could use both arms to push him off! No matter how she struggled, she could not dislodge those hands from around her throat. She couldn't breathe. Her vision blurred as she felt consciousness slipping.

Her right hand found the door handle. With a desperate burst of adrenaline, she twisted her body hard and managed to yank the handle and push the door open. She drew in a breath and screamed for help.

He hit her then. The side of her head hit the metal doorframe before she slid to the ground. The pain was bad, the blackness heavy. The intense blackness erased the pain. When she opened her eyes, the pain was even more agonizing. She was lying on coarse, damp earth. She couldn't raise her head. All she could see were his sandaled feet and hairy legs as he stood over her, cursing and holding something metallic in his hands. As she watched helplessly, he plunged the hypodermic needle into her thigh. The large diamond in the cobra's jaws caught the light.

Milly fought her way out of the nightmare, gasping for breath, shaken to the marrow of her bones, and fiercely angry.

It was... Damn! Who? She fought to bring back the dreadful scene but the nightmare had dissolved into the night.

Milly's shrill scream jolted Bret out of a semi-doze. Trying to sleep just a few feet from Milly's bedroom wasn't easy. Pausing only for the split second it took him to grab the revolver from under his pillow, he tore into her bedroom.

The first strands of daylight streaming through her window made it unnecessary to turn on a light. One glance told him that Milly was alone in the room. She was sitting up in bed with both hands around her neck and moaning.

"Milly, I'm here. It's all right. I'm here," he said. He sat on the edge of her bed and put his arm around her.

"Bret!" she whispered hoarsely. "Oh, Bret. I was there! I know what happened."

The horror of what she must have gone through was in her voice and in her pale, lustrous eyes. He pulled her trembling body into his arms and held her close.

"I'm here, love," he said, nuzzling the top of her head. "It's over now. You're awake."

"Hold me tight," she said, burrowing closer into his embrace. "Tonight was even worse. It lasted longer. He had his hands around my neck and he was choking me again and again. Then I broke away and screamed. Then he hit me and I hit my head on the doorframe and fell out of the car onto the side of the road." She raised one hand to rub her temple and seemed surprised that it didn't hurt.

"No. He didn't hit me," she realized. "He hit Yvette. I felt it at the time but it was Yvette he killed."

She was quiet for a minute before she spoke again. "I felt her life ending."

He would remember the horror and grief in that whisper for the rest of his life.

Her breath was hot against his bare chest. He couldn't prevent his body's automatic reaction but he shifted his hips in the hope that she wouldn't feel it.

"I saw the hand that held the hypodermic needle."

"A hypodermic?" That surprised him. Yvette's ghost had been bloody and dirty. He'd expected more violence rather than drugs.

"Yes," Milly leaned away from him so that they could make eye contact. "After I... Yvette...got the car door open, he hit...her. Her temple struck the door frame and she was knocked out for a minute. When she came to, she was lying on the shoulder of the road. She looked up long enough to see him plunge a hypodermic needle into her thigh. And there was something else. Oh, Bret, what was it? I have to remember."

"It will come back to you," he murmured.

She was trembling violently. "Then there was nothing...not even blackness." She wrapped her arms around his waist and pressed herself against him so tightly it was as if she wanted to be absorbed into his body. "She...died."

He had to kiss her. He needed to connect more deeply with her and take away the bleakness in her eyes. At the first touch of their lips, she moaned. His hesitant nibble on her luscious lower lip undammed the torrents of emotion that both of them had been attempting to hold back. He had wanted her from almost the moment they met and had dreamed about having her half-naked body wrapped around him like this. Their tongues met and tasted eagerly while his hands roamed and stroked the silky skin of her back.

"I want you tonight, Bret," she whispered.

And he wanted her. He knew that she desperately needed to be held and really believed that she was ready to be loved right now.

He let her feel his heavy erection against her belly. "You can tell how much I want you, love. But you're upset. I'd be taking advantage tonight. The nightmare has you so stirred up."

"No. No. It's not the nightmare that has me stirred up." Her gray-green eyes were almost slate gray with passion.

"When we make love, Milly, I don't want there to be the slightest question about why. What you experienced tonight was so emotionally wrenching that you aren't thinking clearly. You're not ready to take this step. You don't know how much I wish I could pretend that you would look back on our making love and chalk it up as necessary therapy. "

He gave her his best brave smile. "It would sure make me feel a lot better. But I don't want you ever to be sorry for making love with me."

He gave her one last hard hug then swung his legs off the side of the bed. As he sat up, Milly clutched his hand.

"Please, Bret. Stay." Her hypnotic pale eyes implored him.

"I can't just hold you, Milly. If I don't leave right away, we are going to make love. I'll be just outside your door."

He attempted to get to his feet but Milly did not release his hand.

"Stay with me," she said, in that husky voice that had cast a spell over him the first time he heard it singing about that old black magic called love.

She smiled slowly at him, then released his hand. Lost in her smile, he watched her get to her knees and tug off her cotton knit pajama top. Her breasts were beautiful, full, round, and definitely aroused. The nipples stood out from the pebbled areolas begging to be tasted.

Milly straddled him and guided his hands to her breasts. Once he felt their weight, he had barely enough willpower to say hoarsely, "Emilienne, love, are you absolutely sure? Because one more second and it will be too late to stop."

"If you stop now, I'll have to kill you," she said arching her back to present her breasts to him.

She wouldn't have to kill him. He would die. He had never needed a woman the way he needed Milly. And he was afraid that it wasn't a temporary state.

He was going to make sure that their lovemaking would be so wonderful that she could not have a moment's regret. He would make love to her slowly, deliciously, until every part of her body sang with ecstasy.

When he took one rigid peak in his mouth and began to suck gently, her low-pitched moan sent an urgent message right to his already rigid member and made him wonder how slowly he was going to be able to go. But he was going to give Milly a night to remember if it killed him.

Milly hadn't known she was capable of feeling so intensely. Every cell in her body was vibrating with intense pleasure and a space inside her that had always been hollow was swelling with whatever it was that she was feeling for Bret. She knew it couldn't be love. Love was the warm, permanent kind of pleasure she had shared with Buzz. This was wild and urgent but somehow essential.

This wasn't a time for thought! Every one of Bret's kisses ignited a little burst of sensation somewhere on her body, each one hotter than the other. The pool of damp heat low in her body was becoming unbearable.

"Bret!" she moaned. "I need you now."

"And I was sure you'd noticed," he said with a laugh. He nipped at the inside of her thigh. "I'm here!"

She reached down and tried to pull him up on top of her. "Inside me," she insisted. "Now, Bret."

"Oh, yes," he said. "Now."

Bret stripped off his briefs, knelt between her legs, then stopped dead. He spat out a fervent curse.

"Protection!" he said.

"In the bedside table," she gasped. "Hurry."

Bret's trembling fingers found the box, fumbled with the condom and, eventually, got it unrolled and in place.

The thought flashed through her mind that she hoped it wasn't too old. It was a fresh box that she had bought not long before Buzz was killed.

At this point, she didn't care if the condom disintegrated. All that mattered was that she and Bret come together as they were meant to do.

As if they had been making love forever, her legs wrapped around him and she reached down to guide him into her.

"Don't close your eyes, Milly," he said. "I want to see into them when we come together."

"Always giving orders," she sighed.

Then, with one powerful thrust, he joined them.

The incredible wave of emotion that swept through her brought tears to her eyes. This was right. This was what poets had been writing about for centuries. Bret's eyes darkened and mirrored the strong emotion she was feeling.

"So right," she sighed as her hips began the sinuous grinding counterpoint to his thrusts.

"Emilienne," he said and the time for words was over.

The intensity of her need built until she thought she couldn't stand it. Then Bret stilled his powerful body and stroked her while she pleaded for him to continue. As he began the escalating movement, the tension built even higher. She reached the ultimate peak and with a scream plunged into black free fall. The velvety blackness was immediately spangled by tiny sparkling fragments of light. She sank into the most marvelous relaxation she had ever experienced.

Bret followed her over the edge and collapsed on top of her. After a moment, he attempted to roll off her. She held him in place.

"Too heavy," he muttered.

"Stay," she said, the word bringing them full circle to the beginning of this amazing adventure. "I like to feel your weight on me."

They let the wonderful lassitude last for a minute or two longer. Then, with her still in his arms, Bret rolled over. Lying on top of him was good, too, but it was the first step of separation. Gradually, the world inched back into their lives.

Bret left her to deal with his ablutions and when he returned he hesitated by her bedside. She raised the sheet to readmit him to her bed. He slid one arm under her and placed her head on his shoulder.

"You pack an amazing punch, love," he said. "I'm still stunned."

Milly smiled into his fine chest hair.

"You have no regrets?" Bret actually sounded worried.

"How could I have? You're a wonderful lover. I'll never forget how beautifully you made love to me."

"That's you, Milly! You can't think that it's like that every time. I've never experienced anything like making love with you."

Somehow she believed him. They had been so much in tune. He'd been right there with her when she experienced her cataclysmic climax and seemed just as shattered by his.

"And we've just begun, love. I'm not letting you go anytime soon." He picked up her heavy braid. "Next time we make love, I'd like to feel your hair loose on me," he mused.

His low voice was beginning to take on a seductive overtone and, amazingly, she could feel him stirring against her thigh. Milly knew that if she turned to him and made love with him again tonight, she would be hopelessly in love with him. She had better call a halt while she still had some shreds of control.

She stretched lazily. That enabled her to move naturally an inch or two from his beautifully muscled body. Her fingers wanted to stroke his chest once more. She wanted to kiss the dreadful scar on his jaw and neck and the terrifying long one that must have almost killed him. It was hard to remember why she needed to distance herself from him. But she did.

"Let's not plan, Bret," she said, trying to sound rational about her totally irrational feelings for him. "Let's just let things happen. You were right earlier. We are both in a highly emotional state. Who knows how we'll perceive our personal relationship in a day or two?"

Bret stared at her in surprise. He looked bewildered by her abrupt turnaround, then he smiled and leaned over to press a surprisingly sweet kiss to her lips.

"Fine, love. I won't push. But don't pretend that this was a just casual 'kiss it and make it better' kind of loving. You and I might just find ourselves in this for the long run."

He got to his feet and strode, unconcerned about his nakedness, over to his briefs which lay on the floor where he had tossed them.

"Get dressed, Milly. We have some serious talking to do," he said, sounding a lot more like his autocratic self. "I'll put on the coffee and meet you out on the patio."

Then without a backwards glance he headed out of the room, carrying his underwear and leaving the door wide open behind him. Milly couldn't prevent a resigned smile as she watched him leave. Even giving it her best effort, she doubted if she would be able to keep many doors closed between them. He was too...too everything. Too dynamic, too attractive, too much a part of her already. She was afraid that a very special link had been forged in the heat of their passion.

The sun was just nicely up and moisture was pearling on the grass when Milly stepped out onto the patio. The ugly duo of reason and caution had begun to make themselves heard while she dressed. They told her she would be a self-indulgent fool to go blithely headlong into any kind of personal relationship with Bret. She knew so little about him. He didn't talk about his past except in vague generalities. She didn't know if he had ever truly loved anyone. She didn't even know if he had ever been married! How could she have slept with a man she didn't know?

How could she have resisted?

She should have.

Refusing to do any more debating with herself right now, Milly caught Bret's eye. His unabashed delight at the sight of her cast all of her very sensible reservations aside. She smiled back.

Two steaming mugs of coffee sat on the enameled tabletop and Bret was wiping the last of the dew off two of the patio chairs. When she sat down in the one closest to the edge of the swimming pool, he dragged the other close beside hers.

"I was tempted to forget I said I'd make the coffee and dive into the pool while I waited for you," he said.

She gratefully took a long swallow of the hot black brew. "You made the right decision," she said. "But you can use the pool any time. I usually have a swim in the evening before I turn in."

"Maybe tonight," Bret said no more than that, but his words conjured up a tempting scene.

She wished she could daydream for a while about a midnight swim with Bret. But the beautiful respite from horror that Bret's lovemaking had given her was over. She had to remember last night's dreadful nightmare and tell him exactly what it had revealed.

She cradled the mug in both hands and concentrated on her coffee for a moment, feeling his eyes on her. The silence demanded to be filled.

"I never saw his face," she began. "Not in any of the dreams. Even last night when I was trying to drag his hands from my throat in the dim interior of his car, I couldn't see his face. Only when he was in the act of killing me..."

"Yvette," Bret muttered, putting one arm around her shoulders. "He was killing Yvette, love."

Suddenly, she stiffened.

"What is it?" Bret asked.

"It's come back. The last part of the dream. I know what I saw. It was Ronald Wilson, Bret."

His eyes flew to her face. "Ronald! You're positive?"

"The hand that held the hypodermic was wearing that creepy pinky ring. I've never seen another one like that flat-faced snake with the big diamond in its fangs."

Bret sat back and sipped his coffee, lost in thought.

"If that's the case, then whatever it was that Yvette was advising Kit against was something to do with Ronald. The prenuptial agreement? Surely, Kit is too savvy to let him talk her into canceling that."

"Ronald is smarter than you think and, believe me, he can be extremely convincing."

"I wondered if you had some personal history with him." Bret had donned the bland look that she had already come to think of as his professional mask.

"A very brief history," she said. She might as well tell him. There was no point in trying to hide it. "And long ago. Ten years ago, actually. At the time, I was studying voice in New York and helping to pay my way by singing with a group. I met Ronald at a legal convention where we were entertaining and I fell hard. For a couple of months, he had me convinced that we would be married as soon as he finished his articling. However, next thing I knew, he had eloped with the daughter of the senior partner of the firm he was articling with."

"It still rankles, doesn't it?" he said. Bret felt an uncomfortable twinge of doubt. He didn't know much about dreams and what caused them. Could her subconscious have planted that clue to Ronald in her dream because of some deep-seated resentment?

"It does not!" Now he was telling her what she was feeling. "I admit that I was devastated at the time. I was hurt and terribly ashamed that I had fallen for his line. But that's long in the past. When I saw Ronald on Sunday for the first time in ten years, I felt absolutely nothing, Bret."

"You pretended you didn't know him. I have to admit, that bothered me at the time."

"I was annoyed. It was childish but I wasn't going to let him maneuver me into reminding him that we certainly had known each other. I hope you didn't think I was in collusion with Ronald to keep our long-dead relationship from Kit." She paused. "I still can't figure out why he would bother lying to her about that."

"There is something fundamentally wrong with a man who would see another woman when he had the chance to have you in his life."

Milly looked to see if he was joking. But he looked perfectly sincere.

"I wonder if he's capable of being faithful to anyone," Bret went on. "Maybe he's been cheating on Kit and is trying to keep her convinced of his admirable character. All Kit ever told me about Ronald was that he was a lawyer from Atlanta. I don't even know what kind of practice he had there."

"Yvette ran into Ronald again when she was getting accredited by the Florida bar association. Ronald happened to be attending the same series of seminars. I think she said he was doing mostly trial work. Criminal stuff. I wasn't all that interested at the time. Then, a few months later, she told me she had introduced him to Kit and they were getting married."

"I wish I had asked more questions over the past few months, but I mostly avoided spending time with Ronald. He's always been a bit slick for me. Criminal law, you said," Bret mused. "That kind of practice wouldn't have much repeat business. Sometimes a long-term client can come in handy when you are doing a background check. However, criminal law would certainly provide Ronald with the right kind of contacts."

"Some who might know how to attach an explosive device to a car's ignition," Milly suggested.

"According to Kit, Ronald has opened a new office in Palm Beach and is doing mostly Schofield Pharmaceuticals business." Bret was desperately trying to remember any bit of background he had on Ronald Wilson. "I think she said he was an only child. And a widower."

"That's right. Ronald told me when you and Kit were below getting our picnic lunch on Sunday that his first wife, Jenny, died five years ago." Milly froze with her coffee mug halfway to her lips. "I wonder how she died. Oh, Bret, the person Yvette wanted you to warn was Kit! Not me, at all."

"That makes sense. Yvette knew me only as Kit's cousin. I had never met you, Milly. She must have meant me to warn Kit. And I haven't been thinking about her at all. I don't even know where she is at the moment."

"It shouldn't be urgent as long as the prenuptial is still unchanged. What would Ronald gain if she died now? For that matter, what did he gain by killing Yvette? She wasn't the only lawyer in the world and apparently she and Kit had come to some kind of compromise agreement." She felt like screaming in frustration.

"I wish we could simply ask her. But what would I say? 'I saw the brand new husband you're crazy about kill my sister. Oh, yes. I saw his ring. In a dream'," Milly said, rolling her eyes at how ridiculous that sounded. "It's even hard for me to believe it!"

Bret put his hands on either side of her face and looked into her eyes. "I know that you saw it, Milly. And, I may be crazy, but I believe you experienced your sister's murder right up to the moment when she died. And you saw Ronald's cobra ring.

"I'll get Jim to put a couple of men on this. We need any information he can find on Ronald - his business, his finances, his social life. Do you know anything about his mother? He seems to be concerned about her. Or maybe that's only part of the good boy image he's trying to project."

"He never mentioned her when I knew him," Milly said. "While you're at it, ask your partner when that security system is going to be installed."

"That's the least of our worries," Bret muttered as he turned to leave.

Milly wondered briefly if anyone was actually trying to get the missing component. Actually, when it came right down to it, she'd rather believe that she had no choice but to have Bret stay in her home a little longer.

Bret's telephone calls took longer than he expected. By the time, he returned to the patio, Milly was sitting on the edge of the pool dangling her feet in the water and delving into the functions of Yvette's electronic organizer.

"According to her calendar, Yvette met with Robert Smithfield three times in the last two months. So what? We know he didn't kill her."

"He is still the tie-in with the construction site," Bret agreed. He pulled her to her feet. "That water does look tempting but we have too much to do today to have a swim now. I want to check that Kit is all right. Then see if the police have discovered anything about the source of the explosives.

"Oh, and I was just speaking to Marie. She says she's been through the papers at the office and hasn't been able to find any hint of where Yvette might be. She thinks we should go through Yvette's New York apartment to see if she left any clue there."

"We can't tell her that wherever Yvette is, it isn't any place she intended to visit," Milly said.

"I did pump Marie a bit about Ronald's life before Kit. She isn't happy that I refused to tell her why I wanted to know but she did come up with an address of his old law office.

"But the biggest news is that my brother, Bart, is arriving this afternoon."

So that was why Bret was looking so much more cheerful.

"The mission he was on was at such a crucial stage that they weren't able to notify him of Will's heart attack until this morning. I told Jim I'd pick him up in Atlanta this evening."

Milly knew how important it would be to Bret to see his brother again.

"How'd you like to go to Atlanta with me? We could see what we can learn from the people in the mall where Ronald had his office."

"What's the point of checking his Atlanta business? Yvette didn't have any connections with him in Atlanta."

"I don't know where Yvette came across it but I have a hunch that she knew something that Ronald couldn't afford to have broadcast."

"Do you mean broadcast to Kit? Do you figure it's a woman? Or something more serious - some kind of crime?"

Something very like pain flashed across Bret's face. "Evidence that he's been cheating on Kit might be the bigger threat. To some people losing the kind of lifestyle that Kit's money offers would be worse than a possible jail term."

Milly had the distinct impression that Bret had been badly hurt by someone who had thought that he was no more than a ticket to a glamorous lifestyle. How odd when his wealth seemed more of a stumbling block than anything else as far as she was concerned.

"What time is our flight?" she said with a grin.

"What, no argument?" He raised his eyebrows in mock astonishment. "Whenever you say, love. You're looking at the pilot."

She refused to let him see how impressed she was by his casual attitude to using a private plane. "Your plane?" she asked.

"It belongs to Will's development company," he replied. "How long will it take you to make arrangements to be gone for the day?"

"Already done," she told him. "Flo talked to Eva and she agreed to take over my duties for the next little while. Eva and Stu together can handle anything that comes up."

"Are they an item?" He really liked the possibility that Stu's interest lay elsewhere.

"Eva would have no objections. And I think Stu might be more interested than he realizes."

By midday, they had landed at the private airfield where they left the Thornton plane, rented a car, and were driving into the Atlanta suburb where Ronald's old law office was located.

Bret wheeled the medium-sized white Ford into the parking lot of an unprepossessing strip mall. At ground level the mall consisted of a convenience store, a unisex hairdressing salon, a small bar and grill, a take-out pizza outlet and a real estate office. The windows in the storefronts looked clean but the whole place was a few years beyond a needed face-lift.

The second floor advertised a family dentist, a massage therapist, a law office and a martial arts club.

"Not exactly Palm Beach," Milly said, then realized how snobbish that sounded. "I mean, Ronald wouldn't want to be forced to come back here."

"Let's try L. R. Swanson, Attorney, first." Bret was out of the car and standing on the cracked sidewalk by the time she opened her car door. By his posture and casual smile, a person would read him as nonchalant and relaxed but Milly was beginning to realize how little his outward appearance meant. Something in the set of his jaw told her how eager he was to talk to the lawyer.

The door to L. R. Swanson's office was open. The little vestibule contained an unmanned desk and three vinyl chairs. As they entered, a tiny gray-haired woman emerged from the inner office.

"Have a seat," she said. "My secretary is off sick today and I just this minute got in from the courthouse."

She disappeared, then reappeared almost immediately in the doorway. "You might as well come straight in," she said.

The office was jam-packed with filing cabinets and overfilled bookshelves. She plunked herself down behind a surprisingly clear desk and focused her shrewd blue eyes on them.

"Now, what can I do for you?" she asked briskly.

Bret decided that no kind of cover story was going to fool this woman. He handed her his business card. "I'm Bret Thornton and this is Milly Brzezynski. I'm with Greco Associates."

"Lena Swanson," she said and extended her hand to both.

"Greco Associates," she said under her breath, reading the card carefully.

"We were hoping to consult Ronald Wilson about a tie-in with a case he handled last year. This is the address we were given. Are you still associated with him?"

"Actually, I do strictly real estate and probate work. Ronny and I were never associated. His office space was taken over by the Tai Kwon Do Club when he gave up the lease. I believe he has opened an office in Palm Beach. Just a minute. I think he left a card with me." She rummaged in her top desk drawer and triumphantly pulled out a business card. "Here you are. His new address. I imagine he will still have his files with him. Even though he's no longer doing criminal work."

"Do you know who might be handling any of his on-going work here in Georgia? Or does Ronald return to handle that himself?" Milly asked.

"I don't know. We didn't talk much when he was just down the hall and I haven't seen him since he gave up the office about six months ago. Sorry I can't help you." She stood up. "Suzy in the salon downstairs mentioned more than once over the years that she cut Ronnie's hair. She might know."

The meeting was clearly over. They thanked her and headed for the neighborhood Cuts 'n' Curls.

"What exactly are you hoping to find, Bret?"

"Ronald wouldn't have been celibate for the five years since his wife died. I want to find the woman in his life."

"You think this Suzy can tell you something?"

"She's going to tell you." Bret loved the way Milly's pale eyes flashed when he made plans for her. "I mean, if you would consent to have your nails done or your hair washed or something, you might find out what we need to know. After all, if the man sat in her chair once a week for years, Suzy would probably know more about him than most people."

"That will take at least half an hour. That is, if she can take me right away." Milly was examining her fingernails as she spoke.

"I can make some calls from my cell. I want to check on Kit again. I can make the purpose of the call Bart's arrival tonight. They have always been close."

Fortunately, Suzy's shop was completely empty and she would be delighted to give Milly a manicure. She was a trim, cheerful woman in her mid-forties. From her freckled skin, Milly assumed that the color of her beautiful, dark red hair was natural.

"You're sure you don't want me to do your gorgeous hair? I'd love to get my hands on that!"

"Every stylist I've ever met has wanted to take her scissors to it," Milly told her. "But I like it this length."

"Couldn't I try some fancier braids in it? I could coil them around your ears." She pursed her full lips. "Or on top of your head?"

"Just the nails today," Milly said firmly.

Suzy was interested in everything about Milly's life. Milly thought it would be a good idea to tell her enough about herself to start the woman chatting about herself. And then her clients.

"Oh, you know Ronny? Isn't he wonderful?" she gushed. "I really miss him. He used to come in every Friday, like clockwork." She sighed.

"He married a friend of my sister's," Milly told her.

"I heard he'd remarried," Suzy said. "It was so sad when his first wife died. Ronny was a wreck for a long time. It was so sudden."

"Was she in an accident?" Milly asked.

"No. She was diabetic and had to be in hospital quite often to get her insulin balanced. She was fine for quite a long time but she must have got casual about the diet. The last time she went into shock, they couldn't save her." Suzy went on at some length about the sadness and unfairness of it all. Ronnie being such a nice man and so good-looking.

"I wished I was ten years younger, I'll tell you," she said. "That man kept himself in such good shape." She gave a low breathy whistle. "I swear he worked out at that health club three times a week. At least."

"The Tai Kwon Do Club?"

Suzy laughed. "Oh, no, A real health club."

"Somewhere around here?" Milly probed.

"Uh uh. Way over the other side of the city. I'm not sure where," Suzy told her. "Here hold your hand in under this. It'll dry the polish faster. My, that's a pretty shade on you. You're sure you wouldn't like a pedicure?"

Hiding her disappointment that she hadn't been able to get any more specific information from Suzy, Milly smiled. "I do love that color and I wish I had time to have my feet done today. But my friend will have done his calls by now and be waiting for me as it is."

She had paid for the manicure and added a generous tip when Suzy exclaimed, "I remember now! The name of that health club was on his duffel bag. The Firm. Isn't that a strange one? Ronnie really liked it. I guess he belongs to a tonier one now that he's in Palm Beach. Well, y'all come back now."

Milly returned Suzy's bright smile with a sincere one of her own and dashed out to tell Bret that she had a lead.

Bret was lounging against the car, obviously enjoying the sunshine as he waited for her, when Milly hurried out of the beauty shop towards him. She had never been able to understand her friends when conversation at all-female gatherings turned to appreciation of male physiques. Surely grown-up women could find more to appreciate in a real man than his body. However, at moments like this, the sight of Bret, hard-muscled and golden, stopped her breath.

"That smile tells me your hour in the Cuts 'n' Curls wasn't a waste of time," he said.

She threw herself into his arms and gave him an enthusiastic hug. "Bret, I've got the name of a place where somebody is bound to know him! The Firm!"

He added a quick kiss to the hug before he asked, "All right, I'll bite. Which firm?"

"The health club he belonged to is called The Firm. I don't know the address but it's at the other end of the city according to Suzy. And Ronald used to work out there at least three times a week. Believe me, Suzy thought 'Ronnie' was wonderful and paid close attention to everything he said and did."

"Well, I know you are wonderful," he said, giving her a hard squeeze. "Let's find that address. We should have time for a fast scouting expedition before we have to pick up Bart at eight o'clock."

A quick check of the yellow pages that miraculously were still in the phone booth at the end of the mall provided the address. Half an hour later, they were strolling through the big glass doors of The Firm.

Large, eye-grabbing photographs in the front lobby illustrated each of the muscle groups. The Firm Glutes glorified perfectly formed male buns sheathed in red lycra. There were two photos for The Firm Abs - one of a tightly muscled male midsection and one focused on the golden ring attached to the smooth skin of a slender female's navel. There were several posters of superbly developed male and female chests titled The Firm Pecs.

Bret gave a low whistle. "Great product advertising," he said.

"It's demoralizing," Milly said.

He gave her a quizzical look.

"Makes me realize that I really have to lose ten pounds," she muttered.

"Are you out of your mind? You don't actually believe you should look like those skinny teenagers in the photos? Emilienne, my love, you have the kind of figure that men dream about."

She would have given him an argument but the tall, blond receptionist whose large Plexiglas desk dominated the lobby had left her computer and was reaching out a hand to shake Bret's.

"Welcome to The Firm," she said. Her smile displayed perfect white teeth while her eyes busily assessed them. She included Milly in the smile. "I'm Valerie. How can I help you?"

Bret returned her smile with a convincing but artificial one of his own. Milly realized that Valerie would be best left to him.

"You're the one who's interested in the facility, sweetheart," she said with a bored sigh.

"My fiancée and I would both like to see what programs you have to offer," he said, stressing the "both" and giving Valerie a conspiratorial wink. "The weight training for me and maybe some swimming for Milly."

Valerie's smile grew broader. "Weight training is my specialty. I'll page Mark from the pool. He can give Milly a run-down of the swimming and aquacise sessions. I'll show you the training area, myself."

"I don't want to take you away from your work," Bret said. "I don't mind exploring on my own."

"Lately, giving a quick tour has been my job, too," Valerie told him with a cute little shrug.

"Employers want more and more from us these days." Bret looked understanding. Milly wanted to kick him.

"Oh, The Firm is great to work for," Valerie hastened to assure him. "It's just that one of our weight room staff died suddenly a couple of weeks ago and we're making sure that we get just the right person to replace her."

"We'll meet back here, Milly," Bret said when the fit and smiling, dark-haired male equivalent of Valerie appeared.

Mark had a wonderful smile that he used well. He sounded sincerely glad to make her acquaintance and delighted to show her the pool area. Milly admired the size of the pool and the flanking whirlpools. He described the sessions that she might be interested in.

"The aquacise is very popular," he said. "There are business women's classes that meet in the evenings, if that suits you."

"Oh, I don't have a job yet," she said. "My fiancé has just been transferred to Atlanta and we are trying to make a decision about where we want to live. Bret feels that it's important to be near his health club and Ronald Wilson recommended this one."

Mark's handsome face clouded over. "We haven't seen Ronnie for quite a while," he said.

Milly pretended not to notice his cool tone. "Oh, you know Ronnie!" she crowed. "Isn't he a riot?"

"Actually, I didn't have much to do with him," he said, leading her out of the pool area to the windows that overlooked a quarter mile running track. "Most of our members like to warm up with a jog or a run around the track. The two gyms in the center of the track are booked most hours of the day and night so there's always something to look at while you jog."

He seemed determined to change the subject. Milly refused to let him.

"Ronnie couldn't say enough about this place. He said the staff was wonderful."

Mark snorted. "Too wonderful!"

"Why would you say that?" Milly didn't have to feign her surprise.

"He was seeing a good friend of mine. One of our instructors."

"He dropped her, did he?" Obviously, the woman in question was someone important to Mark.

"She died." Mark took a deep breath. "Sorry. He's a friend of yours. I shouldn't have said anything."

"That's all right. Ronald isn't really a friend - more of a social acquaintance, I'd say. He can be funny at a party but I never knew anything about his private life. I'm the one who's sorry that I reminded you of your loss."

"I don't need much reminding. Nancy hasn't been gone that long." He was silent for a moment, then turned a bright smile on her. "Well, what do you think? Do any of our programs interest you?"

When Milly didn't answer immediately, he added, "What do you say I give you a couple of guest passes?" They were heading back to the reception desk. "You and your fiancé could come back and spend the day with us and try out some of the facilities. Then you could make a more educated decision."

"I'd like that," she said.

Bret was still listening to the receptionist's animated sales pitch when they reached the desk

"Mark has offered us a free day pass to the club, Bret," Milly said, sliding a possessive arm through Bret's. "I think we should come back."

"Fine with me, Sweetheart." Bret flashed a triumphant grin at Valerie. "This club could be right for both of us. We'd better hurry if we're going to meet Bart's plane."

As soon as they got into the rental car, Milly filled him in on what Mark had told her about Ronald's involvement with the dead instructor.

"Ronald seems to leave a lot of dead women in his wake. I wish I'd had the nerve to ask Mark how she died. But I could see that he was sorry he'd said as much as he had."

"I couldn't get the smiling blonde robot to tell me anything," Bret admitted. "The minute I mentioned Ronald's name, she closed her mouth like a steel trap. For some reason, she hates his guts."

"We have to make sure we don't come back on Mark's day off. If I give him a few hours to try to sell me on The Firm, I think I can get him to talk about this Nancy. At least, I'll get her last name."

"That information would be in their personnel files. Shouldn't be too hard to get. I'll give that a try tomorrow." Bret looked at his watch. "Looks as if my plan to take you someplace special for dinner is not going to work out. We'll be lucky if we have time to get a burger at a drive-thru before we meet Bart."

"That's fine with me. We've used the time well. We know a lot more about Ronald than we did this morning. We didn't learn anything that even hinted why he killed Yvette, though." Milly stared bleakly out the window.

"I have a hunch that Ronald's womanizing is at the root of it all. It sounds as if he was still seeing this Nancy while he was courting Kit. Maybe Yvette caught wind of that."

"I'm sure that Yvette hasn't been to Atlanta in years. I talk to her once or twice a week and always know what part of the country she's in." Milly threw up her hands in disgust. "I wish we had her journals."

"If she did find out about Nancy, it wasn't until after the wedding or she'd have at least tried to stop it." Bret scowled at the road ahead. "The timing is all wrong. Maybe we're on the wrong track."

With the heavy traffic out to the airport, they didn't even have time to hesitate at a drive-thru for a burger before Bart's plane was due in. They dashed into the arrivals area on the stroke of eight. Twenty minutes later, Bart came down the corridor towards them. Milly had no doubt who he was. He was thinner and his blond hair was a trifle shorter than Bret's but the same deep blue eyes beamed at them. Even being a twin herself, Milly found the sight of the two men in the same place uncanny.

"Bret!" the mirror image said, as he clasped his brother in a hard embrace. The two men looked intently into each other's eyes for a moment. Then Bart turned his attention to Milly.

"Yvette!" he said, sweeping her into his arms and planting a solid, friendly kiss on her mouth. "Great to see you again. What are you doing with this ugly guy?"

Milly didn't know what to say. Many times in the past, she had been mistaken for her sister and played along for a mild joke. But to play that part right now would be obscene.

"I'm not..."

Bret came to her rescue. "Unhand my woman," he said, slipping his arm around her waist. "This is Milly, Yvette's sister."

Determined as she was never again to be any man's "woman", Milly had to admit that she liked the solid feel of Bret's strong arm claiming her.

"This is wonderful." Mischief danced in Bart's tired eyes. "Why don't we set up a double date with Yvette and see how many people pass out or, at least, swear off drinking when they see the four of us."

"Let's get out of here," Bret said, picking up his brother's bag. "We can talk on the way to the air field where I left the plane."

Bart picked up on the unusual tension in Bret's voice and flashed him a quizzical look. Whatever he saw there made him drop the subject of Yvette.

"How is Will?" Bart asked.

"He's fine, Bart. He gave us a real scare but he's recuperating. He went back home again today, I understand. You can see for yourself."

"I have been in transit for more than thirty-six hours and I have an urgent need for real food and a solid eight hours sleep in a stationary bed that's long enough to stretch out on," Bart stated. "Besides, Will would be asleep by the time we got there and I wouldn't be able to see him until morning anyway. Tell you what. I'll stand you both to the best dinner in Atlanta."

Bart's imploring smile was almost as appealing as Bret's. Whatever possessed their parents to name twin sons Bret and Bart? She would have to ask.

"And a room in the best hotel in the city. You could share with me, sweet lady, or with Bret. Or have your own room even. Please, Milly," he pleaded. "This is one exhausted, starving man you are toying with."

"Toying? I haven't said a word." Milly couldn't help returning his smile. "He's your brother, Bret. You deal with him," she said.

"You're a tough negotiator," Bart said with a sigh. "All right. If you don't want to go to a restaurant, I'll go so far as to settle for a room service supper. Stop coaxing me," Bart went on.

Bart would play the clown if he were dying and Bret suspected that he had come close to doing that on this latest mission.

"Are you all right?" he asked. "Jim refused to tell me what you were up to. All he would say was that you were at a delicate stage of negotiations and couldn't come home when Will had his attack. It was more than that wasn't it?"

"My hosts just couldn't bear to see me leave. Hey. I'm fine and back in the good old U.S. of A.," Bart said. "Not to worry, Bret. I haven't lost anything vital. A little baby fat." He beamed another megawatt smile at Milly. "But women prefer their men mean and lean, don't they, Milly?"

Bret could see from the gray tinge of his skin that his brother was at the end of his endurance. Milly didn't look too averse to the idea of staying over in Atlanta until morning. He met her eyes. She gave a tiny nod and that endearing little shrug that he was becoming fond of.

"Why don't you call Flo to tell her we'll be at The Grove midmorning tomorrow. All right, Bret, choose your hotel. You can call and make reservations."

It was almost ten o'clock before they got to eat their evening meal at a linen-covered room service table in the three-bedroom suite Bart had booked in the "best hotel in Atlanta".

None of them did justice to the meal.

Bart looked regretfully at the large portion of steak that remained on his plate. "I've been looking forward to that piece of meat for weeks and now I can't finish it."

They poured their coffee from the insulated carafe and took their cups to the comfortable sitting area. Bart settled himself in the maroon velvet-covered wing chair and Milly and Bret sat on the love seat.

"So, Bart, where were you?" Bret asked quietly.

"Africa. But it's not an amusing story." Bart frowned. "If you'll forgive me, I'd just as soon not talk about it yet."

"You two want to talk more freely," Milly said, getting to her feet and stifling a yawn. "I'm ready to go to my room anyway."

Both men said simultaneously, "Don't go." Then burst out laughing.

"Sometimes you get us in stereo," Bret said. "We don't sing or dance but our comedy routines are famous." He reached over and clasped his brother's hand. "It's good to have you back, bro."

Bart swallowed hard. "Thanks," he said. "Seriously, Milly. I don't have any objection to talking in front of you. I'm still too close to the situation even to tell Bret what happened. But tell me. You and Bret are being very strange about Yvette. What is going on?"

Milly sat down again.

"Yvette has disappeared," Bret said, before she had a chance to speak. "She had a seat on a morning flight from Palm Beach to New York ten days ago. She didn't make the flight. The evening before, she arrived at The Inn near the Palm Beach airport and no one has heard a word from her since."

"She didn't check out?"

"Apparently, she didn't spend the night there," Bret said.

"Of course, you've notified the police," Bart said.

"Now that it's pushing two weeks since she disappeared, they are beginning to take it seriously. But as there was no sign of violence in the room, at first, they thought she'd simply taken an impromptu extension on her holiday. Milly and her aunt and Yvette's law partner have been on their case a lot and they are making an effort to find her."

"What do you think happened?" Bart asked. All traces of lassitude had disappeared as he focused all his attention on Bret's words.

"She's dead," Milly said quietly. There was not a trace of doubt in her voice.

He whipped around to stare at her. "What makes you so sure?"

Bart was going to think they had both lost their minds. "You had better get comfortable, bro. This is going to take a while. Maybe you should begin with your dreams, Milly."

"Dreams!" Bart snorted and shook his head in disbelief. "Bret, I don't have the energy for this. No fooling around. Just tell me what happened, for God's sake."

"Dreams," Bret repeated firmly. "The dreams are important. Try to keep an open mind."

He hated to put Milly through this again and she looked as if she'd rather be any place in the world than here. "Tell him, Milly. It's the only way."

She squeezed her eyes shut for a moment, took a deep breath, then opened them to gaze directly into Bart's eyes.

"I'm not a person who dreams a lot, Bart," she began. "And I never remember much about the dreams I have. But a week ago, I had a dream that was too real. I was sure that I was actually being choked to death. A little before midnight, I woke up gasping for breath and my throat hurt terribly. I couldn't stop calling Yvette's name."

As Milly described the nightly dreams with their increasing clarity of detail, she became more and more distraught. Her grip on Bret's hand was becoming painful. He wanted to tell her she didn't have to continue but her story was obviously convincing his skeptical brother. He watched the doubt gradually fade from Bart's eyes.

"Milly, I'm so sorry. No one should have to endure that kind of physical and emotional pain." He turned to Bret. "I had a similar kind of experience when you came so close to buying it in St. Thomas last year.

"But Ronald? Not that I've ever liked the guy. I wouldn't be surprised to hear that he'd been cheating or stealing. But killing? I can't imagine him killing Yvette. Not doing it himself. He'd be more likely to hire someone to do the killing."

"Maybe he didn't have time to make the arrangements," Bret said.

"It was Ronald. I saw his ring. He knocked her unconscious. Then finished her off with some kind of injection." Milly's carefully measured speech showed that she was running out of patience. "You can believe it or not Bart. It's up to you."

Bart exhaled a long slow breath. "Well," he said. "Welcome to the Twilight Zone."

"You don't know the half of it," Bret told him. "The rest of this story is going to require a real stretch of the imagination. I've heard that saxophone that Milly heard in her dream. In broad daylight, in the middle of the day. And..." He couldn't meet Bart's eyes. "This is the kicker. You're going to have real trouble with this. I have actually seen Yvette's ghost. More than once."

"Come on! I warn you. This is not the time to try to pull my leg. My sense of humor is nonexistent tonight."

Bret swore under his breath. "Don't be an idiot! Do you think I would joke about this?"

Bart passed the back of his hand over his weary eyes. "Bret, don't do this to me. I know, with Milly so upset, you wouldn't joke about seeing Yvette's ghost but I can't believe what I'm hearing. Somehow, since I saw you last, you've developed a strange imagination."

"Just shut up and listen, Brother Who Knows Everything. My first experience came on Monday night after my regular visit to Will. I was driving by that abandoned retirement community site just beyond Pioneer Grove when the sound on my stereo went crazy. The country song stopped dead and a wailing saxophone started up. It sounded to me like one of Stan Getz' best riffs. At the same time, the temperature in the cab of the pickup plunged. Then, when I got to the south boundary of the property, everything returned to normal. I put it down to some kind of electronic glitch in the stereo. But that was just the beginning."

By the time Bret had finished, Bart was wide-awake.

"So," he said, "you're both convinced that Yvette has sent messages to Milly, indicating that Ronald is the murderer. However, Bret is the only person she has appeared to, as far as we know. She has told him to warn Milly of danger. She's not very helpful, is she? Why do you suppose she hasn't given you one solid fact to give the police?"

Bret opened his mouth to speak but his brother held up his hand to stop him. "Don't interrupt. My brain tells me that you've both lost your grip on reality. Nevertheless, my gut feeling is that these weird things really did happen. Maybe I'll have to see for myself. Excuse me now, I'm going to climb into that unmoving bed for at least eight hours. Maybe a night's sleep will clear my head."

With that, Bart headed towards the bedroom where he'd left his bag. "Oh, good night, Milly," he called over his shoulder.

"I guess there's no point in telling him that she never appears when there is anyone else around," Bret said.

He reached for her then and she came naturally into his arms and raised her face for his kiss. This kiss was different from the others they had shared.

The spark of passion was there, all right, but they were both content simply to take comfort from each other. They sat for a while just holding each other, not wanting to say good night.

Finally he pulled her to her feet and began to walk her towards her bedroom. "Come on, love," he said. "Time for bed."

Milly was so tired that she was weaving slightly.

"My room? Your room? Or both?" he asked.

"Both," she replied. "For a few good reasons."

He was sure they were reasons he didn't want to hear. Before she could say more, Bret kissed her soundly.

"See you in the morning, love." He wheeled and quickly entered his own bedroom.

He was surprised to find Bart, clad in one of the hotel's complimentary terry cloth robes, leaning against the doorjamb of the bathroom.

"About the ghost," Bart said, then rubbed his eyes. "My God! We're calmly discussing a ghost. Anyway, unless both you and Milly have lost your minds, there is something going on at that construction site. And if that is the case, you and I had better make an attempt to contact the only source of information again. Tomorrow night we'll try to talk to the ghost. All right with you?"

"Fine. But up until now, she has only appeared to me. We can go but I don't think we should tell Milly beforehand. I don't want to get her hopes up."

Bart yawned widely. "You forget. I'm the charming twin. Yvette will talk to me."

If he hadn't thought it would knock his brother flat, he would have given him the playful shot in the arm that comment deserved.

As it turned out, he and Bart could not seek out the ghost at the site the next evening. From the moment his feet hit the floor, nothing worked out according to plan.

Bret pulled on the clothes he had worn yesterday. As he gave himself a quick shave with the disposable razor provided by the hotel, he whistled softly. Milly would still be asleep and he was looking forward to kissing her awake. He liked the thought of her, warm and tousled from sleep.

As he crossed the living room towards her bedroom, he caught sight of Milly sitting, fully dressed, looking out the window.

"Morning, love," he said, leaning over to kiss her. Milly turned her head slightly so that his kiss caught her on the cheek.

"Good morning," she said.

From the way she refused to look him in the eye and continued to gaze out at the uninspiring view of rooftops, he deduced that she was having serious, if delayed, morning after regrets.

"I'm ready for some breakfast," he announced. "Shall we go down?"

He knew he sounded a little too hearty but he didn't dare ask her if anything was the matter. Something obviously was.

"You go ahead, Bret," she said. "I have already eaten."

That sounded even worse. She had been up for hours deciding that their lovemaking had been a dreadful mistake. He tried to tell himself that it was just as well. Their relationship had moved much too quickly. Hell, it had galloped.

He didn't want to but he left her there staring at nothing. He did some thinking of his own while he ate breakfast.

Milly was wrong. Their lovemaking had been too special to treat like a forgettable misstep. He was no novice and he had never experienced anything like it. Bret was determined to explore what they had found. Maybe if they made love again, they would discover that the magic had been a fluke. He smiled at that little piece of self-delusion. But he and Milly were going to be lovers again and, if he had anything to say about it, again and again. He wasn't going to let her slip away from him.

When he returned to the suite he hoped he would find Bart up and about; however, Bart's eight-hour sleep looked to be turning into twelve.

"If he's that exhausted, we shouldn't wake him," Milly said, with a resigned sigh. "I haven't read the paper yet anyway."

She moved to the sofa and began to sort the newspaper on the seat beside her.

"Can I have this section first?" Bret asked, reaching for the Sports section, and taking it to one of the club chairs a few feet away.

The strained silence was broken only by the sound of turning pages. But a person can only concentrate on the newspaper for so long without at least making a comment to the only other person in the room.

"All right, Milly. Why..." Bret began.

"Bret, we have to talk." Milly said at the same time.

They both laughed uncomfortably.

"Oh, hell, Milly," Bret said, getting up and moving to sit beside her. "I can see that you're determined to put the brakes on. I guess you're right. We've become too close, too fast. But please don't lose sight of the important part. The closeness is real. I don't want to lose it."

Damn the man! He knew exactly how to deflate her. In her mind, she had been rehearsing a really good rejection speech about the unnaturally sensitive state of their emotions and misread signals that had led them to share the best sex she had ever had. She was going to thank him sincerely but insist that it would never happen again.

But Bret had zeroed in on the real truth of the matter. There was much more to their relationship than good sex. How much more, who knew?

"Bret, we can't." She didn't know how to say this. He was looking at her as if her words were vitally important to him. "I mean, I can't handle a relationship right now. I wish we could have met a year from now. But not now."

She threw up her hands and looked at him helplessly. She was doing this so badly.

He began to reach for her but stopped himself and grinned sheepishly. "That's how this whole thing started, wasn't it, love? I can't help wanting to comfort you when you are upset," he said. "But, I do understand. I'm a little stunned and uncertain myself. The attraction between us is overwhelming. We'll just have to cool it."

"Is that possible, if we keep spending so much time together?"

"We'll make it work. I'm making you the boss. I'll let you draw the line this time."

The corner of his mouth twitched a little. She couldn't prevent a tiny half smile at the absurdity of this conversation.

"You'll let me be the boss?" she said.

"I'm handing over the reins of power. I'm serious, love. What do you want me to do?"

"To start with, you can stop calling me 'love'," Milly exploded.

"Done!"

"And no hugs."

He pulled a face.

"And absolutely no kisses," she said firmly.

"I can do that," he said, exhaling a deep breath. "The first kiss has to come from you, boss."

"And don't call me, boss."

"Okay." Bret began to count off on his fingers. "No Love. No Boss. No hugs. No kisses. Got it. Can we shake hands occasionally?"

"Only if we come to an agreement," she replied with a smile. Bret would be so easy to fall in love with!

Bart finally woke up but things did not move along any more quickly after that. Because they were late when they got to the airstrip, it took much longer to file a new flight plan than Bret had anticipated. As a result it was almost one-thirty by the time they landed in Palm Beach.

When they dropped Milly off at the restaurant, they discovered that a sous chef and one of the kitchen help had been injured in an automobile accident the night before and Flo desperately needed Milly in the kitchen. Bret had no worries about leaving her for a few hours if she was with Flo. Besides, he thought grimly, Stu had volunteered to peel and chop vegetables and would be sure to look out for her.

His and Bart's brief visit with Jim at Greco Associates lasted much longer than he had anticipated. Jim had read the debriefing that Bart had undergone in Paris and apparently needed a few points clarified. Then Bart informed him that he was probably going to turn down the offer from a new government agency and was seriously considering becoming an associate in Greco Associates. The three men had embarked on a long enthusiastic discussion of new directions the company might go with the addition of Bart to the mix.

When they finally arrived at Will's house, Anna greeted them at the door. Tears filled her eyes as she wrapped Bart in a wordless embrace. Then she held him at arm's length.

"Look at you! You need a keeper," she accused. "And your brother looks only a little better. You are both staying for dinner. Come see your father." With that she turned on her heel and led them to the ground floor den that had been converted into a temporary bedroom for Will.

Bret was surprised to see Kit there. She was talking animatedly to Will who was laughing at something she said.

"The boys are here!" Anna announced. "They'll be joining us for dinner. Are you staying, Kit?"

"I was hoping you'd ask. Ronald's mother has had another crisis and he has gone up to see her," Kit said, as she got up to meet them.

When she greeted Bret with a kiss, he could sense the tension in her. He wondered why she wasn't with her new bridegroom visiting his sick mother. He'd like to think that Kit was annulling her marriage and not going to have anything further to do with her murdering husband. No. It had been obvious at various pre-wedding activities that the two women were not fond of each other. That's probably all it was.

With this marriage to Kit, Ronald had gained everything an ambitious man could want. He had moved up into the top levels of a major law firm, belonged to the best golf and sailing clubs, and lived in one of the ocean front mansions of Palm Beach. Ronald wouldn't harm her. At least, not while the prenuptial agreement was in effect.

"Good to see you, Bart," Kit said. Her welcoming smile faded to a frown when she saw how thin and tired he looked.

"Are you all right?" she asked.

"Not to worry. Just too little sleep," he said, leaning over to kiss her cheek.

Bret wondered at the awkwardness between them but Will demanded the spotlight.

"I'm fine, too," he said, testily. "How long are you staying this time?"

"Maybe for good," Bart said.

"That's what your brother said. I'll believe it when I see it."

Bart sat down and gave them the sanitized version of his mission. "I'm sorry that I couldn't get here sooner, Will. I was involved in negotiations to free some hostages. There were women and children involved and the terrorists threatened to kill them all if the government changed negotiators."

What he had told Bret and Milly earlier but didn't add now was that the terrorists had decided that Bart would be a more valuable hostage than a group of useless women and children. There had been some extremely tense days and nights before the backup plan had been implemented and he was rescued.

"Well, I'm glad you finally made it." Will extended his hand. "Now, Bret, what's this I hear about somebody blowing up my Jaguar in the hospital parking lot?"

Bart wheeled around. "What?"

"Someone blew up Will's car?" Kit exclaimed at the same time. "When? You were driving it on Sunday, Bret."

"Not long after we left you. Luckily, I used the remote to start the engine. No one was hurt."

"But you could have been," Will said. "What have you been up to lately? I thought you were out of that business."

"I am."

"Fill me in here," Bart snapped. "I haven't been home twenty-four hours and I discover that Yvette has gone missing and now someone is trying to kill you?"

"Now, calm down. I don't know that anyone wants me dead," Bret said. "I can't think what anyone would have to gain by killing me. The police seem to think it was an act of random vandalism."

"Sure," Bart muttered. "Have you got any of the lunatic fringe on your case these days, Will?"

"Everybody loves me," Will said with his expansive salesman smile. "I haven't stepped on any sensitive toes in a long time...that I know of."

"Then I expect the police are right," Bart said, with a look at Bret that clearly said, "And I want to hear all about this later."

"Enough unpleasant talk." Anna arrived just in time to change the subject. "Time to eat."

"Where's Mrs. Foster?" Bret asked, glad of the diversion and grasping desperately at a new topic.

"She's having dinner with her son. She'll be back later this evening." Will accepted his cane from Kit. "The woman can't stay away from me."

"You are her job, you old fool," Anna snorted.

"I prefer to think she stays because of my charm." He winked at Bret. "Let's go eat."

With everyone making a solid effort to avoid topics that might distress Will, the meal passed quite pleasantly. It was obvious, however, that the company was tiring him and after they finished dessert, he announced that he was on his way to bed.

"I have to admit that I'm not quite up to par yet. But next time you come for dinner, Kit, I'll whip us up one of your favorite Grasshoppers. We can relax and sip and chat."

"I doubt that you'll ever be allowed to have heavy cream again," Anna told him.

"Maybe I'll just have the crème de menthe and crème de cacao then," he retorted.

"We may both have to switch to something else, Uncle Will," Kit told him. "I'm finding that just one Grasshopper makes me awfully sleepy these days. But we will sit and chat."

"Are you staying here, Bart?" his father asked.

"Not tonight. I thought I'd bunk in with Bret. Do some catching up," he replied.

Will would have certainly been surprised to learn what they were actually planning for the rest of the evening.

"Mind if I go along with you?" Kit asked. "Ronald won't be home until late and I'd like to hear what the two of you have been up to."

"I'm not staying at my house right now," Bret warned her. "I'm spending a few days in Pioneer Grove."

"At The Grove," Bart said, arching one eyebrow.

"So that's how it is." Kit's teasing grin made him realize how unnaturally all of them had been behaving. "I'd like to see Milly again."

"All right, Kittle, come along," he said.

"That will be like old times," Anna said with a satisfied smile. "The three of you heading out together. Bret, Bart and Kittle."

"I'll follow you," Kit said, once they were outside.

"I didn't see your little red toy when we came in," Bret said.

"I'm driving Ronald's car. He insisted on buying the Rolls and now he takes my lovely little car every chance he gets and leaves me to drive the black beast."

"Everyone should have your troubles," Bart said.

Obviously they were not going to accost the ghost that night. Bret couldn't say that he was sorry. He could see, however, that his brother had keyed himself up for the experience and was disappointed. Bret pointed out the sign advertising the projected development.

"Doesn't look like much," Bart grunted as he peered out the window.

"This is where the music usually kicks in," Bret pointed out as they crossed the southern boundary of the site.

"Nothing," was Bart's only comment.

"I told you that I've had the experiences only when I was alone. No. That's not quite right. Milly was with me one time when we heard the sax." He paused. "And the next time we passed there was a van following us and we didn't hear anything."

"You figure Kit's car has spooked the spook?"

"This joking is compulsive, isn't it? Have you thought of getting professional help?"

"What do you say?" Bart ignored his comment. "Do we come back later?"

"Let's do it tomorrow night. They have a big anniversary party booked at The Grove and Milly will be too busy to think much about where we are."

"This close surveillance you're doing sounds to me like more than concern about Milly's safety. How serious are you about her?"

Bret could feel his brother's gaze burning into him.

"I'm not sure." He had been asking himself the same question. "She has made it very clear that she's not looking for a long term relationship. And I'm not about to get burned again."

"You're not suggesting that Milly is anything like Sandra, are you? Sandra was a self-centered, shallow social climber. I never understood what you saw in her. When she came into a room, she didn't look for people. She looked for a mirror. Milly seems to be a capable woman with her feet firmly on the ground. She pays attention to people. If she decides that you are the man she wants, your money and social position will have very little to do with it."

Bret chuckled. "She's her own person, all right."

"Damned sexy, too. I've never known you to get so involved with a woman, Bret. Certainly not this fast."

"Lightning strikes fast," Bret said. "Did I say that?"

They both laughed. But he had said it. Worse than that, he knew it was true. He wasn't in danger of falling for Emilienne Brzezynski. He had done it. Damn.

When they joined Milly in the bar, she was polishing glasses and chatting comfortably with Stu.

"Tell me it isn't true," Stu exclaimed. He closed his eyes, then opened them again. "There can't be two of you."

"'Fraid so, Stu. This is my brother, Bart. And my cousin, Kit," he added as she slid onto a bar stool beside Bart.

"Courtesy cousin only," Kit told Stu with a smile. "I am really not related to those terrible twins. You can trust me."

"My daddy told me never to trust a woman who said I could," Stu responded with an appreciative smile. "But I'll make an exception in your case."

"Not related?" Milly raised her eyebrows.

"Will was married to my mother for a while," Kit explained. "The marriage didn't take but the uncle/niece relationship did. And, lucky for me, it came with two hell-raising cousins."

"I think it's time we sat down and had a drink, cousin," Bart said. "You said we had some talking to do."

Kit grabbed at Bret's hand and said to Milly, "I would like to talk to all three of you if you don't mind."

"Just give me your orders and I'll join you with the drinks in a minute," Milly said.

"I'll have a glass of white wine," Kit said.

"Just a draft for me," Bret said. "Your corner booth?"

Bart indicated that he would have the same and followed Bret to the table.

Milly arrived almost immediately with their drinks, and waited for Kit to speak. Kit didn't waste any time with preambles.

"I'm concerned about Ronald," she said. "He hasn't been himself since the wedding. He's short-tempered and preoccupied and seems to be avoiding me. The minute I mention that I'd like to visit Uncle Will, he says that's a great idea because it will give him a chance to do something he really needs to do - work at the office or visit his mother or some other thing.

"I offered to go with him tonight but he said his mother told him having me around upsets her. You'd think I was the one who makes her eat food that throws her blood sugar off."

"Mother-in-law problems can put a strain on the best relationships," Milly said.

"I don't think that's it. His mother's attitude is nothing new. Ronald definitely has something on his mind. And it's not me."

"Do you think that he resents your cutting your honeymoon short to come back because of Will's heart attack?" Bret asked. "He could be trying to pay you back for relegating him to second place."

"That's possible." Kit stared into her wine glass for a moment. "But there's something else. This morning a policeman dropped by while we were having breakfast. He wanted to ask Ronald about some woman who had committed suicide in Fort Lauderdale. They found Ronald's office phone number on a slip of paper under the telephone in her hotel room."

Kit was on the verge of tears. Milly reached out to her but Bart was there first. He put his arm around Kit's shoulders and said, "There could be a lot of reasons for that, Kittle."

"Ronald insisted that her name didn't mean anything to him but that he'd look it up in his files. He was pretty sure that she had never been a client but she might have gotten his name from someone he had defended."

"Do you remember her name?" Milly asked. How many dead women was Ronald associated with? This couldn't be the recently deceased aerobics instructor from The Firm, could she?

"Let me think." Kit shook her head dismally. "It was one of those half-comical names like Ramsbottom or Bottomsley, I think. I was too shocked to think that the police were there in my breakfast room asking rude questions about my wedding night to listen very carefully."

"Is that when this woman died?" Bart asked.

"Yes. On our wedding night," Kit told him. "So Ronald couldn't have had anything to do with it. But the policeman was really unpleasant. He asked me some very personal questions. Ronald told me I didn't have to answer anything. But I started remembering things."

"Oh, sweet little Kittle, let me guess," Brat said with a resigned sigh. "The minute the police left, you hit Ronald with a major inquisition, didn't you? And he took objection to it. Probably stormed out of the house."

"Well, the letters were pretty suspicious," Kit said defensively.

"Letters?" Bret asked.

"A couple of letters that looked as if they had been written by a schoolgirl arrived the week before the wedding. You know the kind of writing. She hadn't dotted the 'i's with little hearts...but she probably thought about it. Anyway, they were addressed to Ronnie Wilson. He insisted they were from a former client who was trying to convince him to defend her again but that he had refused the case. I guess I shouldn't have brought that up again this morning."

"I don't see why not!" Milly wished that she could tell Kit what she knew about her precious Ronald. "Any woman would wonder what he was up to."

"I feel so guilty doubting him like this. After all, I promised to love him and honor him. That means I should trust him, I guess. But this isn't the first time over the past year that I wondered if he might be seeing someone else. He always convinced me I was imagining things."

Kit pushed her hair nervously off her face. "Milly, you must think I'm some kind of ditz, telling you such personal stuff. But Yvette is the only friend I can talk to honestly. And I can't get in touch with her." Her eyes glistened with unshed tears. "I'm sorry. I don't know what I expect you to say."

Milly reached over and took both of Kit's hands in hers. "Maybe that I know how much Yvette cares about you and that makes you important to me. If I can help in any way...even if it's just to listen, I'm here."

"Thank you." Kit took a deep breath and went on, "Yvette tried several times to talk me out of marrying him, you know. She told me that he cheated on you while you were dating a long time ago."

"Kit, we weren't married. We were together for two months ten years ago. That's insignificant ancient history."

Kit looked her straight in the eye. "You denied that you knew each other the other morning on the boat." She had obviously come to the same conclusion as Bret had.

"Pride. He pretended he didn't know me and I refused to remind him. It was childish but it was the equivalent of yelling, 'Liar', sticking my tongue out and waggling fingers in my ears. I wish now that I had done that. It would have been more dignified than going along with his lie."

She demonstrated and the ensuing laugh released much of the tension.

"I'm sorry to unload this on you," Kit said. "But we've been married less than three weeks and I don't know what to do. I don't seem to do anything right as far as Ronald is concerned. You two know how I hate fighting. Maybe I should go away on my own for a while."

That sounded like a bad idea. Yvette had told Bret to warn Kit of the danger.

"Why don't you stay here?" Milly suggested. "Our guest cottage will be empty for another day or two." She hoped that Bret had caught the implied dig at his security company's slowness.

"Tell you what, Kit." Bart placed the glass containing his half-finished beer firmly on the table. "I've decided to be your house guest while things are awkward with Ronald. You have lots of room and I promise not to intrude if your relationship gets back on track."

"Yes." Kit's eyes brightened. "That would work. You could be a buffer."

"What happens if Ronald decides he doesn't want a buffer and tries to kick him out?" Bret asked.

"It's still my house." The way Kit lifted her chin and glared at Bret made Milly realize that Ronald wouldn't find his new wife easy to dominate. "The only part of the expenses that Ronald looks after is Gord's salary."

"Gord? Is he new?" Bart asked.

"Gord Ingles. He's new to my household. He's been Ronald's driver and general gofer for years," Kit said impatiently. "But, of course, you can stay, Bart. I want you there."

"Well then, Kittle. Hand me the keys. I drive the Rolls tonight. And I want a comfortable bed and a midnight snack."

Kit grinned as she dug in her purse and handed him the keys. "I suppose you'll insist on brownies and ice-cold milk. I can provide that. But only if you promise to stay within the speed limit on the highway."

"Well, I might be willing to compromise on the temperature of the milk," Bart said, hustling her out of the bar. "Say good night to the nice people, Kit."

Bret's gaze as he looked after the disappearing couple was thoughtful.

"She really has always been like a sister to you both, hasn't she?" Milly said softly.

"I always thought so," Bret said.

As planned, at eight o'clock on Friday evening, Bret met his brother at Will's. On the drive from The Grove, he hadn't seen or heard anything to suggest that Yvette's spirit still lurked around the construction site. He was afraid that their mission was doomed to disappointment.

True to his promise not to leave Kit unprotected, Bart had convinced her to spend the evening with her uncle while he and Bret went off on some undisclosed "business". There were definite advantages to having a reputation for doing the kind of work they had done in the past. One was that people assumed that if you didn't explain where you were going, it was because you couldn't. However, he thought ruefully, in their wildest guesses neither Will nor Kit would ever speculate that they were off to interrogate a ghost.

Ronald's Rolls was pulling up to the front door as Bret arrived. Had the honeymooners made up? Then Bret saw that the driver was not Ronald. A thin, middle-aged man with a long, dark ponytail was sitting behind the wheel.

Kit and Bart got out of the car and waited for Bret to reach them. Kit brushed a kiss on Bret's cheek and called to the driver.

"Gord, this is Bart's brother, Bret. And this is Ronald's assistant, Gord Ingles."

Bret went over and extended his hand in greeting.

Gord reached out the window to accept it and said quite pleasantly, "Never would have guessed the relationship. Confusing though. With the names."

"My mother had a thing for TV Western heroes. Are you coming inside?"

"No. I have a couple of errands but I'll be back before they're ready to leave."

Bret raised one dark inquiring eyebrow at Kit as the Rolls pulled away.

"Ronald insisted that Gord drive us," she explained.

"Everything okay?" he asked.

"Not really but we're being civil. I'm glad Bart is there. Ronald hasn't complained but he is not happy about it."

"That's understandable," Bret said.

Bart said nothing.

He and Bart ducked in long enough to tell their father they were just passing through and left Kit with him.

"Don't get your hopes up," Bret said once they got on the highway. "Nothing happened when I passed the site on my way down."

"I suppose we do have to give it a shot." Bart definitely seemed be having second thoughts. "But, I have to tell you, Bret, I'm feeling more ridiculous by the minute. Where I should be is with Kit."

"Fill me in on the situation at Kit's," Bret said. Bart was anything but relaxed but he did look a bit healthier than he had when he got off the plane.

"Not wonderful. But it could be worse," Bart said. "Ronald has been home only long enough to sleep since he stormed out of the house yesterday morning...and that was in a guest room."

"Some honeymoon," Bret commented.

"Yeah," Bart said with some satisfaction. "Kit is still angry and very confused about why he is reacting this way. But I'm glad she hasn't questioned why you and I are so concerned about her marital problems. Because there is no way in hell that I'm going to leave her alone to wait for the bastard."

Even though Bart questioned the existence of the ghost, he apparently didn't doubt what Milly had told him about Ronald being Yvette's killer.

The rest of the drive was silent. As they neared their destination, Bret sensed his brother's understandable uneasiness. He was either about to encounter a ghost or was going to have to accept that his twin brother had lost his grip. Bret hoped they'd see or hear something to reassure Bart about his sanity. Bart had been fidgeting and casting surreptitious searching glances at him ever since they left Kit at Will's. It was a measure of how nervous he was that he had not made one wisecrack since they left West Palm Beach.

"Open your window." Bret didn't know if that would do any good but the window had been open the first time he encountered the ghost.

"You've developed a liking for bugs?" Bart grumbled, but opened his window anyway.

Bret had prepared himself for a no-show. But, as the pickup crossed the southern fence of the construction site, he felt the first clammy tentacles of cold air on the back of his neck. Something was going to happen after all. Given the way Yvette had faded out the last time he had seen her, he had been afraid that her spirit was gone for good. His eyes flicked over to Bart.

Bart stiffened perceptibly as the first icy current drifted in through the open window of the pickup. He gave an exaggerated shudder and grimaced back at him.

"Unusual weather we're having!" To say that Bart's impersonation of Bert Lahr's Friendly Lion was shaky would be too kind.

Suddenly, the rapid-fire delivery of newscaster on the twenty-four hour news station stopped in mid-sentence. The silence was like a vacuum, compelling and waiting. The saxophone delayed a full ten seconds before it began to fill the void with the familiar riff. The music did not have the force of the first few performances Bret heard but it was intense enough to make Bart sit bolt upright.

"Christ! Bret," he breathed. "It's happening."

Although he still could see no sign of a white figure among the shadows, Bret pulled off onto the shoulder and came to a stop.

Turning off the lights, he peered intently into the gloom. Nothing moved. Finally, he indicated to Bart that they should get out of the truck.

Having Bart with him made this a little less terrifying. The two of them moved a few feet from the pickup and scanned the dark site. In the pale light of the fingernail moon, large tarp-covered piles of lumber and concrete blocks loomed. Silent hulks of tractors and cranes added distorted angular limbs to the surreal landscape. Still there was no movement. Not even a breeze stirred the dried grass on the clumps of earth. The only sound was the faint wailing of the saxophone from inside the cab of the truck.

"Nobody home." His brother's quip lacked verve.

Something caught the corner of Bret's eye. Over there, by the bulldozer, about a hundred feet away.

"There," he whispered, pointing at a vacillating point of light. Some glowing pale shreds of fluorescence seemed to be wavering across the broken earth.

Bart's hand flashed to the back of his belt where he would normally have kept a weapon. When he realized what he was doing, he gave Bret a self-conscious grin.

Bret could understand his brother's reaction. Both of them were out of their element here. He took a deep breath, then started to move cautiously towards the luminous whirling wisp. Bart followed as close as a shadow.

They had taken only a few steps when the amorphous glow popped up directly in front of them. Suddenly, it took the shape of Yvette's semi-transparent face. Some of the floating shreds of light could be mistaken for arms and shoulders but no one would mistake this apparition for a live woman. Her face still held its elfin shape, but the lips were pale and the large eyes were empty. She opened her mouth but no sound emerged. The floating banners that were her arms beckoned to them to follow her.

"Yvette! We need your help," Bret croaked. "He's going to get away with it."

The movement of the tattered banners became more urgent.

Using every bit of courage he could muster, Bret forced himself to follow deep into the site. His brother was silent but Bret could sense him moving along close behind. As they moved, the wisps of fog he was following slowly disintegrated until they were almost invisible. Finally, the being stopped at the edge of a large excavation and pointed down into it. He could barely make out the outlines of what appeared to be several large tarpaulin-covered mounds of building materials.

The being emitted disjointed fragments of sound as if it were trying to speak. However, the hollow keening sound formed no actual words this time, only something that could have been interpreted as, "erse" or "urse" or even "hurts". Having made that useless pronouncement, the swirling fluorescent fog vanished.

Bret stared at the empty air for a second, then down into the dark excavation.

"Is there any point in climbing down there to check out those dark piles of materials?" he asked.

Bart's face was a pale blob in the faint moonlight.

"We don't have a flashlight," Bart whispered hoarsely.

That was a good enough excuse. He'd sure rather leave it to the police to discover what he was pretty sure they would find under one of those tarps.

"Right!" Bret said. "Let's go."

Giving up all pretense of bravery, they ran for the truck as fast as the rough ground allowed. The tires spat bits of earth and Bret cursed as the pickup slewed, then straightened enough to wheel back onto the highway.

"If it helps your self-esteem at all, Bro, this doesn't get any easier the second or third time around," he said when he thought his voice would be steady enough to speak.

Bart shook his head slowly from side to side. "I don't believe it," he repeated again and again.

"It's a safe bet that Yvette was trying to point out where her body was buried," Bret said when he could gather his thoughts. "But what are we supposed to do now? Call the police and tell them that a ghost told us where to find her body?"

Bart snorted. "Fat chance! I know how much attention I'd pay to a couple of kooks who told me that. I'd check their blood alcohol levels first. Then try to find out what they'd been smoking."

"Probably the best way to get the police there is with an anonymous telephone call," Bret agreed. "I can't believe I've sunk to this. Not only seeing ghosts but acting like a gutless wonder who's afraid to stand behind his statements."

"I don't see that we have much choice. The police will act a lot more quickly on an anonymous tip than they would on the word of a couple of self-admitted crazies," Bart said.

A minute later, Bart broke the silence to say, "I know something about the saxophone music, though. I heard it before."

Startled, Bret asked, "When?"

"When I was driving Kit home in Ronald's car last night, I played the CD that was in the stereo."

Bret hit the steering wheel with the flat of his hand. "And that corroborating evidence proves exactly nothing to anyone but us!"

A few miles down the road, Bret pulled up to a phone booth in the lot of a darkened service station and made his brief call. Although he wished he could warn Milly that the police would be contacting her, it would be best if she didn't appear to be expecting their visit. The most he could do for her was to be by her side when they broke the news.

And he was going to be there. The delay in installing the security system today had been legitimate. The component they needed actually was on back-order. However, he was going to make sure that part didn't arrive any time soon. Milly's attitude yesterday morning had said clearly that she wished that they had never made love. If he let her, she would pretend that it had never happened.

But the vivid memory of Milly's passionate kisses wouldn't allow him to accept that they were never going to make love again. For the time being, he wasn't going to crowd her but she wouldn't be able to take a step without finding him right there beside her. He almost laughed when he thought how that would drive her crazy. Until they found out exactly what had made Ronald kill Yvette, he couldn't be sure that Milly was safe.

Thank goodness she would be busy for most of the evening with the anniversary party. Besides, the Grove had a group playing in the piano bar on

Friday nights and stayed open until after midnight. Milly had promised to stay there until he returned. Much as he didn't like the thought, he knew that Stu would look after her until he got there.

He dropped Bart off at Will's and broke a few speed limits getting back to The Grove. The way her eyes lit up when she saw him was gratifying but she still managed to find tasks that kept her from spending very much time with him until she and Stu had finished their usual closing routine.

"Ready to go home, sweetheart?" Bret asked her cheerfully.

She froze him with a look. "When is that security system going to be finished?" she said. But he got the distinct impression that she was only going through the motions of rejecting his presence.

"Soon." He'd better not try to warm up the atmosphere tonight. Tomorrow was another day. "I'll be out of your house soon, Milly."

But not out of her life. And from the softening he saw in those lustrous eyes, she knew it.

On Saturday mornings, Milly usually slept in because she knew she would be working late that night in the piano bar. However, like everything else in her life, today was different. Flo was still short staffed. She'd found a replacement for one of the kitchen helpers but the sous chef was under doctor's orders to stay off another day. That was why Milly found herself once again peeling and chopping and stirring sauces with Flo instead of enjoying a brisk swim and a leisurely breakfast on her patio.

She took another purple eggplant from the pile, peeled, and proceeded to dice it for tonight's ratatouille. The good thing about this turn of events was that she could avoid Bret for a few hours. He had offered to help out but Flo told him in a few choice words what she thought of amateurs in her kitchen.

She had tolerated Stu yesterday because she was desperate but today she was keeping both men out.

If Bret didn't have her so off balance, Milly would find the way Bret and Stu bristled when the other was around kind of amusing. Bret obviously thought that Stu was interested in her romantically. He couldn't know that it was Yvette who had always owned the bartender's devotion. Stu was protective of Milly but there had never been the slightest spark between them.

Bret was another story. Talk about sparks! She had never been this wildly attracted to a man. She tried to put it down to emotional turmoil. But why try to fool herself? She was in real danger of falling deeply in love. The crux of the matter was that she could lose all the autonomy she had painstakingly built up over the years. It had taken ten years to become a self-sufficient individual.

She hadn't realized until she was twenty-two years old that she'd been taking the easy route all her life. Yvette had always been the dominant twin. She was happiest taking the lead and Milly was always content to follow. The separation from Yvette when Milly had left New York after the fiasco with Ronald had been extremely difficult for both of them.

However, it had shown Milly just how little she had ever relied on her own judgment. Traveling alone and singing at little clubs and resorts all along the Atlantic seaboard had forged her backbone.

Her friends would have been surprised to learn how much her marriage to Buzz had helped her growth into an independent woman. Sure, she allowed him to make most of the decisions in their married life, but she had been conscious of giving her permission. She had loved Buzz dearly but even when they made love, she had always chosen to hold something of herself back.

Making love with Bret the other day had been beautiful. It had also been profoundly disturbing. Absolutely nothing--no self-consciousness, no restraint--nothing had separated them when they had come together. It was as if they had absorbed each other's souls in those ecstatic moments.

Well, it would never happen again. She liked the Emilienne that she had become. There was no way that she was going to relinquish complete control of her life and allow herself to be absorbed by any man. Unfortunately, she had to accept the fact that with Bret there could be no partial surrender. Not because he would demand everything. She honestly would be unable to hold anything back.

Luckily, Bret seemed to be just as wary of her ever since they made love. Good. Everything would work out if they simply avoided each other.

Against her will, the image of Bret's deep blue eyes with their thick lashes invaded her mind, then his whole face with his lips set in a tempting smile as if he were about to kiss her. The image slowly expanded to include his beautifully muscled, golden body.

"If you are finished the eggplant, you can get started on these carrots, Milly." Flo's voice jolted her from her daydream.

 She picked up her peeler and reached for the carrots. She had to think of something else. What was she going to sing tonight?

All the damned songs were love songs! How about a happy little ditty like "I Don't Stand A Ghost of a Chance With You"? The ghost part was kind of appropriate. But there had to be something more upbeat than that. She peeled faster.

After several hours of non-stop effort, she and Flo headed out to the patio with a cup of coffee. Bret was sitting at a shaded table talking into his cell phone.

"That means his fingerprints are on file." He noticed them and smiled broadly. Milly felt her heartbeat speed up. She had no control over that but she kept her returning smile subdued. "Yes, go ahead. I'll check with you later," Bret added before breaking the connection.

"Mon Dieu," Flo exclaimed. "Have you been here all morning?"

"Couldn't think of a nicer place to make my calls. Now I get to share a break with two beautiful women."

"I'll get you a coffee," Flo said.

"I can get it myself," Bret said getting up.

"Don't be silly. I told you to stay out of my kitchen," Flo insisted with a broad grin. "Talk to Milly."

"I wish she wouldn't do that!" Milly said.

"You mean the obvious matchmaking?" Bret said. "I don't object. Flo's not blind. She can see the sparks we generate when we come near each other."

"Bret, you said you wouldn't."

His face was a picture of injured innocence. "I didn't call you 'love'. Or hug you. Or kiss you, although it's very tempting. Or even call you 'Boss'."

Milly glared at him. "What did your partner have to say?" she asked, just as Flo deposited Bret's coffee on the table.

"Jim got a list of Ronald's Atlanta clients. They're mostly minor league criminals. He did have one interesting piece of information about Gord Ingles, though. Apparently he was suspected of arson in connection with a factory explosion in Atlanta four years ago. Seems Ronald's man Gord was in the navy and knows a lot about explosives."

He gave that a moment to sink in. "It was lucky for him that his boss was able to provide him an airtight alibi for the night the factory blew up. Ronald testified that they were on a business trip to New York together."

"And he's still Ronald's driver," Flo mused. "Sounds like he owes Ronald a big enough favor to do almost anything for him. All we have to do now is find a witness to put Gord in the hospital parking lot before your dad's car exploded." Flo threw up her hands and rolled her eyes heavenwards at the impossibility of the task.

"We haven't had any luck with finding witnesses," Bret said. "But now we know someone to focus on. I'll put a man on it. He can get a photo of Gord and see if anyone at the hospital can place him there."

"It wouldn't hurt to pass it around the hotel, too," Flo suggested. "He might have hung around there to catch you collecting the luggage."

"We can't prove that Ronald killed Yvette either," Milly muttered. "He doesn't have an alibi for Sunday night but I saw it in a dream wouldn't cut any ice with the police. They don't even know she's dead."

Bret hoped that his face didn't show the guilt he was feeling for not telling her that the police probably did know precisely that. That, in fact, they could be turning up at any time to inform Yvette's next of kin that her body had been found.

"We'll keep working at it, Milly. Eventually, we'll get a break," he said.

Milly looked so desolate that Bret felt like saying to hell with not taking her in his arms. Flo saved him from breaking his promise by giving her niece a fierce hug.

"Viens t'en, Emilienne," Flo said briskly. "We have to get back to work."

"True. I'd better finish my kitchen chores because I have to spend some time at home at my piano working on whatever I'm singing tonight," Milly said.

"That's fine," Bret said. "I've set up my laptop in the spare room and I'll be working there this afternoon if you need me. I'll be around but not under foot."

Bret watched as Stu carefully polished the same highball glass for the fourth time. During the two hours Bret had sat at the bar spinning out two drafts of beer, Stu had managed to extract more information about Bret's family and life than the most highly trained interrogator would be able to in two weeks. The bartender's manner was gradually becoming a little less hostile but out of the corner of his eye, Bret caught Stu studying him intently any time he thought Bret's complete attention was on Milly at the piano.

In the spotlight, wearing another silky blouse with a plunging neckline, black this time, Milly was so beautiful she took his breath away. He had heard her practicing the songs again and again this afternoon. They all sounded wonderful to him the first time through. But his Milly was a perfectionist, going over each of the love songs until she thought it was right.

And until Bret, unseen in the guest room, was an emotional wreck. Tonight, he was trying not to listen too carefully.

"So," Stu said with studied casualness, "you planning to be around much longer?"

Bret looked him squarely in the eye.

"Yes," he said.

Stu held his gaze. "She's a good woman. I wouldn't like to see her hurt."

Bret decided it was time to state his position. "I'm more likely to be the one who is hurt," he said with a twisted smile. "I'm hoping for the long term here."

Stu inclined his head slowly twice.

"Well," he said briskly. "Would you like a real drink, Bret?"

"Thanks, but not yet."

Apparently satisfied with the exchange, Stu wandered down to the other end of the bar.

Bret allowed himself to concentrate on Milly. Her low voice was throbbing with emotion as she sang about loving someone and wanting him badly. Every atom in Bret's body responded to the desire in the song and in Milly's expressive voice. But the song was a sad one ending with the words of its title, I Don't Stand A Ghost of a Chance With You.

He was going to do his best to prove that the song was wrong. There had to be a chance for the two of them. No woman had ever thrown him for a complete loop like this before. Plain and simple, he needed her in his life. Of course, he thought, stifling a laugh at his uncharacteristic acceptance that an approachable spirit world existed, it was a ghost that had given them the chance.

Milly was finishing up her first set with an upbeat jazz medley, when Theo and another uniformed man arrived. When Bret saw Stu ushering them into Milly's office, he knew why they were there.

"Get Flo, will you, Stu?" he said, as he hurried to be by Milly's side when they spoke to her. "I suspect this is really bad news."

Stu's solemn face told him that he had guessed the officers' mission.

"Right!" he said as he rushed away.

Milly didn't resist when Bret put his arm around her waist to slow her progress towards her office. She seemed to sense his urgency.

"Milly," Bret said, "there are a couple of men here who want to speak to you and Flo."

The heavily lashed gray-green eyes that she turned to him were full of anguish. "They've found her," she whispered.

Bret nodded soundlessly and they entered her office.

Theo approached her with both hands extended. Tonight, the deep lines of his square face were softened in compassion.

"Theo," Milly said, grasping his hands. "What is it?"

"I'm sorry, Milly," he said. "But they've found Yvette."

Bret's arm tightened around her waist.

Flo, looking wide-eyed and frantic, rushed into the room with Stu at her heels.

Theo let go of Milly's hands to grasp Flo's for a moment. "I'm so sorry Flo. They've found your niece."

Theo did not attempt to soften the blow. He told them simply that, in response to an anonymous tip, they had found Yvette's body under a tarp on the construction site. Their best estimate was that she had been killed about two weeks ago. They were treating her death as a homicide but so far they had no suspects. The investigation was barely begun.

"I want to see her," Milly said.

Flo said, flatly, "No, Milly. You don't want to do that."

"Under these circumstances, I don't think it's advisable, Milly," Theo told her.

Bret said nothing but waited for Milly to realize on her own that the Yvette they had found would have little resemblance to the sister she knew.

"The suit and shoe she was wearing were the ones you described in the missing person's report," Theo said. "And I'd like you to look at this Polaroid shot of her personal effects. One of the crime scene officers took an extra one for you to look at tonight. You can come down to the station and identify the items tomorrow some time."

Theo was obviously trying to ease the task as much as possible for Milly but there was no way that identifying Yvette's watch and rings could be made easy.

"They're Yvette's," Milly said in a faint whisper. "Can't I see her to be sure?"

"It would be no comfort to you," Theo told her kindly. "And this should be plenty of identification. Of course, we'll run a check on her dental work to be sure."

Flo put her arms around her niece. "We knew this was coming, chère."

"But this makes it real, Flo," she said. They both stood there with their arms around each other and tears pouring unchecked down their faces.

The men watched knowing there was nothing they could do to ease their pain.

Theo turned to Bret. "I hope you can convince Milly not to view the body," he said quietly.

"Count on it," Bret said.

Eventually, the police left. Then, leaving Stu and Eva to close up, Bret took the two women back to Milly's cottage. For lack of any better idea, Bret poured them each a drink.

Milly stared blankly into the glass she held. She'd known Yvette was gone, but the full impact of this official recognition of her death was beginning to hit her. She wasn't going to give in to another bout of crying. That would start Flo again. And Flo hated tears.

Then it sank in. The police had received an anonymous tip about the location of the body!

"Bret! You're the one who called the police!" Milly accused, welcoming the anger. "Why didn't you warn me?"

"I had to do it this way, Milly. Bart and I went to the site last night and the ghost pointed to a spot down in an excavation. We didn't want to disturb any evidence that was there so I called in a tip."

"You let them surprise me with this."

"Your reaction was real and honest, Milly. Neither of those cops is going to wonder if you knew anything beforehand."

Milly glared at him. "Here's something else that's real and honest. I hate liars. And you purposely lied to me. You pretended that you and Bart had given up on the idea of returning to the site."

"I did what I thought best." Typical.

"So much for discussing our plan of action," she said, getting to her feet. "I'm going to bed now and I don't want to see you here in the morning."

Of course, he was still there, solid and stubborn, when she got up.

When she stumbled out of her bedroom, he poured her a cup of coffee and put it on the kitchen table. He had enough sense not to touch her.

"You're still here," she said taking a sip of the scalding hot coffee.

"Nothing has changed, Milly. I'm not leaving until we're sure you are not in danger." He looked into his own coffee cup. "I want you to know that I didn't like deceiving you."

If she were honest, she would admit that he looked truly sorry.

Milly didn't have the strength to fight him. The night had been long and restless and the day loomed ahead in an endless gray fog. "Stay, then. I don't care."

When she and Flo paid an early morning visit to the police station to identify Yvette's personal effects, Bret insisted on driving them. He did not try to take over but stayed very close when she had to examine her sister's watch and rings.

Eva and Stu were waiting by the door to Milly's bungalow, when they returned. Eva's dark eyes were red and swollen and Stu's eyes were suspiciously red-rimmed.

Eva hugged her close. "Oh, Honey," she said, "I'm sorry. But at least, the waiting and the wondering are over. The strain you've been under has been dreadful."

Stu gave Milly a big hug.

A few minutes later, he cornered Bret. "If you need any help in nailing that bastard that killed Yvette..." His voice caught. "You know you can count on me. I hope to hell you need a little extra muscle to get what you need out of him."

Flo rejoined them. "I've sent everyone home and put signs in the window saying that The Grove is closed for the next two days."

"We'll have to close again for the funeral." Milly's voice was lifeless. "Whenever the police let us have it."

Milly and Flo spent the rest of the day receiving a constant stream of people who had come to express their sympathy.

A weeping Kit arrived with both Ronald and Bart in tow. A third man, whom Milly suspected was Ronald's driver, Gord Ingles, followed them in.

Milly was almost at the end of her endurance by the time they arrived but she looked hard and long at the man who had probably tried to kill her and Bret with the car bomb. Gord was a little under medium height, with close-set brown eyes and wore his brown hair in a long ponytail. Even in his neat, dark twill pants and uniform shirt, he didn't look quite respectable.

Kit hugged Flo. Milly could see from across the room that Kit was incapable of speech at the moment. Ronald stood quietly behind her, his handsome face the picture of sympathy.

When Kit moved on, Milly couldn't take her eyes off Ronald's performance. It was like being fascinated by a snake charmer. Every atom of his body seemed to radiate sincerity and compassion. The man could have had a great career on the stage.

He said something quietly, probably offering the usual condolences but Flo stiffened and glared at him. Milly didn't hear what Flo muttered in reply but whatever it was it made Ronald drop his act long enough to look sharply at her. Bart was there in a flash. He whispered something in Flo's ear. She nodded abruptly and turned away from Ronald.

Milly did hear what Bart said over his shoulder as he took Flo's elbow and led her quickly out to the patio.

"I'm sorry. I'm sure you understand but Flo has had all the company she can handle for a while."

Milly hoped Flo hadn't said anything that would alert Ronald that they knew what he had done.

She could see Bret, who was never far from her side, out of the corner of her eye. She marveled at the way he was able to hide his hostility. Of course, she marveled at a lot of things Bret was able to do. He certainly hid his desire for her well. Had it evaporated overnight? No matter how he felt, his presence gave her the strength to face Ronald right now.

When Milly saw Ronald approaching, looking sad and sympathetic, she clenched her fists and prayed for the strength to keep herself from attacking him physically. She wanted to scream, "You killed my sister!"

"I'm sorry about Yvette," the murderer said, not quite meeting her eyes.

When he took her hand between his and pressed it in an imitation of compassion, his cobra ring grazed her skin. A wave of dizziness swept over her. She felt nausea rising in her throat.

"Thank you." She was surprised that she was actually able to speak.

Bret slipped one arm around her waist. "You look exhausted, Milly. I think you should go lie down for a few minutes," he said and led her, unresisting, out of the room.

Bret closed her bedroom door behind them and opened his arms. She stepped into them and burrowed close.

"Shouldn't," she murmured.

"This is a Time Out, love," he said, holding her tightly. "I'm proud of you, Emilienne. You kept your cool. You almost passed out but you didn't give away anything. We'll find a way to get him. I promise."

He sat down on the ridiculous satin chaise longue she had purchased when she'd redone the bedroom and lifted her onto his lap.

"Don't say anything, love. Just relax here with me," he said quietly.

He leaned back and pulled her against him. She nestled close with her cheek against his chest. Lying there listening to the strong beating of Bret's heart, she found herself thinking that the purchase of this idiotic chair hadn't been such a bad idea after all. Even if this was the only time it was ever used, it was worth every penny she'd paid for it.

Bret's low voice was soothing. "We'll stay here for a few minutes. He'll probably be gone by the time we get back."

She allowed herself the comfort of his embrace, trying not to think about anything. Not about Yvette's murder, not about her impossible relationship with Bret. Nothing.

And Bret's prediction was right. When they returned to the living room, Ronald and his driver had left. Bart and Kit had waited to have a brief conversation with her but left soon after to inform Will that Yvette's body had been found.

Over the next few hours, she was vaguely aware that Bret and Theo spent a lot of time in serious conversation out in the privacy of the patio. That was a good thing. It was time to get some input from Theo. She wondered if Bret was telling him about her dreams. She could just see Theo's no-nonsense face if he did. She'd bet anything though that Bret wouldn't mention seeing the ghost.

Finally, at nine o'clock that night, Bret locked the door behind the last guest.

"Time you two got some sleep," Bret announced. "We have chores to do in the morning. Yvette's apartment has to be gone through to see if we can find anything there that could connect to Ronald. Flo can you be ready to leave for New York at seven o'clock? Milly?"

"No," Milly exclaimed. "Not tomorrow. I can't deal with her things tomorrow. And Flo hates flying."

"Oh, sweetheart," Bret said. "I don't think waiting will make it any easier."

At the endearment, she darted a look at him. "The Time Out is over," she said.

She knew how silly her on and off demands that he keep his distance had become. They both knew that she wanted him. And she knew he wanted her. Only she, however, knew how much it would cost her to give in to that desire.

"I didn't call you, 'love'," he said easily. "But about the trip to New York, maybe you're right. It can wait another day. I did say I'd meet Theo tomorrow at the Sheriff's Office if I could. You and Flo can take it easy tomorrow and we'll leave for the airport at the crack of dawn on Tuesday."

"All right. I'll fly," Flo decided. "I'll close my eyes a lot but I'll do it. I'm going home to pack." She leaned over to give Milly a kiss. "See you in the morning, Emilienne."

She was halfway to the door when she returned and kissed Bret on the cheek. "You, too, mon cher."

"I have some calls to make," Bret said. "So, I'll say good night, too."

"Bret," Milly said, not wanting to be alone just yet. "Did you catch that little scene between Flo and Ronald?"

"I saw it but I don't know what Flo said to him. She looked as if she wanted to kill him. It's a good thing Bart was on the spot. But I believe, even when she's this upset, Flo's too smart to give anything away."

"I hope so."

"That's one of the things I want to talk to Bart about. And if he's still at Will's, he can tell him I'll be away for a day or two. Good night, Milly."

"Good night." Although she desperately wanted him to hold her again, she didn't have the courage to ask him to stay.

With The Grove closed and Bret gone for most of the day, Monday crept by. She told herself that it was the prospect of relief from boredom that made her pulse speed up when he returned.

"We're flying out of here on a commercial jet at seven o'clock tomorrow morning," he told her as they sat with their after dinner coffee in Milly's living room. "You okay with that?"

"I guess so. I'd be happier waiting another few days but I have to admit hanging around The Grove and doing nothing is dismal. I'm surprised you made reservations with a commercial airline."

"Now don't get the wrong idea. It's not that flying in to a major airport makes me nervous," he told her with a grin. "It's that commercial pilots are paid big bucks to deal with that kind of traffic. Who am I to deprive them of the pleasure?"

"Did you get to talk to Bart about yesterday?" she asked.

"According to Bart, when Ronald said, 'I'm sorry about Yvette,' Flo said, 'I'll bet.' It wasn't what she said. It was the way she said it that made Bart hustle her out of there for a breather."

Milly wondered what Ronald made of her reaction. She hoped he didn't feel threatened by Flo now! She could see that Bret, too, was perturbed by the possibility.

"I want to talk to Theo again. He's not as resistant to the kind of information we have as I would have expected. He's ready to move officially as soon as there's a real case against Ronald. Do you think he noticed that bit of by-play between Flo and Ronald?"

"Probably. I wasn't looking at him. I was too wrapped up in preparing to face Ronald myself."

"I'll mention it. I get the impression that Flo is important to Theo," he said, once again punching in the numbers on his telephone and beginning to pace the room.

She left him to it.

Tuesday, everything started out well. Their flight was on time and their cab driver no more hair-raising than most. Even the New York traffic had no major delays.

At Yvette's building, they stopped at the superintendent's apartment before going up to the tenth floor. When Bret had called him from Florida to say that they would be at the apartment for a day or two, the super told him to stop by to pick up a couple of parcels which he had been holding for Yvette.

"Those are probably the boxes of wedding and cruise clothes she sent on ahead," Milly said. "She always hated coping with more than one bag when she traveled."

Bret picked up one of the boxes. "This is all clothes?" he asked, struggling a little under the unexpected weight.

"You must have the box she packed with all her shoes and the souvenirs. Yvette bought a lot of souvenirs on the cruise," Flo told them. "The big jade chess set she got Marie would be in there. It's pretty heavy."

Bret merely grunted as he hoisted the box onto one hip, then into his arms.

"I'll take the clothes box," Milly said.

Flo fumbled in her purse for Yvette's keys and hurried ahead. By the time Bret and Milly caught up to her, she had a key in the third and last lock of Yvette's apartment door. She pushed it open and stood aside to allow them to deposit the boxes inside. The scene inside almost made Milly drop the box she was carrying.

"Mon Dieu!" Flo exclaimed. "What's happened here?"

The place had been ransacked. Every piece of furniture had been turned upside down. The cushions had been tossed onto the floor. Two walls of bookshelves were bare; dozens of books scattered across the floor. Yvette's prized roll-top desk gaped open. Its shelves had been emptied, the drawers had been pulled out and their contents thrown around.

"Her stereo system and television set are still here," Bret pointed out, pulling his cellular phone out of his pocket and dialing 911. "Don't touch anything. Let's leave it as it is for the police."

It was quite a few hours later when the police finally left. They had no way of knowing when during the past three weeks the break-in had occurred. The intruder had forced an entry by breaking the glass in the balcony door. He had done a very rough search of the apartment, but hadn't gone in for wanton destruction. And nothing obvious was missing.

He had not found the small safe, hidden under the living room rug, where Yvette kept her jewelry and a few papers. He had taken all the boxes off the shelf in her walk-in closet and emptied them on the floor but he had not disturbed the clothes that hung there. He had stirred the lingerie and clothing around in her dresser drawers but hadn't bothered to dump them. The object he was looking for must have been large enough to find quickly.

The officer agreed that the intruder could have been looking for Yvette's journal but thought that it was more likely that he was looking for cash or drugs.

They were able to lift a few fingerprints off the desk and the dresser but did not offer much hope that they hadn't been made by Yvette herself.

Milly closed and locked the door behind the policemen and leaned against it.

She opened her mouth to speak but before she could, Flo said, "You don't have to say it, chère. We are not sorting anything tonight. We have to clear off the twin beds and the couch though if we want to sleep lying down."

"Just prop me up in a corner," Milly said. But she was already piling clothing on the easy chair in the corner of Yvette's bedroom. "Why don't you see if you can find something simple to eat?"

"Some hope," Flo said with a sad smile. Yvette had prided herself on the fact that she didn't cook.

"I'll help Milly with the beds," Bret said. "Don't look so surprised. Nobody makes your bed in the military."

Being this close to sheets and beds and Bret at the same time was not a good idea. Desperate for any topic of conversation, she asked, "What branch of the service were you in?"

"Air force, to begin with," he told her. "Then a number of other branches."

"You're as secretive as Buzz was," she muttered.

"For the same reason, Milly. I'll tell you anything you want to know, if I can."

"Who cut you so badly?" she blurted.

"A very nasty man named Joseph," he said. "He wanted me to tell him something I didn't want to tell him. I'm not sure whether or not I did eventually."

It hadn't been easy for him to tell her that. She wondered why he had.

"Thank you," she said and reached up to touch the scar on his jaw. "I shouldn't have asked."

"You are important to me, Emilienne," he said, turning abruptly to begin putting a fitted sheet on the other bed.

It was close to midnight before they went through the motions of eating some canned soup and crackers and heading for bed.

Milly awoke with a start when she heard the apartment door closing.

"Breakfast delivery!" Bret's voice announced.

She heard Flo speaking to him in the tiny kitchen not far away. The rich smell of coffee encouraged her to open her eyes. She quickly closed them again when she remembered the chore that was in store for them today. However, it was only about fifteen minutes later that she headed into the kitchen, freshly showered and determined to try to be a support to Flo.

"Morning!" Bret proudly pointed out the food laid out on the table in the dining alcove. "Bagels, croissants, Danish. My idea of breakfast."

"Beautiful," she said accepting a steaming cup of dark roast coffee from Flo. Suddenly hungry, she bit into a flaky croissant. "Mmm. Nothing but delicious carbohydrates and fat."

She could see that Bret and Flo had already cleaned up the mess the intruder had left in the kitchen. That left the rest of the apartment.

By early afternoon, they had straightened the furniture, divided the books into various boxes according to their destinations and Milly and Flo were sorting through Yvette's clothing at top speed. Now that she actually doing it, Milly grudgingly admitted that Bret's insistence that the three of them fly to New York had been a good idea. Until the coroner's office released Yvette's body for burial, Milly would continue to be in a state of limbo. For two weeks now, although in her heart she knew her sister was dead, there had always lurked a tiny measure of hope that the murder existed only in her nightmares. Packing up Yvette's clothes and books was lending a measure of reality to her death.

"You're sure you don't want to keep any of Yvette's clothes?" Flo asked for the third or fourth time. "Some of the casual clothes she bought for the cruise would fit you."

"I can't, Flo." She had to admit that much weakness. "Someday, I'll be able to wear her jewelry and enjoy thinking about her wearing it. Wearing her clothes would be more than I could ever handle."

"Bien!" Flo shoved the pile of brightly colored cottons firmly into one of the boxes in the middle of the floor. "Goodwill will be happy to get them."

"I just talked to Theo," Bret said as he rejoined them in the bedroom. "After you told him about the arson case against Gord Ingles, Flo, he did some digging. The explosive device used in that factory was definitely similar to the kind they figure was used to blow up the Jag. And, the case against

Gord was a strong one. As a matter of fact, it was only Ronald's alibi that kept him from being arrested. Theo said the arson squad were convinced he was guilty."

"That evidence must still be available," Milly said. "Surely someone can match it with the fragments that they found at the hospital."

"The case is still open," Bret agreed. "And Theo is on it. Oh, and Kit left a message on my voice mail to say she was thinking about you and Flo and wishing you strength to tackle today's task."

"How did she know we were coming here?"

"When they dropped in to talk to Will last night after they left your house, he told them we were heading here this morning. Kit was in a pretty good mood. Ronald actually spent some time with her and Bart last night. Even dropped in at Will's for a while."

"That doesn't thrill me a lot. I wish we could keep him away from her." Milly sighed. "But, I'm afraid she loves him. She's going to find it hard to believe he killed Yvette." And they seemed to be a terribly long way from proving that.

She was grateful that Bret was trying to make conversation. She and Flo weren't contributing much to it.

"Time to break for some dinner?" Bret asked. "I know some great restaurants not too far from here. Or there's one of my favorite delicatessens a couple of blocks down the street."

"I don't know that I could face fine dining right now," Milly said. "You and Flo could go, if you like."

Flo snorted. "Nonsense. Take-out deli sandwiches sound good to me. Why don't the two of you get a breath of air--or what passes for air in this city--and pick up some food? I'll tackle that box of shoes and cruise souvenirs that Yvette shipped home and put aside anything you have to make a decision about. Go." She shooed them out like a couple of chickens.

Rather than argue, Milly grabbed her purse.

"I guess we're going for a walk, Bret," she said with the first weak smile she had managed since Theo Parsons had announced the news about Yvette's body.

The air was warm and had that particular golden quality that was the exclusive property of a late afternoon in the city. Slanting sunbeams cast long shadows ahead of them as they hurried along. As most of the office workers had left for home and the evening's activities had not yet begun, the sidewalk was relatively uncrowded.

Bret took her hand and pulled her to a halt. "There's no hurry, Sweetheart. Slow down. I haven't had a minute alone with you all day."

As she swung around to face him, she noticed a thin, pony-tailed figure she thought she recognized ducking into a doorway across the street.

"Could that be Gord?" she gasped.

Of course, when Bret turned to look, there was no sign of him.

"He was in the doorway of that apartment hotel." She pointed and took off at the dead run. Bret ran with her. There was a small break in the traffic on their side of the street but they were forced to wait a long time in the middle of the road for the steady stream of oncoming cars to pass. By the time they got across, the vestibule was empty.

"I'm not even sure it was him," Milly said with an embarrassed grin. "There are lots of thin men with ponytails. I guess your bit of news about his almost being arrested for arson put him in my mind. You don't think he could be the one who searched Yvette's apartment, do you?"

"It's possible. Ronald knew we were coming here. He might have sent Gord here last night to see if Yvette sent the journal home with her other stuff," Bret said.

"That's a pretty tight time line," Milly said. "I don't know if Gord could have figured how to get into the apartment and done the search that quickly. Besides, Ronald has been concerned about the journal for a long time."

"Let's get our food and get back to the apartment." Bret looked concerned. Did he think that Gord might have hidden some kind of bomb in the apartment?

The deli was fragrant with spices and garlic and had a long line-up of customers waiting for the few tables. Milly was glad that Bret had called ahead and that their massive deli sandwiches and containers of soup were waiting for them.

Flo buzzed open the lobby door for them and had the apartment door wide open when they arrived. She was grinning from ear to ear and waving a small red notebook.

"I found the journal!" she cried. "It was in the box with Yvette's shoes and souvenirs."

Bret picked Flo up in a bear hug and swung her feet off the floor. "Now, we've got something!" he said. "It wasn't destroyed in the explosion. It must have been some other book that the chamber maid packed in Yvette's bag."

"I figure the journal Yvette was writing in at the hotel was a fresh one. This little treasure would be the one she had finished." Milly could hardly contain her excitement. "Have you read any of it, Flo?"

"I waited for you. Believe me, that wasn't easy. But Sit! Sit," she commanded, shoving the notebook into Milly's hands.

"Hold it for a minute, Milly. I'd like you and Flo to take the journal out into the hall and wait down at the end for a few minutes while I check out the apartment," Bret said.

Bret did suspect that Gord had left a bomb! The memory of watching the Jag explode flashed through her mind.

"You don't have to do that yourself. Call the police. They have people who know how to deal with those things," Milly said, tugging Bret's arm. The man was like a rock and just as immovable.

"There may not be time for that," he said.

"What's going on?" Flo asked. "I'm not moving until you tell me what's happened."

"Milly thought she saw Gord on the street. If she's right, I want to make sure he didn't leave us any surprises," Bret said. "Now get moving both of you."

Milly wished she knew what exactly Bret was looking for so that she could help him. But the urgency in his voice told her the best thing she could do was get Flo and the journal out of there.

"If you find anything, promise you won't touch it," she insisted.

"Milly," he bit out. "Get out of here."

The ten minutes after Bret shut the door firmly between them were possibly the longest minutes of her life. She and Flo waited a few feet down the hall straining as hard as they could to hear what Bret was doing inside the apartment. They could hear nothing. She was desperately afraid that the next sound they would hear would be the roar of an explosion. She suddenly realized what losing Bret would mean to her.

Finally, he opened the door and announced with a sheepish grin, "False alarm."

Milly threw her arms around him and kissed him. She could sense his relief in the way he clasped her tightly and responded to her kiss. It felt so good to kiss him again.

"I guess Gord was satisfied with his search and figured he had blown up the journal with the car," Flo said.

"The journal!" Milly exclaimed. "Let's see what it has to say."

Flo and Bret followed her to the dining room table and sat on either side of her. Milly turned the slender red book over in her hands and took a long shuddering breath. She had seen slim red volumes like this one so often in her sister's long, slender fingers - fingers that were so like her own.

"Are you sure you don't want some privacy, love?" Bret asked. "This isn't going to be easy."

"I want you both here," she insisted. She was sure of that. "I'll skim over the entries as quickly as I can and when I come to anything I think is important, I'll read it aloud. Then you two can fight over who reads it next."

She turned to the first closely written page. Yvette's small, tidy handwriting gave her a bad moment. She blinked back the tears, swallowed hard and began to read silently.

The first entry began on the day the ship left Fort Lauderdale. It was Sunday, a full day at sea. They were not due to dock at Cozumel until the following noon. Yvette liked to write down the names and descriptions of people she met as soon as she could so that she remembered them later. She sure had met a lot of passengers. Pages of them. A nice chubby man who promised to teach her how to play blackjack that night. A conceited Frenchman in a minuscule bikini who tried unsuccessfully to impress her with his well-toned body. A little boy who was excited about the first flying fish he had ever seen. Yvette described them all in loving detail. Flo had met a good-looking older man who had invited her to attend the Folkloric Show ashore with him the next night in Cozumel.

"You didn't mention the handsome widower, Flo."

"Just read!" Flo said.

Milly skimmed on. Yvette didn't think she'd go to the Folkloric. She'd had enough socializing at Kit's wedding. She went on and on about that! The attractive twin best men had been good company. Bret was a wonderful dancer. Bart was so funny. Apparently, Bret and Kit's opinions that Yvette had not displayed any romantic interest in anyone at the wedding were right on target.

"You are a great dancer and Bart is funny," she reported.

"Keep reading," he said.

Reading Yvette's thoughts was almost like having her there. A swelling sense of loss threatened to wreck her concentration. She caught the phrase, '...have to talk to Ronald."

"Oh, this looks interesting. She finally mentions Ronald," she said. "She's writing about the wedding. She says, 'Kit deserves to be happy and she thinks that Ronald is what she wants. But the more I see of him, the less hope I have for that marriage. I didn't trust him when Milly was involved with him ten years ago and I haven't changed my mind. He wears a different face with every person he talks to. And that mother of his is going to be a real cross to bear. I have a real bad feeling about this.

'Oh, it's too lovely out here on deck with the sparkling Caribbean all around me to think gloomy thoughts. Maybe it'll work out. Ronald likes Kit's money well enough. I hope that it's enough to make him try to keep her happy. He acts as if he's crazy in love with her. It could be true.

'I'm still questioning my eyesight about Saturday night, though. I must have been seeing things.

'I am definitely going to have a talk with Ronald about it. That was so strange. Completely impossible!

'Maybe he has a twin. There are enough twins around here, me and Milly, Bret and Bart. Now, there's a thought. One of the Thornton twins might be exactly what Milly needs right now. Bart would cheer her up. No, Bret would be better. There's something deep and serious in Bret that I think would appeal to her. Yes, Milly and Bret would have more in common. First chance I get, I'll introduce her to Bret.'"

"Mon Dieu!" Flo exclaimed. "And she did it, too."

"So that's why she chose me to see her ghost," Bret said under his breath. Combine that with the spell that Milly had cast over him the first time he saw her and it was almost enough to make a guy believe in magic.

The three of them sat stunned for a minute. Finally, Milly turned back to the journal again.

"Not another mention of Ronald," Milly said, when she reached the end of the journal. She handed the book to Flo.

"I wish she had been more specific. 'I'm still questioning my eyesight about Saturday night.' What do you suppose she meant by that? Did she think she'd seen Ronald? That was the day of the wedding...'"

"She said, 'Maybe he has a twin.' That 'he' sure sounds as if she meant Ronald. But it couldn't have been. He and Kit were in the Bahamas. It was their wedding night." Bret was almost shouting in his exasperation.

"Yvette was sure she'd seen somebody getting on an elevator who couldn't possibly be there that night," Flo said slowly.

"Were you there when she saw him?" Bret asked.

"I had gone on ahead to open the door while Yvette stopped to get a couple of sodas at the pop machine."

"Then he couldn't think you had seen him."

"She was alone," Flo said. "I wish I had seen him. I wouldn't have recognized him at the time but I'd be able to identify him now."

"I don't like the thought that he might think you'd been with Yvette. Or that she had told you what she had seen."

"She could easily have told me," Flo said. "She was upset about it even though she put it down to being overtired. She'd had a very big day."

"With all the preparations and parties connected with the wedding, she'd been running for days," Milly agreed. "After she left the wedding luncheon, she rushed to my place to change out of her wedding clothes and pick up her luggage for the cruise. She barely took a minute to say goodbye to me. Then she had Stu drive her directly to Fort Lauderdale."

"When he dropped her off at the hotel where we were staying that night, the Bon Voyage party some of my friends were throwing for me had already started," Flo explained to Bret. "Yvette and I didn't stay late because we were sailing the next day."

"Did she mention Ronald at all, Flo?" Bret asked.

"I'm getting to that! She never mentioned his name." Flo shook her head. "But when we got back to the room about eleven-thirty, she was muttering something about everybody having a double somewhere in the world. And saying over and over, 'But that's impossible!'"

"She was awfully proud of her powers of observation," Milly said. "And her memory. Thinking she recognized someone and knowing she had to be wrong would really annoy her."

"She never said who she thought she'd seen." Flo frowned in concentration. "And I was so tired after getting everything organized at the restaurant so that I could be away for a week and then packing for the cruise that I didn't pay much attention. Yvette wondered, at the time, if fatigue was preventing her from seeing as clearly as she should. But she brooded about it."

"Yvette wasn't one for imagining things," Milly said. "All the same, I can't see how Ronald could be on his honeymoon in the Bahamas and in Fort Lauderdale at the same time. We've been dealing with so much spooky stuff lately that I have to ask myself, 'What if he could be in two places at one time?' But why would one of the places be Fort Lauderdale?"

"Whoa, Milly. I have enough of a problem dealing with the ghost of your twin sister. I understand how close your ties were. I can maybe buy that as an extension of extrasensory perception. A lot of very intelligent people think there is something in that. I'm still struggling with my own contact with her ghost. But I'm not about to accept the paranormal as the answer to everything."

"All right. Forget the being in two places at once. Let's concentrate on Fort Lauderdale," Milly conceded. "Remember, the police told Kit that they found Ronald's office number in the hotel room of some woman who committed suicide in Fort Lauderdale."

"Ronald had a girlfriend in Atlanta. Do you figure he had another one in Fort Lauderdale?" Bret asked.

"At the same time as he was courting Kit?" Flo sounded incredulous.

"Three women does sound a bit excessive. We need to dig a lot deeper into Ronald's private life."

"Do you suppose it's time for a little fitness training?" Milly suggested. "I'm curious about the dead fitness instructor. Do you think she might possibly be the woman who committed suicide in Fort Lauderdale? But it's a long way from Atlanta to Fort Lauderdale."

"The people we talked to at The Firm knew Ronald well enough to hate him. Let's find out exactly why. You tackle Mark and I'll attempt to get something about the dead instructor out of the blonde icicle."

Milly turned to Flo. "Could you handle flying back to Palm Beach alone, Flo? Or do you want to come with us? I think Bret and I should talk to some people at that health club in Atlanta."

"I need to get back. We can't keep the restaurant closed forever. I wouldn't be of any use to you in Atlanta and it's about time I sat in a plane without someone holding my hand. When it comes to that, if it would help us find out something that would point the police in that monster's direction, I'd fly all the way around the world alone," Flo vowed.

"If you're going alone, I'll get Bart to meet your plane," Bret said.

"That would relieve my mind." Milly remembered the searching look that Ronald had flashed at Flo after she'd rebuffed his expression of sympathy.

Mark was as charming and attentive as he had been a few days earlier but his friendly smile dimmed considerably every time Milly mentioned Ronnie. She wished it were in her nature to be more subtle. She was at a loss to know how to get Mark to talk to her but she had to try. He was her only hope of getting the details of how Nancy died.

Milly's energy was fading more quickly than her optimism. Earlier, she had romped quite easily through the moderately paced aquacise class that was composed mostly of vastly overweight middle-aged women. Then she'd been passed over to Valerie for a couple of hours to have her levels tested on different exercise machines. Her only break had been for the half hour she'd had with Bret. Over an extremely light lunch in the Club restaurant, he admitted that he hadn't been any more successful than she had.

"Maybe we're being too devious," Milly suggested. "Maybe we should ask them straight out what happened to Nancy."

"Valerie hasn't given me an opening. The only time she mentioned the instructor who died was last week when she explained why she was doing the tours of the weight room," Bret said. "I don't think that she's going to open up to me at all. She's a very careful woman. I think I'll strike up a conversation this afternoon with a couple of the guys who are working out. Maybe they can tell me something about Ronnie's love life."

Deciding that Mark was still her best bet, Milly went back to the pool. The minute he saw her, he made her jump back into the pool and swim lengths. He said he needed to judge what level of swimming class she should join but Milly wondered if he suspected she was a phony and was seeing how far he could push her before she admitted it.

Finally, he called her out of the pool. For a few minutes, they discussed her possible program over an icy glass of bottled water. When that topic was exhausted, she knew she had to ask him directly.

"I haven't been able to get your friend...the instructor who died...out of my mind," she began. "Can you talk about it? I mean, how she died?"

She was doing this all wrong. She not only sounded dim-witted but also completely insensitive.

"Oh, I'm sorry, Mark. That was unfeeling of me."

Mark's dark eyes studied her shrewdly as he took a long drink of his water. He seemed to come to a decision and placed the glass firmly on the table.

"Tell me, Milly," he said softly, "if that's really your name. What is this all about?" His face was stiff with anger as he leaned his elbows on the table and thrust his face close to hers. Suddenly, his muscular arms and shoulders appeared tense and menacing. "You aren't really interested in the swimming program. What are you doing here?"

She met his eyes and hoped that he would believe that she intended to tell him the truth. "I know it's hard for you to talk about it but it's very important to me that I find out how your friend Nancy died."

He waited. "Are you some kind of reporter?"

"Good heavens, no. This is very personal. Ronald Wilson killed my twin sister," she blurted. "I can't prove it but I know he did."

She had startled him. His expression was still hostile but her bald statement seemed to defuse his anger a little.

"How did he kill your sister?" Mark asked.

"He strangled her." That seemed to be the shortest version of what had happened.

"The police said Nancy killed herself," he said. "But that rat killed her."

Mark put his head in his hands. Then the story burst out of him.

"Nancy broke up with Ronnie when someone showed her an engagement notice in the paper. He was marrying some rich woman from Palm Beach. Nancy was miserable at first but she was getting used to the idea when she found out she was pregnant. She was determined to let him know he was going to be a father. Ronnie was hard to catch up with. He had moved out of his apartment and had closed his office here but she got in touch with him somehow."

"I expect he denied the baby was his," Milly guessed.

"No. He was sneakier than that. He called her and said he realized that she was the woman he loved and he wanted her and their child. He said it would take a few days to make the arrangements and to break the news to his fiancée but he promised he would cancel the wedding and marry her. Nancy was walking on air."

"You think he was just delaying the breakup until after the wedding?"

"I think that was his idea. But Nancy wanted to meet him sooner and wrote him a couple of letters at his fiancée's address. Nobody could convince her she shouldn't believe a guy who was living with another woman."

"And one he was engaged to!" The poor woman must really have loved him. Milly had never been that trusting in her life.

"When he invited her, she rushed to Fort Lauderdale for their big reconciliation. I couldn't talk her out of it. Apparently he didn't show. I saw in the paper that he got married after all. Nancy died on his wedding night."

Mark blinked hard. "They don't know exactly what killed her. Her heart just stopped. They said she had taken some kind of sleeping pill. Not enough to kill her. Barely enough to put her to sleep. And she died in her sleep."

Milly didn't know what to say to him. He was suffering and terribly angry.

"At least they didn't call it suicide. There were half a dozen more sleeping pills loose in her purse that she could have taken if she had wanted to.

"But it doesn't make sense. Nancy was a health food nut. She didn't own any kind of drugs. Wouldn't even take aspirin. My God! The woman was an aerobics instructor. Her heart had to be in great shape. They tried to tell me that athletes sometimes drop dead of no apparent causes. But I'm not convinced.

"I don't know how he did it but Ronnie killed her. From what I can find out, he was out of the country. Maybe he hired someone else to meet her and trick her into taking those sleeping pills. And something else they didn't find in the autopsy."

So that was why Ronald had killed Yvette! Somehow he had managed to come to Fort Lauderdale to kill his pregnant lover. And Yvette had seen him.

Where was Kit when this was going on?

So many questions were tumbling around in her head that she didn't know exactly what to ask him next.

"I wonder. Did Ronald have any close buddies here at the club?" she asked finally.

"No buddies," he said thoughtfully. "But he did date Valerie for a while before he began seeing Nancy. And she's sure no fan!"

Milly didn't think she would want the icy-eyed Valerie as an enemy.

"Do you know if he answered Nancy's letters?" Even a note with the date he planned to meet her would help. Even one in Nancy's handwriting.

"I think he phoned. But he might have written. My sister and I packed up her stuff from her apartment," Mark said. "I have to work until eleven tonight but I could look through it tomorrow morning and send you anything that looks helpful."

Milly gave him her business card and jotted her home phone number on the back.

"I can't thank you enough, Mark," she said. "And I'm sorry I wasn't open with you from the start."

"Just get him," he said, pushing back his chair and standing up.

"Oh, you never mentioned Nancy's last name," Milly said.

"Higgenbottom. Nancy Higgenbottom."

"Valerie wasn't about to enter into any conversation that didn't involve my biceps and my abs," Bret told her in the taxi on the way to the hotel that afternoon. "I did meet a talkative guy in the whirlpool though. He thought Ronnie was a 'hell of a guy' and said he sure had a touch with the women. But we knew that. He didn't mention Nancy by name and apparently didn't know she was dead. What did Mark have to say?"

"He's convinced that Ronnie killed her." Milly raised an eyebrow in the direction of the cab driver who was suddenly fascinated by their conversation. "I have a lot to tell you when we get to the room. Two rooms," she corrected herself.

Bret gave her one of his infuriatingly tolerant looks. "Not likely," was all he said.

None of her reactions to Bret were moderate. How could she yearn so intensely to pummel him for his superior attitude and, at the same time, need to kiss that annoying mouth until neither of them could speak?

"No one knows where we are," she argued. "I'm perfectly safe."

"And I'm going to keep you that way." He spoke as if the subject was closed.

She protested again when they registered.

"Okay," he said to the smiling registration receptionist. "Can you give us adjoining rooms?"

"I have a two bedroom suite," he said.

"Even better," Bret said.

When they finally got to the suite, which looked very like the one they had stayed in the previous week with Bart, she couldn't hold back any longer.

"Do you remember Kit telling us that the woman who died in Fort Lauderdale had a name with something like 'Bottom' in it?"

"And Nancy's does?" Bret guessed.

"Higgenbottom," she said, triumphantly. "And she died of heart failure. In a room at the same hotel in Fort Lauderdale where Yvette and Flo stayed!"

"Heart failure!" Bret exclaimed. "An aerobics dancercise instructor in her mid-twenties died of heart failure?"

"Mark said they couldn't find a cause of her death. Her heart simply stopped. The autopsy showed that she had taken a sleeping pill or two. Not an overdose. No alcohol. They called it death from natural causes."

"That's too convenient. He must have done something." Bret frowned in thought. "You saw a hypodermic in your dream. I wonder if they found any puncture holes."

"I don't think so. Mark would have mentioned them. But he also said that Nancy never took any kind of medication. That the sleeping pills could not be hers."

"We'll get Theo to check that autopsy report," Bret said.

"At the same hotel where Flo and Yvette stayed," Bret mused. "That's too much of a coincidence. Ronald killed her and then he killed Yvette because she saw him there. We know she saw him. The journal entry doesn't actually have a sentence that states Ronald was there but it comes close enough to get the police looking into it if only Ronald couldn't prove he was on his honeymoon with Kit."

"I'd be very surprised if Flo hasn't shown the journal to Theo by now. He's no fool. He'll pull out all the stops he can to prove that Ronald was in Fort Lauderdale."

"But you saw the way Kit was looking at him when we were with them on board The Sprite. I'd say Ronald had definitely been with her on their wedding night," Milly said.

"Yeah," Bret agreed. "I'd never seen Kittle blush before."

"Do you think he knows anything about hypnosis?"

"Milly, when we find out what happened that Saturday night, we're not going to find any hocus-pocus. He more likely drugged her. What we need to do is find out where exactly they were in the Bahamas, then ask around the private airports and see if anyone knows anything. I wonder if Ronald is a pilot."

"He wasn't ten years ago. That doesn't mean he isn't now. Kit would know."

"I'll call Bart. He can work flying into the conversation somehow." Bret flipped open his cell phone and began to dial.

"While you do that, I'll have a fast shower and change for dinner," Milly said.

Her day of unaccustomed exercise had exhausted her and she knew Bret was tired enough to suggest room service. But there was no way she was going to spend any more time alone with him in this hotel room than she had to. She had made up her mind that she couldn't risk making love with Bret again. She might possibly survive that one extraordinary night with her heart intact. Any more and she would never get over him.

He flashed her a knowing glance and nodded his acceptance. She suspected that all he was going along with was the dinner. He looked like a man who had his own ideas about the rest of the night.

She hadn't packed very much for the trip to Yvette's apartment but she did have her serviceable black sheath and the Mexican silver and turquoise earrings and necklace that Flo had brought her back from the Yucatan. In spite of everything, she felt a small thrill of excitement at the thought of going to dinner with Bret. She took extra care with her makeup and dabbed a little Je Reviens behind her ears and at her wrists. It was a sophisticated perfume with a lingering musky scent but it went with the mood she wanted to enjoy for a little while.

When she heard Bret's light knock on the partially open door to her bedroom, she checked her appearance in the full-length mirror beside the door. She hadn't realized just how form fitting this dress was. And she hardly recognized the bright-eyed, glowing woman who was wearing it.

"Ready, Mil...?" Bret stopped in his tracks in the doorway. In his dark suit and white shirt and tie, he was gorgeous. The heat in his gaze almost scorched her. "Oh, yeah," he said.

He let his eyes trail slowly over her. His smile told her that he really appreciated the way she looked.

"Oh, yeah!" he drawled again and took her hand. "Well, let's go dazzle the natives."

She didn't know if they impressed any natives of Atlanta but they certainly dazzled each other. The restaurant Bret chose was elegant and quiet. The silver shone, the crystal glistened. The string group who played dinner music was talented and unobtrusive. Afterwards, Milly couldn't have said what she had eaten but she knew that every bite had been delicious. Every leisurely sip of wine had been perfect.

It was an evening out of time - an evening of sensations, tantalizing aromas and tastes, lingering touches, long sensual looks. Milly was in a Bret-induced daze. The only fact that stood out clearly in her mind was that she and Bret were meant to make love tonight. She no longer had the strength to resist. She couldn't even remember why resisting was so important. Her state of mind was still dreamlike when they returned to the suite.

Bret closed the door behind them and pulled her against his wonderfully muscled body and kissed her slowly, deeply, thoroughly. She kissed him back with all the passion she had been trying to suppress. He took off his jacket and tore off his tie. Milly undid the top buttons of his shirt.

Everything was perfect. She inhaled the subtle scent of his aftershave and Bret's warm, clean body. The heavy curtains were drawn against night sky. The only lamp that they had left lit in the large elegant room cast a faint golden glow on the ivory satin upholstery.

The winking red light on the telephone was glaringly out of place.

"A message," she murmured against the scarred skin at the base of his neck.

"Later," he said, lowering the zipper in the back of her dress and pushing it off her shoulders. His lips followed his hands across her shoulder and top of her breast.

"Flo," she gasped, struggling to regain her sanity. "Flo is the only one who knows where we are."

Bret swore under his breath and kissed the nipple of the tantalizing breast that he had just bared. "Don't lose my place," he said.

Milly stood where he left her for a moment but by the time he had reached the telephone and retrieved the message, she was by his side.

The message was brief and disturbing. "Bart wants us to call," he told her gently. "Flo is in hospital."

Milly reached for the receiver but Bret was already dialing.

"Extension seven-three-one," he said. While he waited for the extension to pick up, Bret explained, "The number Bart left was the Healing Springs Hospital. This extension number must be Flo's room." He turned his attention back to the telephone. "Stu? This is Bret. Hold on. Here's Milly."

He handed her the receiver. "I'll get on the extension in the other room," he said.

When he picked up the receiver in the bedroom, he heard Milly saying in total disbelief, "Burns and a concussion?"

"What happened, Stu?" Bret cut in.

Stu's gravelly voice was angry. "Someone tried to kill her! That's what happened. Some son of a bitch set a bomb in Flo's cottage. It's only blind luck she didn't go straight in after she turned the key in the lock. She and

Bart had picked up some cases of china and glassware on the way home from the airport. I got to Flo's place to help them unload as she started to unlock her door.

"Bart called out to her to ask which was the box she wanted him to put in the garage. She headed back down to the car to point it out. She hadn't got halfway down the walk when the explosion blew out her front door. There must have been a very short delay on the circuit. Just long enough for Flo to get right inside the house after she unlocked the door. Some chunks of wood hit her on the head and some of the burning stuff caught her dress on fire."

"But she's going to be okay?" It was more a prayer than a question.

"The doctors say she was very lucky we got the flames out as quickly as we did."

And darned lucky that Flo had not gone directly into her cottage. Milly could not have stood losing Flo too.

"The doctor who saw her didn't think she needed to be in Intensive Care but Bart arranged to have a private nurse in her room around the clock. He's got a guy from that security outfit you work for, Bret, posted outside the door."

"Oh, Stu, I should be there," Milly said. "They're all strangers to her."

"Don't worry, Milly. I'm staying right here."

"Were you and Bart hurt?" Bret asked.

"Minor burns. That's all. The explosion was mostly inside the house."

"Thank goodness for that," Milly said. Flo's house was furnished with lovely antique pieces. She could imagine how distressed Flo was going to be when she learned that her precious heirlooms had been destroyed.

"We'll get the next plane out of here," Milly said.

"Where's Bart now?" Bret asked.

"As soon as we got Flo admitted and talked to the attending doctor, he went back to The Grove to talk to the police. He's okay. He was on the other side of the car when the bomb went off. He tossed me a blanket he had in the trunk and I rolled Flo in it."

"We'll be there as soon as we can," Bret told him.

He hung up and flipped open the telephone book. "I'll get us a plane," he said.

Milly changed quickly into casual clothes and began to pack.

It was dawn before they actually boarded the small private plane which Bret had cajoled an old buddy into lending him. But the long wakeful night had been nothing like the magical one they had almost had. This attack on Flo was almost too much for Milly. Having Bret close was the only thing that held her together.

Bart was waiting for them at the airfield.

"The doctors tell me they are treating Flo's condition as serious because of the concussion but it's not critical. They're keeping her as sedated as they dare. You know how painful burns are and she has one massive headache. The good news is that she is conscious much of the time. The skull didn't fracture and they don't think there's any brain damage."

The dismay she was feeling must have showed on her face because Bart hastily reassured her, "She's going to come out of this, Milly."

"Pray God!" Milly exclaimed. "Do the doctors think she'll be terribly scarred?"

"She was lucky she was wearing a big-brimmed hat. It started to catch fire but Stu snatched it off her and saved her face from being burned. Not even her hair caught fire. The backs of her legs and her arms are blistered but the doctors don't think the burns are deep enough to scar badly. She can thank Stu's quick reaction with the blanket for that."

"Have you had a chance to talk to Theo?" Bret asked.

"Theo is pretty well convinced that this is connected to the bomb in the Jag. He's determined that Gord won't slip out of this one. He had him picked up for questioning last night and he's working on getting a search warrant for his apartment."

"I'm sure Ronald is already at the Sheriff's Office trying to get his flunky out," Bret said bitterly.

"At least, he's making sure that he keeps silent," Milly said. "Gord must have a lot of confidence in Ronald's ability to keep him out of jail."

"He did it before."

"Theo's been around for a while," Bart tossed in. "He'll do his best to keep Gord long enough to get him to talk. If he can, he'll juggle him around from one station to another until he gets what he wants out of him."

"Yeah, and Gord might even try to make some kind of deal," Bret said thoughtfully. "If I were Gord, I'd start to wonder when it was going to be my turn to be excess baggage to Ronald."

Bart wheeled them past the hospital parking lot. What had been left of the cars had long since been taken away but the charred stumps of the stand of palm trees stood as mute reminders of Gord's earlier work. He dropped them off at the front doors.

"I'll see you upstairs," he said.

Milly looked tired and fragile. Not much of her fire and strength was apparent but Bret knew that it lurked not far below the surface.

This was his fault. If he hadn't been dragging his feet about getting the security system installed, they might have caught Gord as he was wiring the bomb. The place was empty - an invitation for a break-in. With The Grove closed and both Milly and Flo's cottages empty, there would have been no one to observe an intruder working on the lock.

"Flo didn't need this," Milly said. "She just lost Yvette and now her home. And she's in pain."

"The pain will be gone in a few days."

He knew she'd gladly take on Flo's physical pain if she could. Lord, he'd accept it himself. Bret wished he could comfort her but he was no good at this. He squeezed her hand. She looked up at him with something--trust maybe, or something more--in those eloquent eyes. He realized with a shock how much he wanted everything she had to give.

He could see her steel herself for the sight of Flo, lying injured in that hospital bed.

Bret greeted the large, good-looking black man who was guarding Flo's room. Saul was a good man who had worked with Bret before.

"I'm the first line of defense," he said with a grin. "The real fierce one is just inside."

When they opened the door to Flo's room, Mrs. Foster blocked their entry.

"Hello, Bret. When Bart asked me to recommend a good private duty nurse, your father insisted that I come. He'll be fine with Anna there," she said. "Milly, your aunt seems to be improving slightly as the day goes on. She will be glad to see you. She's resting now but you can peek in on her for a minute. I sent your friend Stu off to have some lunch. The man has been here since she came in."

She preceded them into the room and checked the drip on the intravenous apparatus. There was something reassuring in the little gray-haired nurse's smile and in her quick confident movements.

Milly sniffed and whirled to look at him with horror in her eyes as she recognized what it was she was smelling. She clearly hadn't expected the faint odor of seared flesh.

Flo lay on her stomach on the hospital bed. Her legs were loosely bandaged from the knees down. And her left arm was covered with gauze. The only tubes in evidence were the ones to the intravenous.

"Does she have to lie like that all the time?" Milly gasped.

"No. No. The more severe burns are low enough on her legs that we can put her on her side occasionally," Mrs. Foster whispered.

"Milly?" Flo said in a thick voice.

Milly took her hand and sat down on the chair beside the bed.

"I'm here. Go back to sleep. I'll be here when you wake up."

"Bien," Flo said and fell back asleep.

"I'm going to check with Saul and talk to Bart about what's been going on here, Milly. I shouldn't be gone more than a couple of hours," Bret whispered before leaving the room.

"That Detective Sergeant, Theo Parsons, was in and out all night," Saul told him. "He seemed pretty broken up about what happened to Ms. Pelletier. He said to tell you he needed to talk to you the minute you got here."

At that moment, Bart joined them. "Theo said he'd meet us at The Grove in an hour," he said. "How's Milly taking this?"

"She's still pretty much in a state of shock. But she was relieved when Mrs. Foster told us she thought Flo was recovering as well as could be expected," Bret told him. "I hate to leave her but I need to talk to Theo."

By the time they arrived at The Grove, someone had nailed plywood across the gaping hole in the front of Flo's neat little cottage and swept up the glass from the walk. Yellow police tape was strung around the whole building. Bret had hoped to be able to report to Milly and Flo on the extent of the damage to the interior. It shouldn't be too hard to convince Theo to allow him inside. The crime scene crew had apparently finished collecting evidence, packed up their equipment and gone.

Theo was sitting on the patio waiting when they pulled in to the parking space by Milly's house.

"Your security system installers just left," Theo told Bret with a snort. "Too bad Flo's place wasn't included."

Nothing Theo said could make him feel worse than he already did. Bret didn't even attempt to justify himself.

Bart came to his defense. "We thought Milly was the target and that having Bret with her would be the most effective way to keep her safe."

"Not 'we'," Bret said. "I'm the incompetent jackass who read the situation wrong. I didn't realize that Flo's attitude would set Ronald off. I figure he must think Flo saw him at the hotel, too. "

"Understandable, I suppose. She was there," Theo muttered. "How is Flo?"

"From what her nurse says, improving a little." That news softened Theo's granite features slightly. "I have Milly's keys and the code for the new system," Bret said. "What do you say we talk inside?"

"I read the journal last night," Theo began the minute they were seated. "I don't know that Yvette's words would be enough for a district attorney to build a case on, but they convinced me. Of course, I knew Yvette well enough to know how observant she was. Now all we have to do is find some solid evidence to place Ronald in Fort Lauderdale instead of on his honeymoon in the Bahamas. Even if we could do that, why would Yvette happening to see him because enough to kill her? I know there's a possible tie-in with the dead Higgenbottom woman but the Fort Lauderdale police say she died of natural causes."

"I can tell you something about that." Bret was glad to have some actual information to pass along. "Ronald and Nancy Higgenbottom were lovers.

According to a good friend, she was pregnant with his child when she died." He told them what Milly had learned at The Firm about Nancy's aversion to drugs.

Theo pursed his lips in a low whistle. "Very accommodating of his pregnant lover to drop dead when he was about to marry another wealthy woman. I did a bit of digging myself after you told me about your suspicions, Bret. The first Mrs. Wilson was a rich woman, too. There was some speculation about her death. Her doctors thought they finally had her diabetes under control. They were surprised when she went into insulin shock. Her father raised a big fuss but no one could prove she didn't accidentally give herself extra insulin."

"I know you don't like considering details from Milly's dreams, Theo, but in the last one, she saw Ronald plunge a hypodermic needle into Yvette's thigh. They weren't able, by any chance, to find punctures on Yvette's body, were they?"

"Not that they could be sure about," Theo said.

"I wonder if they found any on Nancy Higgenbottom?"

"I haven't seen the autopsy report but if he was involved in the first wife getting an extra dose of insulin, maybe..." He took out a pad of paper and jotted down a few words. "I'll call my buddy in Fort Lauderdale and have him look into it. Of course, we still have the little question of Wilson being out of the country with his brand new wife."

"Why is everyone so hung up on his being in the Bahamas?" Bart asked. He looked truly bewildered. "Hell, I've made it from West End on Grand Bahama home to West Palm Beach in a little over three hours. And Ronald could make better time in The Sprite than I do in The Two. Add three quarters of an hour to get him to Fort Lauderdale. He could do it."

"You figure Kit went along for the ride?" Bret's sarcasm masked his frustration.

"I don't know," his brother said. "What if he drugged her?"

"Without her being aware that she woke up with a drug hangover? Kittle is a lot swifter than that."

"Well, I've decided to go back to her house and see what I can find out," Bart said. "That is, if I can weasel my way back in."

"I didn't know you'd left."

"Ronald was getting a little hostile about me hanging around," Bart admitted. "And Kit thought she had made her point. She thinks they'll be able to talk better with me gone. So I wasn't happy about it but I bowed out before I went to the airport to pick up Flo."

"Is your cousin at all aware of your suspicions?" Theo asked.

"Not enough. I've tried to be available if she needs me without upsetting her more than she already is," Bart said rubbing his temples. "She suspects that he was seeing another woman just before they were married. I haven't told her anything about Yvette's ghost. And I sure haven't said, 'Milly dreamed she saw Ronald kill Yvette.'"

"You going to tell her about the journal?" Bret asked.

"Probably."

"She should be alerted to the possibility that he's a murderer," Bret said.

"Damn it! It's not that easy," Bart blurted. "When I so much as suggest anything negative about Ronald, she accuses me of being jealous!"

Bret had seen his brother in some tense situations but he had never seen his laid-back composure crack like this. He must be deeply upset about Kit. And their relationship was more complicated than he had ever imagined.

"Kit has spent a lot of time at The Grove with Milly this week," Bret said. "Maybe Milly could talk to her."

Bart pressed his lips together in a tight line and frowned. "Yes," he said abruptly. "Kit feels comfortable with Milly. Admires what she's done with The Grove. Yes. That would work."

"I should be getting back to the hospital," Bret said, looking at his watch. "What are the chances of taking a look at the damage inside, Theo?"

"I can take you in. But I don't think Flo should be told much about it for a while. The blast was confined mostly to the living room and that's a disaster." Theo face was stiff with anger. "We'll get that bastard Ingles this time. We picked him up for questioning on the strength of a couple of similar components in the two explosions. Deputy Purdy is having a chat with him down at the Sheriff's office as we speak."

Bret hoped Theo was right.

The following Thursday morning, Milly sat at the shaded wrought iron table on her patio and waited for Bret to arrive with Flo and Mrs. Foster. In the week since the explosion, Flo had made a remarkable recovery. Her burns were still painful and restricted her movement quite a bit but the headache returned only when she overexerted herself. Flo insisted that she didn't need a nurse, but Bret and Will overruled her objections. Two Thornton men were too much even for Flo.

The sound of hammers from the workmen renovating Flo's cottage was loud out here. For the next week or so, Flo and Bea Foster would be living in the guest cottage. Security was tight at The Grove, these days. The guest cottage had state of the art technology installed and Greco Associates' men patrolled the grounds. It was like living in an armed camp.

Gord Ingles was still in jail. Despite Ronald's best efforts, bail had been denied. The judge felt that the violent nature of the charges indicated that he should be held until the preliminary hearing. As far as Milly knew, Gord was still maintaining his silence about the bombings. Ronald was still enjoying a privileged life in Palm Beach.

The one thing that had fallen perfectly into place was the re-opening of The Grove. Stu continued to be invaluable running the bar area and Eva had taken over Milly's duties as hostess. She was even doing some of the paperwork. The senior sous chef had assumed control of the kitchen and was quite happily doing a repeat of last month's menus.

She seemed to have everything pretty much under control. Everything, that is, except Bret. And, perhaps, her stubborn self. Bret had made no secret of the fact that he was determined to resume the lovemaking that was so rudely interrupted a week ago in Atlanta. She had told him she was relieved that they hadn't made love. Her excuse was that the timing was all wrong for them. He gave her that knowing look that showed he knew she was afraid and said he'd wait.

The problem was she knew he'd wait as long as it took. She also knew that her need for him was not fading with time. She remembered, all too clearly, the magical evening they had spent together in Atlanta. But the real world was awfully real right now. She needed to find a way to control her life.

Bret drove past in the silver Jaguar that replaced the one that had been destroyed. His smile said that he was glad to see her. He gave her a crisp wave and pointed the way to the guest cottage.

Her unconvinced heart leapt.

The guest bungalow was the closest building to The Grove, directly across from Milly's cottage. Milly saw Flo glance down past the pool to her own house, then quickly avert her gaze from the raw wood of the new front door and the unpainted siding around it.

Bret lifted a wheelchair out of the trunk.

"That wheelchair is Bea's idea. Not mine," Flo complained. "I can walk perfectly well."

"You don't have to use it indoors. Those legs have done enough bending for the day. She flatly refused to come home in a comfortable ambulance," Bea Foster added for Milly's benefit.

Flo muttered something about "more extravagance".

"I was planning to make the ride your birthday present," Bret said with a laugh.

"My birthday isn't until December." Flo glared at him.

"Now I don't know what to get you," he said with a chuckle as he scooped her up in his arms and deposited her gently in the chair.

He turned and gave Milly a quick kiss on the mouth. "Hello, love," he said.

Visions of being greeted like that every day for the rest of her life tantalized the imagination. But what would it cost her? Even though they had joked about her being the "boss", that was the last thing she wanted. Nevertheless, with Bret she could no longer be self-contained. If she gave in to the feelings that were tugging at her, she would leave her heart with no protection. Her essence would be totally his. He wouldn't have to demand it. She would surrender it. And when he left, she would have nothing.

Bea allowed them to come inside long enough to assure themselves that Flo had everything she needed but she soon ushered them out. "She needs her rest. Come back after she has had a good sleep," she said. "She doesn't have any idea how much this ordeal has taken out of her."

When they reached the end of the walk, Milly started to turn towards the restaurant. "You must be ready for a cold drink," she offered.

"Let's sit by the pool," Bret said. "I'll get us each a cold soda from the cottage. Would you rather have a beer?"

"Soda's fine," she said. She had the feeling that the less time they spent in the confines of the cottage the better. The little house felt crowded with Bret there. His vitality filled it to bursting. And her bedroom was too full of steamy memories and dreams of his loving.

"Have you heard anything from Theo?" she asked when he emerged with the sodas.

"Nothing new. Gord's still refusing to talk but Theo says he's showing signs of cracking. Ronald is still free as a bird."

Bret sat back and she couldn't mistake the hungry look in his eyes. Her fingers itched to join the breeze that ruffled his thick blond hair. She didn't want to react but she could feel her treacherous body heating as his hot gaze slowly swept over her. When it lingered on her breasts, she stifled a gasp. His smile became more intimate and dangerous.

"You've been avoiding me, love," he said.

She should tell him forcefully that she was going to continue to stay out of his way. But then she would have to explain about eavesdropping on him and Bart. She hadn't intended to pause outside the window of the cottage but she hadn't been able to resist. She hadn't realized how much both brothers missed the excitement and variety of the lives they had led with the agency.

She wasn't certain about which brother had been more enthusiastic about the news that the mysterious agency had been reactivated under another name. They were both considering accepting their invitations to sign up again. Their voices were so similar.

One of them--she thought it was Bret--was saying that he had given the security business a good try but he didn't think he could face staying in Florida much longer.

The other twin replied that it was ironic that they were both back here doing exactly what Will had been suggesting for years.

Then they must have moved farther away from the window because she could catch only the occasional phrase. But she did hear something like, "...care too much about that woman...too many complications. Have to get away before it's impossible to make a rational decision."

Well, she was going to make a rational decision, too. And that was not to get any more involved with Bret!

"Bret, we are living in the same house." That sounded almost as if she had her emotions under control.

"Looks that way to an outside observer," he said.

Bret had decided he wasn't going to let her off the hook this time. She was going to have to face that he was a major factor in her life. The sexual attraction between them was so strong that you could almost see it vibrating in the air. He didn't know where it was leading them but he was damned if he was going to go along with pretending it didn't exist. Why should they? They were independent adults, responsible to no one.

"If you are trying to drive me crazy, love, you are doing a good job of it. I can't think of anything else but you." He reached across the table to take her hands. "Milly..."

When he saw Eva running across from The Grove, waving a manila envelope, he felt like cursing. Then when he realized what he had almost said, he was glad for Eva's interruption. Milly, too, seemed relieved.

"Just adding another duty to my job description," Eva said. "Short run courier service. This just arrived, Milly. For you, marked, 'Personal'."

She handed the envelope to Milly. "Gotta run," she said, "Stu is helping me with the invoices."

She winked at them and headed back to the office without even pausing a moment at their table.

"It's from Mark Sanders," Milly exclaimed as she tore open the envelope.

"Who?"

"Instructor at The Firm."

Inside was a sealed envelope and a brief note.

She read the note aloud, "I hope that you and your fiancé are having more success than I am. My sister and I looked through the box of Nancy's papers. But we didn't find a word written by Ronnie Wilson.

"Would this letter addressed to him help? Both of us can vouch that the address is in Nancy's handwriting.

"Please keep me posted. Mark Sanders"

Across the envelope, someone had written in a bold hand, "Return to Sender."

"Yes! The address sure looks like the handwriting Kit described." Bret grinned and reached for the letter. "And I'd be willing to bet that Kit wrote the Return To Sender."

"Shouldn't we be careful how we touch this? Or do you think too many people have handled it already for it to matter?"

"It's the handwriting on the letter that's probably the best proof of the connection between Ronald and Nancy," Bret said. "I'll get it to Theo this afternoon."

"You just missed him," Milly said. "Now that Flo's here, he makes sure that his deputy is in place. He insisted on doing a security check several times a day at the hospital."

"I told him we were doubling the security patrols of our men today. Having Theo drop in will keep them all on their toes."

"Ronald still thinks she's a threat to him."

"I don't think he's aware that we're on to him. But if he tries to get at her now, we'll get him."

"Is Bart having any luck in Fort Lauderdale?" Milly asked.

"He swears he and two of our investigators have covered every marina in the area this week and haven't found the one where Ronald docked The Sprite. Bart suspects that he left it at someone's private dock."

"That means it could be anywhere. All Ronald would have to know is that the person was away on holiday. It could be anyone from one of his clubs or a client. Anyone."

"He'll find out. Bart's good and he's determined."

"I guess that's why I haven't seen more of him. Kit's been here almost every day without him. I can see why she and Yvette were such good friends. They both have the same kind of zip."

Bret seemed about to say something then stopped himself.

"I keep thinking that someone must have noticed Yvette leaving The Inn," he said after a moment. "The investigators from the Sheriff's department say no taxi picked her up. Our guys double-checked that. Went to all the independents and couldn't find anyone who had picked up a fare that looked like Yvette that night. What do you say you and I go back to The Inn for an early dinner and ask around?"

"I guess it's worth a try."

"I wonder which restaurant Yvette would have chosen."

"Yvette would eat in the more casual one. She did fine dining only for special occasions and rarely used room service. Thought they were extravagant."

Milly tried to put their dinner date in Atlanta out of her mind. At least, this would not be another white linen and crystal type of restaurant.

She made the mistake of meeting Bret's eyes. Not for the first time, she wondered why she was fighting so hard to resist him. Maybe what she needed to do was give in. That possibly would get him out of her system. Who was she trying to fool? Possibly? Not probably. Not likely.

"Later, then," he said.

She watched him leave with the promise of those words warming her like a caress. She was a fool.

Bret whistled under his breath as he strode towards his car. Milly wanted him. Her expressive face was an open book. Every emotion she felt was written there. And she knew as well as he did that tonight they were going to make love. Tonight would not be the last time. Not by a long shot.

He called the Sheriff's office from the car and was told that Detective Sergeant Parsons would be expecting him in half an hour.

Theo Parson's office was very much like the man himself, plain, uncluttered and efficient. Theo, himself, was seated behind his desk in his shirtsleeves. His jacket was on a hanger behind the desk.

Bret didn't waste any time getting to the point of his visit. "I have a letter here that proves there was a relationship between Nancy Higgenbottom and Ronald Wilson," he said. He tossed the letter on Theo's desk.

Theo looked at the envelope, then at Bret. Then he waited.

"I don't know how much of this you know," Bret said. He began with the visits to Atlanta and finished with the note Milly had received from Mark Sanders.

Theo called in two deputies to witness his slicing open the envelope. He used long tweezers to slide out the three sheets of flowered stationery it contained.

"Thanks," he told the men when they had signed an affidavit to that effect. "I'll lift the prints myself."

Finally when the long painstaking procedure was finished, Theo allowed Bret to get close enough to the pages spread out on his desk to read what they said.

"Keep your hands behind your back," Theo said. "We don't have to get too close. The writing's big enough and the ink is dark."

Theo looked as uncomfortable as Bret felt about reading the young woman's love letter.

Nancy Higgenbottom had been painfully gullible and desperately in love. She wrote a dozen different ways how much she longed to be with Ronnie again. She went into embarrassing detail about how she was going to ensure that Ronnie enjoyed what she referred to as their pre-honeymoon in Fort Lauderdale.

It was at the bottom of the second page that she wrote, "You won't be sorry that you dumped that Schofield woman. She has money but she was never right for you, Ronnie. You would have been miserable with her. You do understand that's why I was going to tell her about the baby. Marrying her would have ruined your life, Honey. You'll be so happy with me and your baby."

Theo shook his head sadly. "Poor silly woman," he said.

"This proves Ronald had a motive but officially there is no crime," Bret said.

"And there is not likely to be. A buddy of mine from the Fort Lauderdale force sent me a copy of the transcript of the autopsy tape. The pathologist did mention one puncture of the skin of her inner thigh but only the one. No old needle marks. As there was no drug involved except for the sleeping pill she had apparently taken, his conclusion was that it was not significant in her death."

"Mark Sanders swears she never took pills of any kind and that she definitely wouldn't start after she discovered she was pregnant."

"He may or may not be right but there were six Seconal capsules loose in the bottom of her purse. No one saw her with anyone and only one champagne glass had been used. The bottle in the ice bucket was half empty. The officers on the scene felt that she had been stood up, drank half a bottle of champagne, took a couple of sleeping pills and died in her sleep."

"Of no perceptible illness," Bret said.

"I hate to admit it but anything else is going to be next to impossible to prove. We'll have to get him for killing Yvette. There's no doubt about that being murder." Anger and frustration rang in Theo's voice. "You'd think someone would have seen her with him at the hotel. But we haven't found anyone who remembers her."

"Milly and I had the same idea. We're going to give finding a witness one more shot. We'll go to The Inn tonight and see if we don't have more luck this time." He glanced at the wall clock and moved towards the door. "I'd better get back."

"Before you go," Theo said. "I do have two pieces of news. One is that we should be able to release Yvette's body for burial early next week. The second is..."

The older man's self-satisfied grin told Bret that he was going to want to hear this.

When Bret arrived at Milly's door at four-thirty, he was jubilant.

"Celebration time!" he said, with a broad grin. "Theo tells me he thinks they've got enough on Gord Ingles to make the charges stick."

"They finally got the search warrant?" Milly couldn't believe that she was actually hearing good news.

"For the whole building. The garage and his apartment above it. They found traces of the chemicals he used to make the bombs in the tool room of the garage. And they found acid burns on some coveralls in his apartment."

They were going to get the monster who had almost killed Flo!

"The clincher is that on Wednesday, a customer who hadn't heard The Grove was closed stopped for dinner. He got out of the car to read the "Closed" sign in the window and wondered what the beat-up white van was doing between Flo and Milly's cottages. The guy was smart enough to copy down the tag number. When he heard about the explosion the next day, he called the Sheriff's Office. What do you think of that?"

They finally had some real evidence. This brought them a giant step closer to getting Ronald.

"Wonderful!" Milly threw her arms around his neck and kissed him.

The kiss was supposed to express her relief and happiness but instantly became much more.

One touch of Bret's lips made all her hard-won resistance evaporate. It acted like a blast of oxygen on the glowing embers she had tried so hard to damp down. Bret's response was immediate and every bit as uncontrolled.

He thrust his tongue deep into her welcoming mouth and his large hands pulled her hips against him. Without a bit of foreplay, she could feel his amazing readiness, hard against her abdomen. Knowing how much he wanted her added fuel to the blazing heat inside her. Milly's breasts tingled and she could feel a hot moistness where she needed him most.

Their kisses became more frantic. She could not touch or taste him enough. Bret's tongue plunged again and again until neither of them could breathe.

Almost before he had kicked the door closed behind them, their mouths still fused in that amazing kiss, she was fumbling with his belt.

She didn't recognize this crazy woman she had become. When Bret broke off the kiss, she moaned in protest.

"Your room," he said.

"Now," she mumbled against this neck.

He picked her up and in a few long strides they were in her bedroom. He set her down on the edge of her bed.

Milly couldn't have said how it happened but the next thing she knew, she was lying on her cool, satin bed spread with Bret's mouth devouring hers again and his smooth, warm flesh pressed full length against her naked body. Shirt, pants and briefs lay in a heap on the floor beside the prim shirtwaist dress she had just finished ironing.

He kissed a line of tantalizing sensations along the side of her neck, and down her right breast.

Her hands moved restlessly on his back when he took the nipple in his mouth. When he sucked hard, the spasm of sweet tension deep in her body made her cry out. She tried to pull him up to reach the hardness that would relieve her fierce need.

"Bret," she gasped. "No more."

"I want to make sure you're ready," he said. His face was rigid with the strain of holding back.

"I've been ready for a week," she said, trying to reach the drawer that held protection.

Bret's hand was there before her. He ripped the package open with his teeth and attempted to put the condom on. His fingers didn't seem to want to obey.

"Help me with this damned thing," he bit out.

Between them they fitted the sheath to him. And between them, with a few strong, intensely satisfying strokes, they ended the sweet torment.

When the storm had passed, Bret shifted their positions and held her on top of him.

"I'm sorry, love," he whispered into her hair after a long while. "You deserve more finesse than that."

"Any more delay would have killed me," she said. "I love...the way you make love to me."

"Let me make love with you again."

She chuckled but then she felt him stirring against her and realized that he was serious.

"We can ease into it this time, love." Bret's voice was low and tempting. "And really enjoy the voyage. Let's stay right here in your bed and save our visit to The Inn for another day."

She didn't ever want to leave his arms. But she needed some time to come to terms with her feelings. She had done exactly what she had sworn she would never do again. And she sure had held nothing back this time. And she was dreadfully afraid that she had slipped down that slippery slide right into love.

"We can still get to The Inn," she said. But only if she moved out of his arms right this minute. Her willpower was next to nonexistent. "Then we can come back here and see how we feel."

"The voice of reason," he said with a wry grin. "All right. Get up woman." He gave her a kiss on the tip of her nose.

Bret watched her stretch and slowly get off the bed. She was beautifully proportioned. Her long braid hung down her back just past the point where her slender waist flared out to perfectly rounded hips. Next time, he thought, she'll take time to unbind that hair. Or he'd do it. "And please, please put some clothes on," he said.

He watched her dress again, this time in a green silk shift that pointed up the green in her eyes. In or out of her clothes, Milly was breathtaking. Only the possibility that he might return to her bed when they returned from the hotel, stopped him from trying to convince her to stay home.

"Am I going alone?" Milly asked pointedly.

He expelled a long reluctant breath and picked his clothes up off the floor.

At The Inn, they walked around the lobby a couple of times and spoke to several of the bellmen but no one remembered seeing a woman who looked like Milly.

The family style, mid-priced restaurant was cheerful with red and white checkered tablecloths. The waitresses wore costumes that reminded him of The Sound of Music. In spite of the fact that they were getting nowhere with their attempt to find the witness they needed, Bret enjoyed his meal. Milly seemed comfortable with him and hadn't retreated into herself as he'd feared she might.

They had finished their main course and were waiting for dessert when a middle-aged waitress whom Bret had noticed glancing at Milly a couple of times, stopped by their table.

"I'm sorry to bother you, dear," she said, "but I've wondered a few times how your aunt is?"

"She's fine," Milly replied, obviously wondering how the waitress knew that Flo had been injured. "She came home from the hospital this morning."

The woman's concerned expression gave way to a smile. "You must be relieved. You were so worried when you got that call about her stroke."

Bret interrupted. "She got the call here?"

"You remember, don't you?" The woman looked at Milly, confused for a moment. "My name is Catherine. I waited on you."

"Actually, I think it was my twin sister who was here that night," Milly told her.

"Oh? You sure look alike," she said looking relieved. "Oops, I have to go. The hostess is waving me back to my own tables."

"Can we talk to you when you finish your shift?" Milly asked. "It's important."

She gave Milly a long look. "Meet me in the donut shop next door at ten o'clock. That's where my husband picks me up," she said and bustled back to the other side of the restaurant.

Two hours later, good as her word, Catherine walked into the donut shop. She stopped briefly to speak to a burly man who was seated with another two men near the door. She picked up the coffee he had obviously bought for her, then carried it over to the table where Bret and Milly were dawdling over what seemed to be their hundredth cup of coffee.

"I can't tell you how much we appreciate your talking to us, Catherine," Bret said, pulling out a chair for her.

"Why?" she said, looking at them suspiciously.

"We'd better introduce ourselves, Bret," Milly said, pulling her driver's license out of her purse and handing it to the woman. "I'm Milly Brzezynski and this is my friend, Bret Thornton"

Bret produced his card.

"My sister, who is the one you waited on, disappeared from the hotel the night you saw her."

"Oh, my dear!" Catherine's hand flew to her mouth. "I didn't see anyone bothering her. She ate alone and she seemed perfectly fine until she got that call."

"I'm so glad you remembered her," Milly said sincerely. "Nobody had any idea why she would leave the hotel until you told us she had a call about my aunt."

"Nobody told you they called to tell her about the stroke, then."

"Their aunt didn't have a stroke," Bret informed her. "She has been in hospital for the last week because of an accident she was in."

"Oh, my goodness," Catherine said. "And your sister was so upset. I heard her cell phone ring and looked over at her. She answered, listened for a minute, then went real pale. She came right over to the table I was serving and handed me a handful of money that more than covered the bill and apologized to me for running out. She said her aunt had had a stroke and a friend was picking her up to take her to the hospital."

"You didn't see her again?" Milly asked.

"Sorry," the waitress said. "I think she was heading for the elevators the last I saw of her."

She agreed to make a statement to the police if they thought it was necessary and gave them her address and telephone number.

"I really am sorry I couldn't give you any more help," she said as they left.

"You don't know how much I appreciate your talking to us," Milly said.

After Bret handed Catherine a couple of folded bills which she resisted taking, they headed back to The Grove.

They were saved the trouble of calling Theo. He was leaving the guest bungalow as they arrived.

"You don't dare go in there on penalty of death," Theo told them. "Bea is on the rampage. According to her, Flo should have been asleep two hours ago."

"How is she feeling?" Milly asked.

"The medication is controlling the pain and Bea tells me that both the burns and the concussion are progressing well but will heal in their own sweet time. Flo's comments in French were fortunately beyond my limited knowledge," he said with a fond smile. "But I got the gist of them."

"Can I get you a cold drink, Theo?" Milly asked. "Or a coffee? We need to talk to you."

"Thanks but I only have a few minutes," he said, heading for the closest table on the central patio.

"Evidence against Ronald Wilson is starting to mount up, though," he began when the three of them were seated around the table. "All we had until this afternoon was Yvette's journal and that letter from Nancy Higgenbottom. But late this afternoon, Gord Ingles changed lawyers. That's significant. And he's trying to make a deal. He wants to avoid an attempted murder charge in return for information about who hired him to do the bombings." Theo rarely showed his emotions but his anger was clearly visible in the rigid lines of his face. "I want to tell you it will be a cold day in Hell before I go along with that. I just hope the D.A. doesn't like the idea."

"Milly and I have something to add to your list. We learned how he got Yvette out of the hotel and into his car." Bret told him briefly what they had learned from the waitress at The Inn.

"If we can find that cell phone, with any luck we'll find his phone number in the memory." Theo sounded more hopeful. "But we've found no sign of her purse."

"She wouldn't leave the hotel without it," Milly said.

"There are two dumpsters on the construction site. I'll have some men to go through them." Theo pursed his lips and blew a long thoughtful breath. "Yes. His phone number on the cell phone would be enough to get his car impounded. Then we could go over it for evidence that he had her there."

"You'll find her blood on the doorjamb," Milly challenged.

"I'm beginning to think we will," Theo replied. "But we have to hold off laying charges until we get unshakable evidence. Schofield Pharmaceuticals has a lot of clout. The D.A. would never go for charging the husband of its Chairman of the Board. And one of its lawyers to boot."

"We have to get a witness that saw him with Yvette," Bret agreed. "He doesn't have an alibi for her murder. Breaking his alibi for the one in Fort Lauderdale isn't going to be easy."

"I don't fancy grilling the head of Schofield Pharmaceuticals about her wedding night, either." Theo got to his feet. "I'll be in touch," he said and left them alone by the pool.

Milly woke with the first rays of sunlight shining on her face through the lace curtains on her bedroom window and a heavy arm lying possessively across her waist. Her cheek on Bret's chest, she could hear his heart beating steadily in her ear. She was snuggled against him, one bent knee across his thighs. She'd known if they made love again she would never want it to end. Even if he broke her heart, she was glad she'd had the courage to risk this kind of love.

She squinted against the strong sunlight and saw her tiny black bikini lying, perfectly dry, on the floor beside the bed. She smiled and sighed a totally satisfied sigh as she remembered the look on Bret's face when she came out of the bathroom wearing it.

"No midnight swim tonight, love," he said, reaching for her.

And that was one order she'd had no problem obeying.

She ran a finger lightly over his smooth chest. Bret was not a hairy man. A fine line of golden hair formed a T that linked his nipples then led directly to the interesting organ that was stirring against her thigh with his morning erection.

She sensed that he was waking and her finger began to trace the top of the T.

Bret murmured something unintelligible that rumbled in her ear. What a lovely way to wake up!

The sound of the telephone on the bedside table was strident and jarring.

She tried to raise her head and winced at the sharp pain. Bret was lying on her hair. When he tried to reach for the phone at the same time she did, he rolled more firmly on her hair.

"Ow!" she cried. "Bret, don't move a muscle."

"Sweetheart, I'm sorry. I'll just lift myself up so that you can get it out from under me."

Every attempt to lift himself off her hair pulled at another strand. The wrestling and swatting and apologizing might have been funny to an outside observer but to Milly, it was no joke.

She yelped again. "Let me do it!"

"Never, never again," she muttered as she struggled to free her too long hair which seemed to have taken on a life of its own and wrapped itself around Bret as if it would never let him go. "I sleep with my hair in a braid. Or I cut it all off."

It took a while to untangle herself while the phone kept ringing insistently and Bret kept apologizing. Finally, she was free.

"Don't you dare answer that phone," she added.

Bret laughed and saluted. "No, ma'am, Boss. I wouldn't dare."

She knew how bossy she sounded but she wasn't ready to explain to Flo why Bret was answering her bedside telephone.

She picked up the receiver. "Yes," she snapped.

"Milly, I'm sorry. Did I wake you?"

"No, no, Kit. I was in the shower." She returned Bret's grin and blew him a kiss.

"I just had a brilliant idea," Kit said. Her voice sounded overly bright to Milly. "Can you get away from The Grove for the day?"

"Possibly," Milly said cautiously.

"Ronald and Bart are playing in a two-ball golf tournament at the country club today and tomorrow," she said. "I thought we'd take advantage of their absence by going out on The Sprite. You and I could spend that long leisurely day at sea that we've been talking about."

"They're partners?" Milly asked incredulously.

"Bart was so surprised to be invited that he accepted." Kit's laugh was more genuine now. "Please say yes, Milly. You said you were nervous about tackling the ocean but the winds are supposed to be light today. And you need to get away for a bit."

Maybe it would be a good idea to get far enough away from Bret for a few hours to regain a little perspective.

"What time and what can I bring?" she decided.

"As soon as you can get here if I'm going to show you my favorite swimming spot. And yourself, your bathing suit and a good sunscreen," Kit said.

When Milly hung up, Bret reached for her and asked, "Who are partners?"

"Bart and Ronald are playing in a two-ball tournament at the country club," Milly told him, enjoying his stunned look.

"That should be an interesting round," he said, pulling her back into bed.

She gave him a long thorough kiss, then said, "That's going to have to hold us for a while. I have to leave. I'm spending the day on the water with Kit and she said to hurry."

"I thought you said you didn't much like boats," he said.

"Kit tells me that if I take a Dramamine an hour before we sail, I'll be fine." She shrugged and reluctantly left his arms and the bed. "I hope she'd right. I got seasick in the Maid of the Mist on the Niagara River."

She quickly showered and dressed in her favorite denim shorts and turquoise T-shirt.

"I have the feeling that Kit wants to talk to me about something. I'm a little uneasy about how much to tell her. Is she safest not knowing what her husband is capable of? Or should she be on her guard?"

"That's the question Bart and I have been struggling with," Bret said. "You saw how Ronald responded when he thought Flo was a threat to him."

"I guess I'll play it by ear," she said. "I'll take my cue from Kit."

"Do you want me to go with you? I really don't want to let you out of my sight until Wilson is behind bars."

"I suspect she wants a girl talk session," she said. "We'll be perfectly safe. Bart is right with Ronald and Gord is in jail." She felt a little shiver tremble up her spine. Well, that was true.

She met Kit on her own property for the first time. If she had been impressed by Will's West Palm Beach home, she was overwhelmed by the Schofield estate. The expanse of prime ocean front property with docking on the Intracoastal Waterway was even more impressive than she had been led to believe. The house itself looked more like a small, elegant hotel than a private home. Its weathered brick would have fit in better on an English country estate than on a Florida beach but somehow over the years it had grown compatible with its setting.

Kit met her on the circular drive.

"Would you like a tour of the shack?" she asked. "Or would you rather wait until you feel stronger. My mother loved this place and insisted in her will that I live here for at least three months a year. It grows on you."

"I've taken my Dramamine. Let's head out to sea!" Milly said. "I can't believe I said that!"

They boarded The Sprite and within minutes, with Kit at the controls, they were heading out the Boynton Beach Inlet to the open sea. Milly was cautiously optimistic that she would survive the trip.

"Where are we going?" she asked.

Kit was obviously in her element here. "Grand Bahama!" she said. "We'll have a swim in my favorite cove and take the tender in to shore for the best conch chowder in the entire world."

Milly wondered why they were headed for the site of Kit's honeymoon. Did Kit simply want her to see her favorite place or did she have another reason?

Milly didn't have time to ponder this question, though, because at that moment they came out into the open Atlantic Ocean. The winds might be considered light but the waves were plenty big enough for her. After a minute or two of anxiously scanning the blank horizon and trying to gauge how large the next wave was that they were going to slice through, Milly accepted that they were not going to be swamped. Then, gradually she began to feel a wonderful exhilaration. The splashing of the spray from the waves that curled off their bow became exciting, the foaming wake endlessly fascinating.

"Do you want to take the wheel?" Kit asked.

"Do you have a death wish?" Milly countered.

"There's nothing out here to hit," Kit told her.

"Another time," Milly said, surprised that she meant it.

Three hours flew by. Much too soon, they slipped around a headland into a calm little bay where Kit dropped anchor.

"Well, here we are," she said. "Paradise. Are you ready for your swim or would you like to sip a cold soda and have a look around you?" Kit indicated a tiny refrigerator.

"I'll have a soda, thanks. I need a minute to think about how wonderful that ride was. Oh, Kit, no wonder you and Yvette spent so much time on this boat. It must be even more exciting when the sea is up a bit."

"You're bitten, too?" They made their way to the deck where they took a couple of deck chairs out of the locker where they had been stowed. "That's great."

The two women sat silently for a while. Milly commented occasionally on the color of the water and the ring of beaches around the little cove. Kit seemed distracted.

Finally, she spoke.

"Milly, you knew Ronald well at one time."

"For a couple of months, ten years ago," she answered.

"We were engaged for a year and I thought he was the man I would spend the rest of my life with," Kit began. "But I'm beginning to think I've made a terrible error in judgment. My marriage seems to be falling apart already. Do you think I can trust Ronald?"

This wasn't something she could answer yes or no. "What makes you ask, Kit?"

"Several times over the past year I wondered why he was unavailable so much of the time. He always had a good explanation. But then a friend told me she'd seen him with another woman in Atlanta. Ronald said she must have been referring to a client he was meeting. I accepted that."

Milly could see that Kit didn't like admitting she'd been wrong.

"Yvette kept saying he was after my money but when he didn't object to anything in the prenuptial agreement, I decided maybe she was a bit jealous of my happiness. I was determined to give the marriage every possible chance. My mother discovered that it's hard for most men's egos to be married to a woman with real money.

"I thought I would avoid part of the problem by giving Ronald a million as a wedding gift so that he wouldn't ever be short of money. He didn't want to accept it at first. Then he was so marvelous about postponing the wedding after Uncle Will's first heart attack that I was convinced that he really loved me. The million didn't matter."

Kit had apparently approached her marriage the same way she would prepare for a tricky business merger. She seemed to have confronted each issue that she thought would present a problem and countered it logically.

"Is the prenuptial agreement what you and Yvette quarreled about? Were you planning to change that?"

"I don't want you to think changing the prenuptial was Ronald's idea." Kit was quick to come to his defense. "That and making him the joint owner of the Schofield house was my own idea. Our five day honeymoon was so wonderful and he was so understanding about cutting it short when Uncle Will had his second attack, I wanted to show him that I wasn't planning to be married six times like my mother. I wanted to make a gesture that said I had confidence in our marriage...without escape hatches."

That Schofield property would bring somewhere in the neighborhood of fifteen million dollars on the current market. Some gesture!

"Yvette fought you on it," Milly said.

"After hours of wrangling with her, I agreed not to tamper with the prenuptial agreement for a year. But I was still going to give him half the house. That's in the papers she was going to draw up for me. I wonder now if I argued so hard with her because I was afraid she was right about him."

"I believe she was," Milly said. That prenuptial was the only thing insuring Kit's safety right now.

"It all comes down to one question. Was he two-timing me with this Higgenbottom woman? She wrote to him at my house and the police found his office phone number in her hotel room. Do you think he's capable of doing that to me?" Her tone of voice said she obviously didn't have much hope that Milly would tell her he wasn't.

"He was seeing her up until a month before your wedding," Milly said.

"How can you be so sure?" Kit was objecting but didn't appear surprised.

"I had a long talk with a good friend of hers. He insists that they'd been seeing each other for years. She told him that Ronald had decided to cancel his wedding to you and that they were getting back together."

Kit looked upset enough without mentioning the pregnancy.

"Well, he didn't cancel it!" Kit stood up and walked to the railing. When she whirled around to face her, Milly could see she was appalled by what she was thinking. "And the woman is dead. My God, Milly! Was she murdered?"

"Not according to the police. Her cause of death is listed officially as 'natural causes'." Milly told her. How much more should she say? "If they had been able to find anything but heart failure, they would have called it suicide. Nancy was stood up by someone she was expecting, drank half a bottle of champagne and took two sleeping pills. Not enough to kill her."

"Maybe the friend you talked to is wrong. Ronald convinced me he didn't know her personally. God! I should be able to trust my husband!"

Milly crossed the deck to her. "I'm sorry," she said.

"I'm getting carried away. I have to think. This is too important," Kit muttered. "If I throw him out now, this will be the shortest marriage on record. Shorter even than any of my mother's."

She stared down into the sunlit green water for a long while, then turned to Milly. "Do you think I should give Ronald a chance to own up to his past?

I know he'll promise to be faithful." Her pretty mouth twisted into a cynical smile. "I haven't signed the papers that give him joint ownership of the estate house yet."

"I'm the wrong person to ask, Kit," Milly told her. "I thought I was unofficially engaged to Ronald when he eloped with his first wife. But, you're right. You shouldn't rush any decisions right now. You might be wise to pretend you don't know anything."

"I don't. I've been trying to hide my head in the sand," Kit cried. "But terrible things are happening. Bret's car being blown up, Yvette's murder, Flo almost being killed. And now you tell me that Ronald's..." She grimaced at the word. "Ronald's lover died in some mysterious way. I don't know how it's all connected but it has to be. And I can't ignore that Ronald's Man Friday, Gord, was arrested for setting that bomb in Flo's house."

"I know you don't want to believe that Ronald has had anything to do with all that. But, just be careful."

"You think he had something to do with Yvette's death?" Kit was clearly shocked at the idea. "Why? Was he having an affair with my best friend, too?"

Kit's voice was climbing in pitch. Her eyes were beginning to glisten with unshed tears.

"No," Milly said putting her arms around Kit's slender shoulders. "No, I'm sure there was no romantic interest between him and Yvette. Not ever. But, I do suspect he is involved somehow. Bret and I have been talking to Flo's friend Theo Parsons who is with the Sheriff's Department. The police are looking very carefully at Ronald's activities. So far they've found nothing to tie him in with the murder. Or anything else."

She gave her a quick hug. "Come on, Kit. Talking about this will get us no farther ahead. Didn't we come here for a swim?"

"Right!" Kit tore off her shorts and shirt. "Last one in pays for the chowder."

Milly, too, was wearing a blue bikini under her clothes but she was slower at stripping down than Kit.

"I guess lunch is on me," she cried as she imitated Kit's shallow dive off the aft platform into the clear water.

Milly was a strong swimmer but her need to expend physical energy at the moment couldn't compare to Kit's. She kept up with the tiny blonde for the first few large circles around the yacht but gradually let Kit outdistance her. This was definitely a time to allow Kit some privacy to deal with the unhappiness that had invaded her life.

After about twenty circles around the boat, Milly hoisted herself up onto the platform and sat quietly watching Kit's energetic attempt to exorcise the devils in her mind.

Finally, Kit swam up to the boat.

"Lower the ladder, would you?" she gasped. "I don't think my arms are up it."

"Feel better now?" Milly asked after a minute.

"No. But I'm hungry," Kit announced with a small smile. "And we have to get dressed. Can't hit Susinna's in a bikini."

"It's formal?" Milly asked in a minor fluster. "I didn't bring a dress."

"The shorts you were wearing are fine. Susinna is big on modesty, though. No swim suits or short shorts."

The tiny village at the foot of the cove had a fairly long wooden pier at which several fishing boats were moored and not much else. A handful of brightly painted wooden houses, a small general store, and an outdoor stall that featured colorfully decorated straw baskets, purses and a few hats were strung along the single street.

The busiest spot was Susinna's Restaurant. It consisted of about a dozen tables in an open-air enclosure surrounded by a picket fence. The number of bicycles and motorbikes leaning against the fence explained why there appeared to be more people in the restaurant than lived in the village. The island beat of the music that poured out of the speakers mounted at the corners of the porch roof was cheerful. The aroma of chowder and hot bread was absolutely mouthwatering.

"Miss Kit!" The loud, chocolate-rich voice belonged to a tall, thin black woman with the warmest smile Milly had ever seen. "You came back."

Kit was enveloped in a big hug.

"This is my friend, Milly, Susinna," Kit said. "We've come for conch chowder."

"Of course, you have," the woman roared and led them to a table. "Welcome, Milly. Sit here near the kitchen so we can talk as I go by. Beer, tea or cola?"

"Tea," Kit looked at Milly, "for two."

Susinna chuckled and hustled off belting out Tea for Two not quite at the top of her lungs, but loudly enough to drown out the calypso for a few bars.

"You did not stop by when you were here with your man," she announced to the world when she brought their iced tea and a large bowl of fragrant chowder.

"We weren't here long," Kit said apologetically. "I didn't know you'd seen us."

"My house is on the headland," Susinna explained with a wink. "I see everything in the bay."

Kit blushed and bent to concentrate on her chowder.

Milly had to agree that it was the best conch chowder she'd ever tasted. When she asked to speak to the cook, Susinna howled with laughter.

"I am the cook, the waitress, the owner. My husband is the fisherman."

Milly looked pointedly at the pretty young girl who was bussing tables. "Ah, that is Alicia. She is my oldest girl. She will cook one day. Now she does dishes."

When they left Milly had Susinna's assurance that if she brought her aunt who was the cook at Milly's restaurant, they would exchange recipes.

"I hope I do get to come back. Susinna is unique and you were right about the chowder," Milly said as they climbed into the tender to head back to the yacht.

Milly wasn't eager to resume their difficult conversation and gave herself over to enjoying the sensation of speeding through the calm waters in the little motorboat.

They agreed that it would be a waste of a lovely afternoon to head back to Palm Beach right away. It wasn't until they were both lying on the deck, slathered with sunscreen, that Kit announced bitterly, "I didn't think anything could make me feel more like a fool."

Coming out of a sun-induced doze, Milly uttered a sound that was a cross between an expression of sympathy and a request for more information.

"Susinna must have seen us on deck that afternoon. I didn't think anyone could see us from shore. But I was so happy that day I wouldn't have cared if I had known. After months of delay, it was my wedding day. We planned to spend our first night as man and wife here in the cove because I love it here and it wasn't too long a long boat ride after the brunch."

She gave a hard little laugh. "We must have put on quite a show. Ronald outdid himself in his loving bridegroom role. We had a swim and drank champagne in the sunshine. Then we made long, lazy love... I mean, we had great sex...on the deck."

Milly wanted to interrupt and say, "Don't bare your soul to me, Kit. You'll probably wish you hadn't. And, it is remotely possible that Ronald does love you. Even rotten men can fall in love." But she couldn't say it. And she didn't believe that Ronald had an ounce of sincere emotion in his whole body. So she closed her eyes and listened.

"Then Ronald laid out the supper that Anna had packed for us. We snuggled on the deck watching the sunset and sipping Grasshoppers. No. Let's be precise here," she bit out. "I sipped Grasshoppers. Ronald sipped cognac. I thought he was being so wonderful to me. He made a full blender full of lovely icy grasshoppers but I only had one glass before I fell asleep. Must have been the champagne and sunshine. Not to mention our wonderful big wedding."

Kit sat up and reached for her T-shirt. "Ronald must have carried me to bed because it was just before dawn when he woke me up to make lo... Oh, shit! This is so depressing. Let's go home, Milly."

"Kit, I wish I could say this is all going to blow over, but..." She sighed. "Yes, let's go home."

All day The Grove had been a hive of productive activity and Bret was not part of any of it. Even Flo had convinced Bea to take her into the kitchen to badger the sous chefs about the weekend menu.

Bret waited. He waited for Bart to finish playing golf and, he hoped, getting valuable information out of Ronald. He waited for Theo to get back to him with further word on the puncture wounds in Nancy Higgenbottom's thigh. He waited to hear that someone had seen Yvette and Ronald together. He waited for Milly to get home.

He swore, he swam, he made phone calls. Finally, about noon he gave up fighting boredom and frustration and made an appointment with the CEO of a small electronics company who wanted Greco to evaluate their security.

The results of that were predictable but at least he would be doing something!

Three hours later, he had a signed contract and a feeling of accomplishment but was back in the holding pattern. He was sitting in his pickup wondering if it was worth going in to the office to hand the contract to Jim as prove that he was still an active member of the company when his cell phone rang. He snatched at it.

"Bret Thornton," he snapped.

"Mr. Thornton." The caller did not identify himself but Bret had no trouble identifying the light, self-important voice. "You left me your card and I think I have found something that will be of interest to you and Mrs. Brzezynski."

"Yes, Mr. Smithfield?"

"Josephine seems to have found a purse. I didn't look in it for identification but it seems quite heavy. I notified the police immediately, of course. I was put on to a Detective Sergeant Parsons who seemed very interested in it. I thought I'd let you know."

"You'll be home for the next couple of hours?" Bret asked, turning the key in the ignition.

When Robert Smithfield stated that, of course, he had told the police he would be home for the rest of the day, Bret informed him that he and Milly would be there as soon as possible to see if she recognized the purse. He was already en route to the Schofield estate.

He tried Kit's cell phone but he didn't have much hope that she'd have it turned on. When Kit went off for a jaunt it was hard to convince her that someone might want to get in touch with her. He was best to drive to the dock to meet the women when they came off the water.

He arrived just as The Sprite was gliding to a stop by the dock. It was a lovely picture. Kit and Milly were two beautiful women. Silhouetted against the rosy sunset-colored sky, both slightly tousled by the wind, they could have posed for a boating brochure.

"Catch," Kit said and grunted as she threw him a coil of rope with a two-handed toss. The weight of it almost rocked him back on his heels.

"You've been weight training again," he said with a laugh.

"No more. I'm going to change my style," she said with an odd laugh. "I'm going to surround myself with muscle-bound hunks to do this kind of thing."

"You'll get no objections from me," Bret replied as he slid the loop over one of the mooring posts.

"Come aboard," Kit invited.

"Another time, Kittle," Bret said. "They've possibly found some new evidence in Yvette's case."

"What?" Milly breathed.

"Smithfield called. One of his dogs found a purse."

"Yvette's?" Kit asked.

"Smithfield was smart enough not to open it up. He's waiting for the police so that whatever evidence is in it isn't destroyed. Milly could maybe identify it without opening it."

"So could I," Kit said. "I saw what she was wearing the day she died."

"No point in taking three vehicles," Milly said. "Come with me."

"I'll follow you," Bret told them.

Milly parked behind the Sheriff department's car in Robert Smithfield's driveway. Bret pulled in behind her. The sound of shrill barking was almost deafening but the dogs were not in sight. The three of them hurried to the front stoop where Theo and Robert Smithfield were talking and looking intently at a filthy, badly chewed, white leather purse. Smithfield had placed the purse on a folded piece of clear plastic in the middle of the stoop.

When they saw it, neither Milly nor Kit had to say a word. They merely looked at each other with eyes that brimmed with tears. Kit nodded.

"It's hers." Milly's voice was barely audible.

"I'm afraid Josephine must have had it buried for a while," Smithfield said apologetically. "I figure she found it in the ditch in front of my house. The dogs don't go off the property unless I'm with them."

If Bret hadn't seen the military precision with which the two little dogs obeyed Smithfield, he might not have believed that statement.

"I saw her digging under a shrub at the back of the garden the other day," he told them. "When I investigated, I found that she was chewing on a woman's shoe. I took it away from her, of course. Then, I'm afraid I threw it in the trash."

He looked very uncomfortable. "I'm sorry. I know I said I'd let you know if I discovered anything but you wouldn't believe the things that I find walking the dogs along the road." He actually blushed. "All manner of articles of clothing, for one thing."

"I'm glad you called about the purse," Milly told him.

"The little devil had buried it in the same place as the shoe and must have taken it out to chew on occasionally. I hope it's still useful to you, Sergeant," he said.

"That all depends on what is inside," Theo said, taking a pair of surgical gloves out of his pocket and pulling them on. "We sure can't destroy much more on the outside of this."

He picked up the slimy purse and flipped up its tooth-marked outside flap. Gingerly, he pulled out a black leather business card holder and a packet of facial tissues. The card displayed in the plastic window read, "Yvette Pelletier. Attorney at law."

Milly stifled a sob.

Theo struggled with the damaged zipper that protected the inner pocket. Eventually, he got it open and pulled out a white leather wallet.

"Flo gave her that wallet for Christmas," she said.

Theo opened the wallet enough to see the wad of bills it contained.

"Robbery sure wasn't the motive," Bret said.

Theo reached down into the bottom of the bag and, very carefully, pulled out a tiny black cellular telephone.

"That's it!" Bret cried. "His number should be on that phone."

"Whose number?" Kit asked.

"We'll know that as soon as I can get all this stuff to the lab and have the technicians check it out," Theo answered and turned to speak to Robert Smithfield.

"You don't need us anymore," Milly said, realizing that Theo wasn't going to say more with Kit present. "Why don't you come back to The Grove with us, Kit? Ronald and Bart probably won't be back from the club until late."

"I think I'd like to go home," Kit said. "I won't be alone. My housekeeper and some of the other staff will be there. I think I need an early night. I'll take a sleeping pill and probably be out like a light before the men get back."

Good. She wasn't planning to confront Ronald tonight.

"I'll take you home, Kit," Bret said. "And Milly can see for herself how much better Flo is feeling after a few hours of barking orders in the kitchen."

Flo was finishing up her supper tray when Milly arrived at The Grove. She was, Milly was glad to see, in a much more positive frame of mind.

"The headache's gone," she said. "I can handle the other when I can think clearly. Tell me. What has put that look on your face?"

Milly told her that she had just returned from identifying Yvette's purse at Robert Smithfield's house.

"Just keep your fingers crossed that they can retrieve the list of incoming calls from her cell phone."

Flo looked perplexed. Of course, Theo had been keeping her pretty much up to date on the Gord Ingles case but she hadn't had a chance to tell Flo about what the waitress had told her and Bret. Or about the letter that Mark had sent. Milly had just finished telling her about what she had learned from Kit that afternoon when Bret arrived.

Bea Foster brought him to the door.

"It's nice to see you, Bret," Bea said. "But you have five minutes before I'm insisting that my patient get some rest. She's already had too big a day."

The five minutes was spent listening to the two middle-aged women argue about who was in charge of Flo's life. But Flo grudgingly gave in and Milly and Bret left when the five minutes were up.

As they left, they crossed paths with the two men who were patrolling the grounds.

"Flo doesn't like the feeling that she's living in an armed camp," Milly said.

"And I'm not happy with the idea that Ronald still thinks she's a threat to him. He must be aware that the web of evidence is coming together. He doesn't want an eyewitness who can put him at the scene of Nancy's murder."

"Murder? Has the medical examiner decided that those puncture marks mean something?"

"Theo is optimistic." He waited while Milly unlocked the door. "You've had quite a day," he said.

"I feel like a wrung-out dish rag," she admitted. "It's hard not to be affected when you're around someone who is as upset as Kit is right now."

"Kit and I had a long talk in the car and I told her as much as I could about our investigation of Ronald."

"Did you tell her about my dreams? And your contacts with Yvette's spirit...or whatever it was?"

"Some of it." Bret took her in his arms and gave her a long, intense kiss. She knew it was not a prelude to anything but simply a necessity for both of them. "It's been a long, long day since I kissed you in bed this morning."

She agreed. "Tomorrow we'll stay there longer. Saturday is my morning to sleep in," she murmured against his chest.

"Sounds like my kind of morning," he said. "Oh, damn! Kit said to tell you she thought the two of you should go back and have another chat with Susinna. Kit said she'd like to leave about nine to catch her at the end of the lunchtime rush."

"What more can she tell us?"

"Kit has been thinking about that Grasshopper Ronald mixed for her and wondered if he could have slipped something into it to knock her out for maybe eight or nine hours. She figures she fell asleep before seven o'clock in the evening. She didn't see a clock when he woke her up but the sun was coming up. She figures he must have put something in front of the clock on the dresser or covered it somehow.

"She told me she fell asleep the week before after he'd mixed one for her. She put it down to exhaustion from all the preparations for the wedding."

"You figure he was testing to see how long she would be unconscious?"

"That's what she thinks now. She is hoping that Susinna or someone else might have seen the boat leave and then come back early that morning."

"So, I guess I only get to sleep in a little tomorrow."

"Why don't we go to bed early tonight." Bret's smile was suggestive. "We need our rest. Who knows..." The smile got broader. "We might just spend the whole night sleeping."

"Who knows?" she replied.

Bret swam lengths in Milly's pool until he could no longer endure the smell and taste of chlorine. Now he paced the patio. Nothing seemed to dissipate the tension that had been mounting in him since Milly left this morning

The strident ring of the telephone sent him racing to the chair where he had left his shirt. He yanked the phone out of his pocket and pressed the talk button.

"Bret Thornton," he barked.

"Ronald slipped away on me," Bart announced, with no preamble. "We're waiting for the last foursome to come off the course because we're in line to win the damned tournament. When he left the bar, I thought he was heading for the men's room. He never came back. We took The Two to the club via the Intracoastal this morning and the boat is gone."

"I'll meet you at the club. Can you get a boat?"

"I've borrowed a speedboat. You bring me a firearm."

"Done."

"Have you heard from Kit and Milly?"

"Not a word."

Bret clicked off the phone and tore into the house to get his Beretta. He commandeered a Smith and Wesson .38 from one of the Greco Associates men who were guarding Flo. The immediate danger, he had a gut-grabbing hunch, was to Kit and Milly.

Susinna must have seen Kit and Milly from the moment they entered the cove--certainly from the time they got into the tender--because she was on the dock when they landed.

"Miss Kit, come ashore!" Her smile was welcoming but her dark eyes held questions and, perhaps, concern. "I don't see you for weeks then two days in a row," she boomed as they strolled back up the dock. "You would like some lunch?"

"Of course," Kit replied. "I'm surprised you saw us come into the bay. I thought you'd be busy with the lunch crowd."

"I don't miss much through the big window in my kitchen," Susinna crowed. "My Jacob he says I missed my calling. I should be a gossip writer for the newspaper."

The island beat was belting out cheerfully from the speakers again today, but the restaurant was almost empty. The only customers left were an elderly couple who were seated at the table nearest the street. They dawdled over their coffee calling out greetings to everyone who passed by.

"Come in the shade, here, where it's cooler," Susinna said. "Now what can I get you? Chowder? Conch fritters? I have a nice chilled gazpacho today."

"A cold soup sounds wonderful," Milly told her.

"Some of my regular customers like it. I make it once a week."

"Why don't you join us?" Kit invited. "We haven't had a visit for years."

Susinna arrived with three bowls of soup, a basket full large hunks of grainy bread and some little pats of butter.

"Now," she said, "tell me why you are sad. What can I do?"

"Oh, Susinna," Kit said. "Thank you but there is nothing anyone can do. My best friend, Milly's sister, died. We are trying to take our minds off that."

"I'm sorry," the older woman said. There was sincerity in her voice. "But where is your handsome man?"

"Playing golf," she said. "How do you know he's handsome?"

"You would choose a handsome man," she asserted. "I envied you that day with your loving man playing in the sunshine."

"I didn't know you could see us." Kit's face was scarlet.

"Don't you fuss. I only saw you kissing and heard you laugh." Susinna patted her hand. Then she grinned and rolled her eyes. "I couldn't see anything at all when you went for your romantic sunset cruise."

"You saw us leave?"

"Oh, yes!" Susinna was vehement about that. "And saw you coming back many hours later. My six month old son had an earache and kept me up on and off all that night."

"You're sure The Sprite left the bay."

"Oh, yes. First, I was surprised that you were leaving without stopping by the restaurant. Then, I was surprised when you came back around five in the morning. I thought you probably had anchored in some other bay for a while."

When they finally had finished their soup and left Susinna with their sincere thanks, they made their way slowly to the outboard.

"I guess I have to believe it now," Kit said quietly.

"Look, Kit." Milly pointed at The Sprite which was riding at anchor in the middle of the bay. Beside it was a smaller yacht with a blue awning over the top deck.

"It's The Two," Kit cried. "Bret must have come after us after all."

"You told him not to come to the restaurant. I guess he figured you didn't mean he couldn't join us in the cove."

"I didn't know Bret knew exactly where this was," Kit said. "But he never does tell all he knows."

When they approached The Sprite's stern, they could see the other boat's tender tied to it.

"He's on board," Milly said. She was anxious to tell Bret that they actually had a witness. She climbed out of the tender and called out his name while they tied up.

He didn't answer.

"He must be below," Kit said.

Milly ran down the few steps ahead of her.

There was no one in the main saloon. A whiff of citrus cologne stopped Milly short. She whirled around.

"It's not Bret!" she whispered. "We have to get out of here."

Kit was right in back of her on the steps but in the time it took for her to turn and start back up, Ronald had emerged from one of the staterooms.

"Stop where you are, Kit," he said almost casually. "Unless you don't mind seeing your friend Milly's blood all over your new carpet."

The revolver he held in his hand was probably a normal size, but to Milly, it looked enormous.

"Over there," he said, waving them over to the brightly upholstered sofa bench that lined one wall.

"The gun isn't necessary, Ronald," Kit said in a voice that was not too steady. "We can talk."

"Oh, Sweetness," he said with a long, deep sigh. "I'm afraid the time for talking is over. I've had some rotten luck and I'm going to have to leave you behind."

He tossed Milly a roll of duct tape. "Tape Kit's ankles together, would you, Mill?"

There was no way that both she and Kit could get out of here before Ronald shot one of them. He had obviously arrived prepared to kill them. Milly decided to play along with him and hope for a chance to get his gun away from him. Buzz had insisted that she take a course in self-defense. However, Ronald was keeping a respectful distance and that training wouldn't help her if she couldn't get close to him.

She knelt in front of Kit and started to tape her ankles.

"Cross them first," Ronald ordered.

Kit crossed her ankles. Milly bound them together with the tough tape and, with some difficulty, ripped the piece off.

"Give the tape to Kit," he ordered.

As soon as Kit had bound Milly's hands and feet, Ronald put his gun down and picked up a folder off the coffee table.

"I drew up this paper I want you to sign, Sweetness," he said. "When you die suddenly and inexplicably, I will be mourning in South America. But I will be your heir."

"You'll never get my money," Kit spat out. "You know the police are going to figure out how you killed the Higgenbottom woman soon. If you kill Milly and me, too, they'll hunt you down."

"Not every country has extradition with the United States, my dear. And I have quite a little bit set aside in offshore accounts. Don't worry about me."

"Worry about you?" Kit turned her head away.

"Sign it, Kit. It's already been witnessed." He picked up the gun again. "Would you rather I shot Milly now? The injection is quick and appears to be relatively painless. I'm sure you would both prefer that."

"The Two is not invisible you know," Milly interrupted. "You'll be caught and identified."

"Ah, that's the beauty of my wife's isolated, virtually uninhabited little cove. Nobody has seen me. All right, time's up, Kit!"

He pointed the revolver directly at Milly's stomach. "No head shot. I'm not going to make this easy for her."

"I'll sign it," Kit muttered. "Give it to me."

Ronald watched Kit sign the paper that no doubt was sentencing them both to death.

"I really hate to have to play the grieving husband again," he said as if Kit had orchestrated this whole situation just to annoy him. "I thought we could make a go of it, Sweetness. I thought I had it all. You have so much money and I discovered that we were extremely compatible, too."

Afraid that Kit was going to explode and precipitate the death scene that Ronald had planned for them, Milly said, "If you're going to kill us anyway, Ronald, I wish you'd tell us how you killed Nancy and Yvette without anyone suspecting that you did it. Or even that they were murdered. Bret and I have chased clues all over the Atlantic seaboard but we are still bewildered."

"No one would have ever known if it hadn't been for rotten luck. Yvette saw me in Lauderdale. Then the masons went on strike."

Kit picked up the beat. "The masons? What did they have to do with anything?"

Maybe if they could keep him talking long enough, Milly could do something. She or Bret would find a way to save them.

She had to stay alive. She hadn't told Bret she loved him.

With Bart at the controls, they made it to the little cove on Grand Bahama in just under three hours. Bret doubted if the speedboat's hull even touched the water during the trip. They must have picked up some time on Ronald. The Two was a considerably slower boat.

Sure enough, when they arrived, both yachts were still at anchor. Then Bart spun them to a gliding stop against the port side of The Sprite and Bret leapt aboard as quietly as possible. Bart fastened a mooring rope to a cleat and followed him.

There was no one on deck or in the cockpit. The boat was too quiet. Bret pulled the Beretta from its position at the back of his waist and tiptoed down the steps into the saloon with Bart on his heels. Bart had the Smith and Wesson in his hand, ready to fire.

Milly and Kit were lying on the long upholstered bench that lined the left side of the room. Ronald was standing between them, in the act of removing a hypodermic needle from Milly's leg.

"Bret!" Milly screamed when she saw him.

With a roar, Bret charged at him. Ronald transferred the revolver he was holding in his left hand to his right as he whirled to aim at Bret. Before he could squeeze the trigger, there was a sharp report. A small red hole appeared in the middle of Ronald's forehead and he dropped to the carpet.

"Help Kit!" Milly said. Her voice was slurred.

Bret picked up the small bottle that was lying on the bench beside Milly.

"Insulin," he said.

"Kit's alive but unconscious," Bart sounded more panicked than Bret had ever heard him.

"Bart, we need honey or sugar to counteract the insulin." He dredged that fact out of the depths of his memory. A long-ago prep school roommate had been an insulin dependent diabetic and had drummed the first-aid treatments into Bret's less than enthusiastic head.

By the time Bret had cut the tape on the women's wrists, Bart was running back from the galley with a jar of liquid honey. He poured some of it into the lid and handed it to Bret.

"Put it under her tongue," Bret said. "In case she can't swallow."

He lifted Milly's head onto his lap and opened her mouth wide enough to slip some honey under her tongue with his finger. Her face was flushed and her heartbeat was too rapid. More honey. A few drops at a time.

"Not too much," he cautioned Bart.

"Please, love, come back to me. Please God, don't let her die." The words repeated over and over in his brain. Nothing was clearer to him now than the fact that Milly was vital to him. If she died, he might as well die, too.

After several interminable minutes, Milly stirred. Her eyelids trembled. She swallowed. Over her murmured protests, he gave her more honey.

"She's coming round," he cried.

"Kit isn't," Bart said. "Damn it, Kit. I can't handle this!"

Kit's eyelids fluttered.

"Thank God! Now, swallow, Kittle," Bart crooned. He put more honey in Kit's mouth.

She mumbled a curse at him. "That's better," he said with a relieved grin. "That's my Kittle."

"I'll radio the coast guard to get a doctor here right away," Bret said. "Keep an eye on Milly."

He rushed out, then returned to the saloon with two glasses of orange juice in his hands. He handed one to Bart. "That's the other thing Timothy told me to give him if he went into insulin shock."

"Timothy?" Bart asked.

"Don't you remember the wimp roommate of the century?" Bret asked as he wrapped his arms around Milly and tried to get her to sip some orange juice. "Bless his little bossy heart!"

"Not bossy," Milly mumbled. "Don't like orange juice."

Lord how he loved this woman! And as soon as she was conscious, he was going to tell her so.

Bart had succeeded in coaxing a little juice into Kit and she was gradually becoming more alert. When she was able to focus enough to realize that her husband's body was lying in the middle of the floor, she suddenly began to laugh hysterically.

In fact, even when the coast guard and the paramedics arrived, she was still having the occasional burst of laughter and saying, "He lied again, Milly. He did. He did get blood on the carpet."

I love you, Milly." It wasn't the first time Bret had said this. Ever since that ugly scene a month ago on The Sprite, he had been telling her that theirs was the kind of love that would endure forever. "I can't imagine life without you."

"I love you, too," Milly said and snuggled deeper into his arms.

They were sitting on the deck of The Two with their after-dinner coffee, gazing out at the moonlit waters of the Intracoastal Waterway. The night was balmy and the strains of an old Sinatra tune were wafting faintly up from the stereo in the saloon. It was a night made for romance.

"Will you marry me?" he whispered.

"Oh yes," she whispered back. Her life would be empty without him.

The emerald ring he slid on her finger was breathtaking. His kiss was even more so. Milly knew that she had never been happier.

The notes of a jazz saxophone crept up on them. This sax was mellow and rich. Its music flowed about them and enveloped them in loving warmth.

"That's lovely," Milly murmured. "I didn't think I would be able to enjoy a saxophone ever again." She held her hand up to admire the way the emerald caught the moonlight.

"I think Yvette just congratulated us on our engagement," Bret said.

"Why do you say that?" Milly raised her eyes to his questioningly.

"I wouldn't have chosen a saxophone to set the mood tonight, love. I don't even own that CD."

The melody swelled for a few seconds, then faded away.

You can find ALL our books on our website at:

http://www.writers-exchange.com

All our romances:

http://www.writers-exchange.com/category/genres/romance/

Growing up in Timmins, in its gold mining heyday, gave Dee Lloyd her love of dramatic scenery, strong men and independent women. It taught her nothing is impossible with determination and hard work. Still in grade school, she told a reporter for the Timmins Daily Press that she was going to be a writer. Many careers--ranging from selling in a music store to teaching creative writing--later, she is doing just that.

Dee is now the award-winning author of seven romantic suspense and paranormal romance novels. *TIES that Blind* won the EPPIE Award for best contemporary romance. Her paranormal/reincarnation/ghost novel, *OUT of HER DREAMS*, was the 2010 EPIC award winner for Paranormal Romance. It was also a nominee for Romantic Times Reviewers Choice Award for best Paranormal Romance.

Dee was married to Terry Sheils, award-winning author of horror, mystery, and fantasy, for over forty years. Dee states, "Writing has always been as essential as breathing in our house."

Dee is a popular speaker at romance and mystery conferences. She teaches online writing courses at Savvy Authors www.savvyauthors.com and Outreach International Romance Writers http://www.oirwa.com.

Dee's life is full. She lives with a wild and wonderful Mini-labradoodle named Meg. Her daughters are supportive and dynamic. And of course, the grandchildren are exceptional. The icing on the cake is the growing number of enthusiastic readers who write to tell her they enjoy her books. Visit Dee's website for news, free excerpts, short stories, and a free downloadable cookbook. Visit her website at http://www.deelloyd.com.

You can keep track of all her books on her Writers Exchange author page:
http://www.writers-exchange.com/Dee-Lloyd/

If you want to read more about books by this author, they are listed on the following pages...

Dangerous Waters Trilogy

{Romantic Suspense}

Dashing heroes set out to protect the women of their dreams as they travel by boat over the Caribbean and the Bahamas, even to a clear lake in Muskoka, where romance--and deception--will take them all into Dangerous Waters.

Book 1: Change of Plans

Mike and Sara didn't plan on falling in love...

Determined to change his image from "Mr. Nice Guy" to "dangerous and exciting male on the prowl" after a near miss that almost had him marrying the wrong woman, Mike is disillusioned and angry with women in general. His fiancée eloped with her boss while he was away completing a contract job in Africa, and he can only think, *Good riddance!* Now all he has to do is find a fun-loving woman to share his honeymoon stateroom...

Sara has never been in love, but she does want a family. She decides to take a cruise so she can consider the marriage proposal of Stephen Cafik, a wealthy electronics engineer whose political career her retired state senator father is encouraging.

But someone else on board the ship has plans--ones that involve killing Sara...

Publisher: http://www.writers-exchange.com/Change-of-Plans/

Book 2: Ghost of a Chance

Bret's well-ordered life is already off the rails when a lovely but bloody ghost confronts him on a dark, deserted road. Recovering from a recent injury that nearly killed him, he's convinced his nerves must be in worse shape than he believed if he's starting to see ghosts.

When Bret steps into the piano lounge, he sees a beauty on the stage, weaving a spell for her audience. Milly's performance doesn't suffer, but she's intensely aware of the stranger's unwavering gaze on her from the audience.

Bret is convinced Milly is the ghostly, bloody woman he saw on the road. But how can she be?

Publisher: http://www.writers-exchange.com/Ghost-of-a-Chance/

Book 3: Unquiet Spirits

Headstrong Kit Schofield heads north to her family resort at Spirit Lake, convinced the hit-and-run that almost killed her was a random act of violence. Not-so-convinced, lifelong buddy Bart Thornton joins her as a self-appointed bodyguard, much to Kit's chagrin--at first.

Two lusty ghosts drop clues about old murders and insist that Kit and Bart are soul mates. One kiss proves it, unleashing unexpected, unwelcome and totally distracting passion between them.

Disturbing old secrets and equally unsettling ghosts lurk in the lodge as well as in the calm waters of the deceptively peaceful resort. In the calm, a deadly, elusive killer strikes again...

Publisher: http://www.writers-exchange.com/Unquiet-Spirits/

Mine

{Romantic Suspense}

Inheriting Pop's property brings Cadie unexpected complications ranging from a devastating, antisocial tenant to a potential gold mine, a silent, deadly enemy, and, as if that isn't enough, love when and where she least expects it.

...Mine by Dee Lloyd sure is one of those books where you wish it were a movie because of all the action and suspense in this one story...

~ *Fallen Angel Reviews*

Publisher: http://www.writers-exchange.com/Mine/

TIES That Blind

{Romantic Mystery}

A body in a garage. A revolver in a locked car. A chance meeting of two old friends on a plane. Is this a happy reunion...or a devious frame-up for murder?

The Risa Vitale that Adam Taggart remembers as a skinny daredevil kid trailing him around the ski club never showed any signs of becoming the attractive woman who greets him as he disembarks from a flight. His uncomplicated happiness at their reunion, however, ends shortly after she offers him a ride. Finding a revolver under his seat and a pool of blood in the back of her van quashes any hope of attraction. The biggest romance killer of all: The dead body of his stepsister in Risa's parents' garage!

Publisher: http://www.writers-exchange.com/TIES-That-Blind/